I0546799

The Legend of Graeme Macpherson

Deb Kemper

Charlie Dawg

Press

This book is a work of fiction. Any resemblance of the characters to people, living or dead is unintentional. Historical facts are as correct as my research material.

ISBN: 978-1944979-17-1

Acknowledgements

When I saw the picture of the castle I knew it was perfect for the cover of this book. Thank you to whoever took the time and trouble to capture the sunrise. I can't find a copyright. I clipped it and tried to chase down the origination only to find a dead end. We were within a few hundred feet of the castle May 2013, in the midst of a snowstorm and failed to get to see it in person that day. We'll return for another go at the wondrous places we haven't discovered yet. We look forward to being in Scotland again soon and often.

Thank you to the Macpherson clan
for use of the official clan crest.

Thank you, Judy Kemper for your expertise and
encouragement. You're a great editor and friend.

Dedication

To my friend and the coolest gal I know, Dede Gross, who taught me, among many other things, that there is no *fear* in Macpherson.

To my husband, Ken, for support, encouragement and love. You fill my life with good things. Thank you for the care you take with my tending. You taught me love and trust. Our relationship is priceless.

American English is not identical to British or Scottish English. I am American and write for a primarily American audience. A lot of words differ in meaning and some in spelling. *Failing to mention this cost me dearly on my last book when someone who didn't know dragged me through the muck.* I can't seem to shake the review, no matter how hard I work at getting it off the record or addressing the issue. It's disappointing after spending more than a year to write and produce a book to be bashed over lack of understanding. I do not presume to be so familiar with the Scottish culture to not make errors. This book is my best effort to date.

You'll find a glossary in back for your convenience.

Prologue
June 1678
Clary Castle Scotland

Wailing became screams of agony. Graeme Macpherson paced the gallery outside his brother's quarters. He stopped and studied the door, willing it open.

She must have flown by now.

The door creaked on iron hinges, slowly swinging into the room. Head bowed, Esperenza Macpherson stepped through, pushing the solid oak closed behind, muffling her good daughter's voice.

She dared meet her middle son's gaze. "She's gone." Holding a delicate linen square to her face, she choked back a sob. "We *must* find the source of this plague stealing our children from us."

He glanced at the door, sighing. "Aye, Mither. But I daen't ken where to begin."

Esperenza shook her head. "Nor I, son. But death has made itself known in our home. 'Til now it's taken only offspring of the poor. We've learned a harsh lesson; it reaches into the castle. Our walls do not diminish its power to destroy.

"Order a conference of physicians and healers within our borders. Bid them come together and discuss a solution. Mayhap we can discover the reason our young and elderly are stolen away for nigh on two summers." Her resolve was felt in her tone. "I'll direct them, just get them here."

"The summons will go out at once." Graeme watched his mother closely.

Her tear-stained face met his eyes again. "No parsons. They'd make certain to spread word that we're convening witches." She took a few steps towards the stairs and turned back to him. "They

1

see nothing good coming from God. They espouse only hateful judgment." She grasped a baluster and guided herself along.

"Dae ye require help up the stairs, Mither?"

"Nay, there's no hurry now" her voice broke, "our precious is gone." Her back straightened as she climbed to her room.

At the landing she stopped to rest on the cold stone, her delicate frame perching near the edge of the tread. Quietly she wept, her head lowered.

Her good daughter's intense lamenting calmed for a moment. Silence prevailed with the family's grief.

Chapter One

May 1985
Clary Castle, Scotland at the Medieval Times Festival

Dusk fell as the Medieval Times parade circled the castle sunwise for the third time. Half the pipe and drum band led the parade; the other half brought up the rear. The squeal of bagpipes echoed off the ancient stone.

Jenna pushed a concealed latch, opening the hidden door into the cold corridor of a secret passage.

"Bran?" She eased inside, gathering her blue velvet gown in hand, and held the door open.

"Aye, I'm here." Bran shouted above the noise of revelry, waving as he appeared ahead of her, having entered from inside the castle.

The comely blonde's face screwed into a frown. She paled. "Where's tha' light comin' from?"

Bran Macpherson turned to see a glow blooming beyond the junction to his right. Reflections danced off the aged grey rock around him.

"Don't ken. I'll just be a moment." He turned to an unexplored leg of the passage.

"Bran, no!" Jenna called sharply. "Don't go in there!"

He stopped as the path curved away. Beyond, he caught a glimpse of luminous treetops swaying in a turbulent breeze through an opening in a rock wall. Strange musical voices enticed him into the radiance.

He glanced back at his girlfriend and threw up his hand, calling to Jenna, in his best actor's voice, "Tell you what, I'll see you at my place—at midnight, sweetheart."

Scaling the tumbled part of the wall into the beckoning radiance, he missed her stamping her foot, shrieking, "Bran Macpherson, you come back here!"

3

****

Bran's ribcage throbbed as he struggled for breath. He opened his eyes, blinded by sharp sunlight. "Hey, buddy," he croaked, "wanna get off me?"

The large owner of the brogue, propped against his ribs, hovered then squatted beside the intruder. "Where'd ye come from?"

"The Medieval Times Festival at the castle." Bran sat up cautiously and glanced around the forest. The sound of rushing water competed with his heart beat throbbing in his ears. He rubbed the back of his head.

"What's 'at?" his host asked with amusement.

"It's where folks dress up like…," Bran studied the man, "you and pretend to be knights and ladies during medieval times. Aren't you part of the festival?" He raked leaves out of his thick chestnut hair and studied his surroundings.

The man's rumbling laughter took him by surprise. "Nay, ye've landed in the middle o' my property and I wanna ken where ye're from. Is tha' plain enough?" He stood straight, all six and a half feet of him, and stepped back.

Bran watched him and scrambled to rise. "I walked down a secret passage in a castle towards a really bright light—and ended up here. That's all I ken. What is this place? I don't recognize a thin'." He squinted in the brilliance of the valley washed in the tangerine and scarlet of receding sunlight.

"*This place* is Alba. Some call it Scotland, lad, and ye're standing in the midst of Macpherson land." He offered his large hand. "I'm Graeme Macpherson, laird of all ye see and more ye daen't."

Bran grinned as they shook hands. "Bran Macpherson."

Graeme's dark eyes narrowed. "Ye're kin? How?"

"I have no idea." Bran dusted off the seat of his trews and glanced past his host to a black gelding tethered nearby, a freshly killed stag draped over its hindquarters. Blood dribbled onto the ground. Steam rose from the puddle in the sinking chill of the evening. "Your ride?"

Graeme turned the direction of the stranger's gaze. "Tha's a horse. Dae they not have 'em where ye're from?"

"Where I'm from?" He circled in his tracks. Nothing looked even vaguely familiar. "I'm from nowhere near here. Really, take me back where you found me and I'll be gettin' outta your way."

"I foun' ye where ye're standin', lad. Ye fell through tha' tree," he nodded at a large linden, "and landed at my feet." Graeme crossed his massive arms and studied the intruder with a frown. "Are ye daft?"

"Huh?"

The Macpherson made a circle motion with his finger near his ear. "Daft, ye ken?" At Bran's blank stare he continued, "Are ye an idiot?"

"No…you're not gonna believe this…." Bran chuckled.

"Try me." His host smiled.

****

Graeme propped his feet on a stool before the high seat. He gazed into the roaring fire in the hearth of the great hall. "So tell me all abou' yer world."

"Uh, what time—uh, year is it here?" Bran studied the soot darkened walls as women bustled past carrying empty serving platters. Earlier the hall brimmed with locals eating their fill from the laird's table.

"May 1680, according to the British tyrants jes' south of us," Graeme growled.

"Oh, well then I guess you have no grasp of cars, um, carriages that drive fast without horses or indoor plumbin' for tha' matter." Bran's notice tracked a tall blonde across the vast room to the kitchen entry.

"Tha's my champion's sister ye're oglin'. Ye better be in fine shape to take on John if ye look her way again," the laird grinned.

"Just admirin' the natives, sire." Bran turned back to find Graeme watching him through narrowed eyes. Smiling his best salesman smile didn't dent his host's veneer.

5

"Carriages wi' no horses?" Graeme scrubbed his rough chin with a hefty fist. "Tell me more." He tipped a tankard of mead to his mouth.

"Tha's just the beginning. The cities are full of tall buildings called skyscrapers, because they appear to touch the sky. Oh, and there are roads and carriageways all over Scotland now.

"Food's changed. We buy it in shops, um somewhat like goin' to market, but in clean buildings. There're choices from all over the world. There's chocolate from Mexico, perfected in Belgium. There's pasta. It made its way to Italy where they reinvented the dish with tomatoes—um, love apples. Let's see, oh yeah, women have equal rights and can hold seats in parliament, vote, even ask a man to marry."

Graeme chuckled. "As lads, my brothers and I had a tutor. He shared the Celt's magical secrets of cairns and how lairds and kings built their towers around them to capture the power. When movin' sunwise round 'em at dusk and dawn you could slip through to the *other side*.

"One very boring afternoon, during one of 'is endless lectures the three of us ran out. He followed at a brisk pace. We passed through the secret tunnel, which was ne'er anyone's secret, and ended up in the midst of a lot of folks goin' into our castle. The people looked strange, grey-coloured. The air was thick. It was hard to breathe. We were in such a fright the tutor caught us standin' there with our mouths agape.

"A woman in odd clothes with hair cut short like a man's patted my head and called me pet. I think she mistook me fer a primate." The Macpherson grinned.

"Did you ever try again?" Bran leaned forward.

"Aye, a few times. Once I went fer a stroll along the roads. Found my way back, by a map in a library." He pondered the memory.

"How'd I fall when I left the passage?" Bran frowned.

"Instead o' turnin' right at the door, ye ran straight off a cliff into the treetop below." Graeme raked his hand through his shoulder length jet black hair. "Ye could've killed yerself."

Bran grinned. "Nah, I'm lucky like that." He drank golden mead from a clay tankard. "How long ago was yer visit to my world?"

"Twenty-three summers, I was seven at the time." Graeme smiled at the memory.

Bran nodded. "That made it around 1958, I think. You see, in the real world it's May of 1985."

"From what I saw o' where ye're from, I'd say this is the real one."

A page approached the dais. Graeme noticed and gestured him up the steps. "Wha'?"

"Lady Ruane summons ye, sire."

Graeme sobered quickly. "Tell 'er I'm comin'."

"Your wife?" Bran watched the page trot back to the entrance and disappear.

"Nay, my brother's. His daughter's ill. I better go see 'bout her." Graeme shrugged broad shoulders. "We've lost most of our young ones for more than four summers. Can't seem to grow 'em much past a bairn. Soon as they leave their mam's breast the plague snatches 'em away, as it daes all the weak." He rose. "Stay away from the women. They're well-armed and can gut ye before ye blink. I'll be back or send a page fer ye."

Bran stood and nodded in deference. "I pray your news is good, sir."

"Thank ye kindly." The grim laird left his randy guest.

****

Wailing pricked Graeme's hearing as he neared his brother's quarters in the west wing of the castle. He inhaled a bushel of air before he opened the heavy oak door.

Tomas glanced up at Graeme's intrusion. Ruane's head lay in her husband's lap. She screamed; her cry muffled in the blanket covering his still legs. He held her shoulders and rubbed her back.

Their mither stepped out of the nursery, wringing her hands. She held herself stiffly, but appeared on the brink of collapse.

She patted her silvering black hair into place and advanced to her oldest son.

"My soul, Graeme's here." Tomas swiped his face and lifted his wife to her feet. His massive upper body had developed powerfully above the arms of the wheeled chair.

Graeme caught Ruane and held her as she lamented the loss of their youngest daughter. "There now, lass. Alicestar rests in the arms of our Lord." He stroked his sister-in-law's dark hair and wondered what else he could possibly say or do.

Their mither sat beside Tomas, propping her head on his shoulder. He leaned against her and wept.

****

"Sir?" A page climbed the steps of the dais where Bran waited, feet propped before the fire.

Bran broke off conversation with an attractive blonde and turned to the young lad. "Aye, news of the laird's niece?"

The boy's eyes dropped to the stone floor. "Aye, sir. The delight of Carny Castle is no more wi' us."

Bran nodded.

The youngster continued. "The laird sends word that I shew ye to yer room fer the night."

Bran considered Jenna waiting for him at his flat. *Serves her right for putting me off. Can't leave 'til tomorrow anyway.* "Lead on then, lad." He stood and turned to the newest object of his affection and winked, using his best actor's voice. "On the morrow, lass."

****

Bran woke in complete silence of early morning. He looked around and remembered the strange events of the day before. He spoke aloud to an empty room. "I really am in bed, in a castle, in the 17th century." He pinched himself. "Yep, still here…unfortunately alone."

He rolled out and slipped into yesterday's clothes and laced his fashionable, period correct brogues onto his feet. He

8

opened the door and thought he remembered the way back to the great hall.

He began the journey to food and lovely lasses.

Chapter Two

Bran waited anxiously as the phone rang. *What'll I say to her so she'll listen? Will she forgive me for standing up her friend...what was tha' girl's name, Lynn? No, Glynn, or was it Glynda? Man, I don't remember. That was two weeks ago. Maybe she forgot. What am I thinkin'? This is Lizbeth.*

"'Lo?" A sleepy female voice responded.

Ah! Karen, that was it.

"Hey! It's Bran. Did I catch you at a bad time?"

"Worked straight through a twenty-eight hour shift. Do you know wha' time it is?"

"No—oh, the clock says 9:15! Jeez, sorry, sis."

"Not your sister, Bran. What do you want?"

"I need to see you. Have a friend you need to speak with soon. Two words for you, Lizbeth—dead children."

She took a noisy deep breath and sighed. "This better be true and brief or you won't leave here upright." She hung up.

Well, at least she didn't bring up whosis. I'm pretty sure it was Karen.

*****

Lizbeth Macpherson

I pulled on a robe, splashed water on my face, and fastened my hair into a clip. I intentionally left lights off and found my way, by the illuminating glow provided by the security on the property. I wasn't ready to wake all the way up. By the time I walked into the living room the doorbell chimed.

Bran peeked back at me from the fish eye safety lens. He smiled, dimples in his cheeks and chin, reminding me of his brother who left me a widow three years earlier. I wanted to strangle him.

Instead, I invited him inside.

10

He began blabbering as soon as he cleared the door. "I promise I won't keep you but a minute. The weirdest thing happened to me yesterday. You won't believe it."

I dropped onto the deep cushioned olive green sofa and propped my bare feet on the matching hassock. "Get to the point."

"Yeah, that. I found an entrance to the past, Lizbeth. There's a tunnel, well a secret passage, really. Jenna and I stole away from the festival for a little break…."

"Makin' out?" My hair began to slip out of the clip. I caught it and pinned it back up.

"Well, yeah, but anyway, it was while the parade circled the castle three times, at dusk. An opening appeared at the end of a hallway where a wall had partially caved in. There were bright lights, wind, and strange music. It was really cool." He smiled to himself and went quiet.

"And this wouldn't wait 'til later?"

"Oh, sorry. So, I climbed the wall and found a short tunnel. I've never checked out that part of the passage before. After I made the other side, I ran in the direction of the light, through a curtain that felt electrified and ran straight off a cliff into a treetop. I landed in front of The Macpherson, *in 1680*, Lizzie!" His blue-green eyes widened, dimples deepening with his grin. He always reminds me of his brother and that stirs the ire I neglected to vent on Garrett.

"Tell me about dyin' children. Tha's what you said on the phone."

"Yeah, I'm sorry. I'm totally tripping on the fact I was actually there. *I* found a *rift in time* and passed through—*me*!" He chuckled before continuing. "So while we were in the great hall, after dinner, food's incredible by the way, a page came for Graeme…."

"Who?" I perched nearer the edge of the sofa.

"Graeme Macpherson, *The* Macpherson to commoners."

"Continue." I leaned back and tried to figure where Bran's tale would lead.

"Their little ones are dyin' from what Graeme, the laird calls a plague."

11

"Tell me exactly what he said." I crossed my arms against the chill that swept over me and glanced around for a throw, fishing one from behind me and wrapped it over my shoulders.

Bran cleared his throat. "He said they were dyin' not long after they were weaned from their mams. A page came for Himself to go to his sister-in-law because 'the light of Carny Castle was no more.' Graeme's niece died. She was the second daughter his brother, Tomas, lost."

"Tomas?" I was up, pacing. "His brother's name is Tomas?"

"Aye." Bran stood and watched me for a moment, completely sober. "This is significant, isn't it?"

"Maybe. Thanks for coming to me with this. I trust you're smart enough not to blab such nonsense around, right?"

"Lizzie, this isn't nonsense!"

"It will be to other people, Bran. So don't talk about it to anyone but me. How can I help them?"

"I thought maybe you could go over, talk with him, ye ken? See if you can run tests, find out what's causing the problem. I can take us over, Lizzie. I ken how to get to the castle now without walking off the cliff again. What do you say?"

I stood there studying him, wondering if he was nuts. My brother-in-law's not famous for common sense or intelligent decisions when it comes to anything but investments. He's a star in the heavens of the stock exchange. His boss and all his shareholders love him. Every other aspect of life completely eludes Bran. He can't even keep a steady girlfriend.

"I'll think about it, Bran. I can't promise anything right now. Mom's in nursing care, barely holding on. I...can't." I threw my hands in the air and took a deep breath. *Why now?*

His voice softened, his great idea shot full of holes. "I understand, sis. I just thought—well, we could change history there, you ken? If you could've heard the way Graeme's sister-in-law carried on through the night. It's the second child she's lost in two years. His younger brother, Niall, and his wife Cora have a baby boy. I looked at the lad and thought...maybe he doesn't have to die."

I couldn't face Bran. I kept my back to him, staring out at the loch behind my house. The wind picked up and created waves, blowing overspray onto my picture window, obscuring my view. Or maybe it was tears.

He left quietly.

Chapter Three

A fortnight later

Bran yelled over the noise of the packed ballroom. He grinned and nodded, "She'll be here. I ken her ways, Graeme. She never misses the festival ceilidhs. She's friends with most o' the folks here." Bran tossed back his second cocktail and glanced around for a waiter. "We've been doing this for years. Lizzie got me started."

Graeme, resplendent in a formal kilt and linen leine, glanced around the room. People in various forms of dress: costumes from the festival, denims and tee shirts, tuxedos and evening gowns pressed his position. He sighed.

Bran snagged another glass from a passing tray. "Don't worry, man. She's coming." He slapped the big Scot on the back as though they were chums.

Graeme turned a cool look on his companion, then back at the milling crowd. He watched the door and wondered if there was more than one exit. He gazed with longing on a track that he knew led to fresh air, or what passed for fresh air in this world.

Then *she* walked through the entrance. Long dark hair caught on the sides away from her oval face.

Tall, look at the curves, mmm.... No mistaken tha' one fer a lad. She's all woman.

He followed her movements. He glanced around to see if anyone else watched or waited for her.

His palms were damp. He cleared his throat and tried to think what he would say to her, should she find her way to where they stood in the midst of the crush.

Um, hullo, Graeme Macpherson. I'm a friend of Bran's. He scrubbed his palms down the sides of his kilt and took a step towards her. *Where'd she go?*

14

He frantically searched the growing crowd for the dark-haired lass who'd haunted his dreams for almost three summers.

This daen't bode well atall.

****

Lizbeth

The crowded room throbbed with dancers and revelers. I looked for my brother-in-law, but didn't spot him right away. A comrade from work grabbed my attention, so I headed her direction, still searching for Bran.

He caught my eye. He was taller than I'd dreamed.

Sounds silly when I put it into words.

Three years earlier we met in a dream.

Most every night we were together.

I directed my steps, bound for him, afraid to blink. Would he be there when I made the trek to the opposite side of the ballroom? Maybe he just resembled...no, this really was *him*.

He looked around, searching for someone. Then he saw me. A throng of people separated us. I pressed my way through as his scrutiny burned across the distance.

Mercy, what a beautiful man!

I plowed through the mass of flesh that kept us apart.

A smile warmed his eyes. Bran spoke to him. He nodded, maintaining my gaze.

A hand clasped my arm. "Lizbeth?" I recognized a friend's voice and shook myself free, surging ahead, towards *him*.

I broke through, at last, only to find Bran with open arms. He said something.

"Charmed, Bran." I pushed past him to reach my goal.

Graeme Macpherson was the most handsome man I've ever seen, almost pretty, long lashes framing black eyes, full lips and when he smiled, a small gap between his front teeth.

It made me smile.

I considered him. He felt real enough when my hand gripped his arm. My breasts brushed his chest and I savored his scent when, on tiptoes, I shouted in his ear. "Lizbeth Walker-Macpherson." I stepped back and offered my hand.

He took it, leaning forwards and yelled back. "Graeme Macpherson, Lizbeth."

My brother-in-law interrupted to say something else.

I ignored Bran and switched to shouting Gaelic. "Are you more comfortable with your native tongue?" He still held my hand.

Surprised, Graeme continued. "Aye, it makes conversin' easier and he daen't ken much. Is my speech so thick ye picked up on it right away?"

"Oh, nay." I raised a brow as I replied loudly in English.

We stared at each other. The air crackled between us, too dense to breathe deeply.

Bran jumped into the lull. "Um, Graeme's an antiquities expert, darlin', should anyone ask." He patted Graeme's broad back.

Neither of us looked away from our mutual assessment to acknowledge him.

After a moment I yelled above the roar of the room. "What kind of antiquities?"

"Coins, mostly." Graeme shrugged broad shoulders. "Some art, seventeenth century is my specialty. Gael or Scots, of course." He glanced down, realizing he still held my hand and awkwardly released me.

"Fascinating...I love seventeenth century art. I can learn coins."

A brief smile flashed over him, brightening his dark eyes. "Tha's good to know...tha' ye're a fast learner."

"I'm gonna get a drink. May I bring the two of you anythin'?" Bran interjected.

We shook our heads in unison.

"How long have you known my brother-in-law?" I stepped closer to his side and spoke above the crowd.

He leaned down to my ear, his breath teasing my skin. "A fortnight. He sort of fell into my lap."

"Sounds like Bran. How'd you meet?'

"I was hunting. He stepped off a cliff into the top of a tree where I'd tethered my horse."

"Ah, one of his adventures, I suppose."

"Is tha' what he calls it? I almost killed him. Had an arrow nocked, about to shoot when I realized it was a man tumbling through the branches screaming."

"You might regret the decision to let him live," I joked, a smile plastered on my face.

"True that, already have twice." He chuckled.

"How long will you be here?"

"I've been over fer a fortnight, so far."

"What're you doing *here* tonight?"

"Waitin' fer ye." His features softened.

My smile faded. "For me?" I laid my hand on my chest as I studied him. "I'm intrigued. Bran said he was bringing you out to my house for the weekend. We have plenty of time to talk." I paused, catching my breath. "Do you dance, Macpherson?"

The bagpiper began a familiar tune. The pipes always bring tears to my eyes. The minstrels' instruments blended into a soothing melody.

"Aye, madam, I dae. Dae ye follow?"

I laughed. "Aye, sire." I offered my hand again. It felt more natural in his grasp than dangling at the end of my arm where it's always hung.

Graeme accepted it, dropping a kiss on my fingertips. His perusal skimmed down the front of me. "Then let's be about it, lass."

We parted the crowd as we walked to the dance floor. Graeme caught my waist, I rested my hand on his belt, and we moved round the floor. A smile warmed his mouth.

I blushed, the heat creeping up my neck to burn my ears.

We moved together, then apart, together again. When he touched me, I felt fire pierce all the reserves I hold onto like life rafts. The heat from his touch warmed parts of me that hadn't seen sunshine in years.

He was really here. Now.

This really was happening.

I had at least tonight with him.

****

17

Bran stayed at the party after running into a former girlfriend who didn't slap him when he spoke to her.

I pointed out my old BMW in the parking lot. "We're over here. Bran will bring out your luggage when he comes."

"Tha's fine." He held my door and circled to the passenger side to climb in beside me.

I cranked the car and waited for it to warm. "What do you think of our world so far?"

"Feels verra strange. I long for a quiet spot about now. Never heard so much racket in my life, except in the heat of battle." His smile took some of the sting out of his answer. "Is it ever *dark* here?"

"Nay. How long can you stay on this side?" I reversed the car and pulled out onto the carriageway.

"A few more days. I had to learn to function here amongst yer strange ways, without losing my mind. My family thinks I'm in Inverness. I need to return soon." He watched me instead of the passing scenery.

"Hopefully I can help. You'll need to tell me everything you can about what's happening. I might be able to offer suggestions without crossing over. If not, I'll need soil and water samples. I can teach you how to gather the information we need...or I can go with you to fetch it myself."

Graeme smiled. "I prefer ye come home with me. I daen't ken what ye dae."

"I'm an environmental scientist. I'm still studying at university for a degree in Pediatrics. What all that means is that I find out what's happening in the air, land, and water that affects the health of children in a bad way. Does tha' make sense?"

"Aye, I ken why Bran was convinced ye could solve our problem. How dae we begin?"

"When we get to my home we'll discuss the changes in your land over the past.... How long has this plague been killing the children and elderly?"

"More than four summers now."

"Consider what's changed in the past four summers on your land. It could be farming practices, things like that. Has there been any alteration to the soil or water in that time?"

"I'll need to ponder that, lass." He scrubbed his chin with his fist and glanced around.

"Take your time. We'll talk it through; see if we can sort it."

We drove in silence for the remaining ten minutes' journey to my home. We crossed a stone bridge over the loch into my neighborhood. Graeme studied the structures without comment, as we passed. A block and a half later we parked in front of my cottage.

The front of the house resembles a small stone bungalow among many similar structures. Inside is a simple floor plan like all the others. I unlocked the front door while Graeme perused the area, his hands in the pockets of his cloak. We stepped inside the foyer. I stopped to put away my purse. He caught my cape at the nape of my neck, his knuckles brushing flesh, and handed it to me. I took his cloak and hung it on one of the coat hooks. He followed me into the living area, open to the kitchen and a small breakfast nook.

"Verra pleasant." He nodded as he spoke.

"Tha's the kind of thing people say when they can't think of anything nice." I smiled at his expression while flipping on a few dim lights, in hopes his eyes could rest from the assault of light pollution.

"Ah, well. Small—," he glanced around, "'tis a bit bigger than a crofter's cottage. At least yer fire isn't in the middle of the floor." He looked doubtful. "Was tha' more acceptable?"

I laughed. "It's fine, sire. Would you like a drink? I have wine and beer."

"Beer then, thank ye." He approached the sofa and sat warily. The soft cushions settled around him. He stretched his long legs out to cross them at the ankle.

The phone rang. I answered in the kitchen. "Hello?"

"It's about time you got home," my brother's sarcastic voice snapped.

"Hello, Aaron. I have company right now. May I call you later?"

19

"We have matters to discuss that can't wait. The bloody roof leaks and the plumbing needs to be replaced," my brother barked through the phone line.

"This is business. I'll speak with you tomorrow." I hung the phone back on the cradle and disconnected the line. It rang again almost immediately. I ignored the phone jangling in the bedroom.

I set Graeme's beer, mug, and my wineglass on the hassock tray and bent to light the fireplace.

"Take it ye daen't have a servant to dae tha'?"

"Nay, a lady comes in to clean for me every sennight. Between work, university, and my hobbies, like the medieval festivals, I'm busy. Then my mother's in nursing care. I take a run by there each day." I rose and looked about. "If you don't mind, I'd love to change from this fairy outfit." I held the sides of the long sheer skirt in my hands.

"Tha's what ye are, a fairy?"

"Aye, a fairy godmother this year. I grant children's wishes and make all their dreams," I shrugged, "come true." *And someday, perhaps, my own.*

I left him, my face burning, and passed through to the master bedroom. I leaned against the door for a moment and inhaled.

Surely this is a dream.

I pulled a green and cream satin paisley caftan from the closet. Graeme liked green. I slipped out of the fairy frock, dropping it into the laundry. The stays and period cotton underwear went with it. Today was my last day at festival for the next several. I'd taken holiday to go with Graeme, if necessary. I also left word I wouldn't be in the lab for a few days. It's my day job when I'm not playing make-believe.

The satin of the floor length caftan felt cold against my flesh. Sliding my feet into my soft brown leather mules, I opened the door to rejoin my guest.

Graeme's head rested on the back of the sofa, his eyes closed. By the time I circled he was alert.

He mumbled, "Ye're beautiful." His full lips parted as he watched me through narrowed eyes.

I paused before joining him on the sofa. "Thank you." I almost smiled. "I haven't heard those words in a long time. My mother has kept my ego primed throughout my life, but she fails to notice these days. Between pain and heavy medication, she struggles." I picked up my wine glass for a taste.

A pad and pen lay beside the tray. I'd begun a list of possible pollutants in Graeme's land. First I wanted to hear what he thought about the plague. I sat back against the arm of the sofa with the pad and pen, pulling my knees up and tucking my caftan beneath me. I gazed his direction.

He watched me. "Tha's a shame; ye should wake to those words every mornin'."

I smiled. "Well, I wake up alone. I had a cat for years. He was old and died. He didn't talk to me though, even on his best day." I glanced down at my list, hoping to cover my discomfort. "Now, what do you think causes the plague? You said the children get sick after they're weaned?"

He nodded. "Aye, they daen't live, maybe a fortnight past. Our mither is," he searched for words and switched from English to Gaelic, "a bit of a healer. We convened with the healers and physicians in our land. She presided over them. There was some talk of ill children downstream, more than usual. I've studied what happened with my nieces, as they were closest to me. We lost Leslie two summers past. Then Ruane, my brother's wife, was loathe to stop nursing Alicestar. She was afraid tha' what happened, would." He picked up his mug and took a long drink, compressed his lips and set it back on the tray. "The only difference I can see in what they did was drink water after leavin' their mams."

I pondered that for a moment. "From a pewter mug or cup?"

He shook his head. "Nay, we have a clay pit in our territory. The healer, Agnes, says it's better for drinkin' and eatin' vessels than metals."

"Tha's a wise healer." I smiled.

"Mayhap, but they daen't stand up well in the midst of a brawl." He cut a sidelong glance my way.

21

I fought a smile and quickly shifted my regard to the pad. "What changes have occurred the past five summers to your property?"

He began to list growth in yields of grain, vegetables. "Some years are verra good, some are no'. The last two have been good. Niall could tell ye more, tha's his part of runnin' the land." He closed his eyes for a moment. "Oh, Niall started keepin' sheep and a few goats. We always had cattle and fowl, but he began raisin' sheep...abou'...four summers ago."

"Is your drinking water from a well?" I made notes.

"Aye, a deep one."

"Do the children eat differently?"

"They may eat vegetables and fruit from the garden and the wild. My chatelaine's a forager for wild things, particularly carrots, mushrooms, and onions. She and the local healer are sisters. They have a grand time with wild herbs and roots. Mary's always lookin' for somethin' edible; her sister Agnes, digs for what she calls useful."

I nodded and wrote down what he said.

His fingers brush across my toes.

"What's this?" He glanced up, amused.

"Um, nail polish. Women paint their toes and fingernails. I don't paint my fingernails because I work with my hands. It wouldn't last and might interfere with chemical tests."

"Mmm...I saw lasses at ceilidh with paint on their fingers and long, claw-like nails." He grimaced.

"Aye, that's a fad; a way of doin' a thing that's popular. A lot of women grow their nails out or pay to have fake ones glued on."

He touched my silver anklet. "Daes someone own ye?"

"It's jewelry...adornment. The idea was taken from slave's anklets, but the decoration was made lighter in weight and pretty rather than heavy iron."

"Ah." He nodded, with a smile.

"Bran gave me the anklet for my birthday last year. It has my nickname engraved on the surface."

He turned the name plate up and read. "Lizzie?"

I smiled. "Aye, my mother calls me Lizzie. Bran picked it up from her."

Dropping his hand, he touched my foot lightly. It was thrilling. I felt a shiver pass through me, though I fought to be still.

"Ye have lovely feet." He glanced up again, smiling. "And yer eyes, I'm curious what color they are."

I wondered if he had any idea what he was doing to me. I whispered, "Thank you, sire. I think my eyes are kind of blue-gray, like storm clouds over the sea. Tha's what my father used to tell me anyway."

He stretched and leaned back into the cushions.

I glanced at the clock. "It's very late for you. What say you to bed and we'll talk more on the morrow?"

He smiled and gave me a quick scan. "Sounds good." He stood with some effort and glared back at the cushions with a frown.

"It takes practice getting up from soft pillows."

He drained his mug and reached a hand out to me. I took it. He tugged, and I was on my feet. I put the pad and pen on the hassock and crossed my arms.

"Come, I'll show you to your bed." I led him to a guest room. "Here you are." I switched on a bedside lamp and turned to him. "Privy's in there." I pointed to another doorway. "If you need anythin' I'm in the room next to you." I jerked my thumb to the right.

"Mmm…I'll manage, thank ye kindly."

I stopped at the door. "Need I wake you?"

"Nay, I rise wi' the sun." He unpinned the brooch holding his breacan across his broad shoulder and grasped his belt.

"Tomorrow, then." I nodded, smiling.

Padding to my bedroom, I closed the door silently, to change into a long-sleeved white gown and brush my teeth. I turned out the light then slid between the sateen sheets of my bed.

Thunder rolled in the distance. Rain fell in sheets, freckling the window panes when a wind gust blew against the house. I watched shadows play across the ceiling as lightning performed a cloud-to-cloud waltz.

23

I must have fallen asleep because I woke from a dream shaking. I turned on my side to gaze out the window across the room. It still rained in torrents.

The man who haunted my slumber was in the next room. Pondering the big question, do I dare disturb him? I was halfway to his door before it struck me what I was about.

Quietly twisting the knob, I peeked inside, and spied Graeme lying on his side facing the middle of the bed. I eased in and soundlessly closed the door. When I turned back he propped on one elbow, watching me in the dim light. His chest was bare, dark against the white sheets.

The curtains in the room billowed in a breeze from open windows on the sheltered side of the house. Our air must feel stifling to him.

I walked around the bed opposite him and he folded the covers back for me. I slipped between the sheets and faced him. He lay back and positioned his right hand flat on the pillow between us. I did the same with my left hand, touching the side of his. He moved his hand to clasp mine.

Closing my eyes, I dozed.

Upon waking again, I looked up to find a large, gorgeous, naked man walking to the bathroom. I glanced at his pillow, still warm to my touch.

He was real.

Chapter Four

Slowly, I opened the door to the living area, unsure whether Bran arrived during the night. As I stepped out I heard his key rattle at the front entry. He stood there agog, hefting Graeme's valise in his hand. I took it from him without a word and placed it on Graeme's bed, closing his door behind me.

Hurrying to the kitchen, I turned on the coffee pot, then on to my room to shower and dress. I pulled on a long dark blue linen skirt and a knit sweater, sliding my feet into the soft brown leather mules of the previous night. When I stepped out, Bran sat on a stool at the bar sipping from a mug.

"Well, I guess you didn't miss me last even', eh?" He grinned.

"Nay, no' for a minute." I stepped into the kitchen for a cuppa.

He folded the newspaper he brought inside and smiled. "I return to Edinburgh today."

"Godspeed. And thank you for introducing us. I'll go across with Graeme…this evening and return to test the soil and water samples we collect. When're you comin' back?" I blew across the surface of the hot coffee and sipped.

"In a few days. If you want me to fetch you from the castle grounds, call my mobile." He stood and stretched. "I'll be off then. You two have fun. You could do with a little fun in your life, Lizzie." He wasn't teasing.

I smiled, sure of his implications as we walked across the room. "I doubt we're thinkin' the same, though. What's fun to me would be boring to you."

Bran paused at the front entry and looked back wistfully. "You may be surprised at tha', lass." He closed the door before I could respond.

Graeme spoke up behind me. "Fine marnin'."

25

"Aye, isn't it?" Responding to the old Doric greeting, I headed back to the kitchen. "Did you sleep well?"

"Aye, ye?" He must be an excellent card player. His eyes didn't reveal a thing though the twitch at the corners of his mouth fought a smile.

"Aye, fairly." I poured coffee and used my mug to hide my embarrassment, handing his over across the bar. "I have errands to tend. I'll return in a few hours and we'll prepare to leave for…your home."

He wore dark jeans and a white ghillie shirt, the lacing on the front placket hanging loose.

I longed to tie it.

Cannot bear anythin' undone.

He caught me gazing at his chest and grinned. "Wha'?"

"Would it be forward if…." I pointed to his shirt. "Things incomplete drive me mad. Would it be a bother?"

He glanced down and laughed. "Whatever ye need to dae, lass." He turned and spread his legs for me to step closer. "My leines have buttons. I daen't ken what to dae with strings. They're fer lasses gowns, are they not?"

Walking around the bar, I stood between his knees and tied the lacing on the ghillie shirt. "There. Here laces are used on both men's and women's clothes."

His hands rested on my hips, his eyes laughing. "Feel better now?"

"Yes." I didn't hurry to leave him, even knowing what could happen.

He watched me try to figure out what to do, smiling, then spoke softly, "Ye feel good in my hands, Lizbeth." His eyes narrowed as the smile faded.

Grasping his wrists, I tore myself away. "Thank you, sir." I beat a hasty retreat to the other side of the bar and refilled our coffee cups as though it was my mission in life.

"I'll change back to my kilt before we leave this even. I saw a few kilts walking abou' when Bran took me round. It's good to ken they're still useful. Breacan's our heritage, our colours worth dyin' fer." He hefted his mug. "I like this brew."

"It's just strong coffee."

"We have it at home occasionally. Our mither's Spanish."

That explained his jet black hair and onyx eyes.

"We dae a bit o' trading wi' the Mackintoshes' shipping company. Mither loves coffee, but only orders it twice a year." He took another long drink, savoring the flavor. "She has an awful fear of liking anythin' too well. Says it canna be good fer ye." He sat his cup on the bar.

Tilting my head, I found my voice. "Do you wanna come with me this morning?"

"Is yer business inside buildings?"

"It is." I grimaced and sighed.

"Then I won't." He pushed back from the bar and stretched. "Yesterday was enough fer a summer or more. I'll explore yer loch while ye're away and feel fitter fer the time out."

"Unlike you, I don't own a loch. I own the house and the property to the edge of the patio."

"Bran told me of yer strange rules. I daen't actually *own* anythin'. The clan oversees everythin' in our boundaries. Ye canna own wha' God made fer everyone."

"I like your way better than the one I'm bound to." *For now, anyway.* I toasted English muffins in the countertop oven and stirred up frozen juice from a can. "Let's break our fast and I'll get busy." I took a deep breath, my back to my guest. "Are ye goin' to say anythin' about me comin' to your bed last night?"

"Ye weren't walking in yer sleep then?" A smile flavored his tone.

"Nay, don't sleepwalk."

His voice was soft, his tone playful. "Ye daen't snore either."

Keeping my back to him, I stopped stirring and poured two glasses of apple juice, retrieving butter and jam from the fridge to sit on the bar.

Scottish men are sexy. Not in the way Italian or Spanish men are, with their fluid movements, but the look in their eyes warns and entices a woman at the same time. The amount of testosterone harnessed in that regard tips the scale. If a woman dares return his smile *and* his wink, she's booked the evening. It's not an especially subtle gaze, but an 'I can be had if you can, darlin'' declaration.

I couldn't meet The Macpherson's eyes but tried to keep a pleasant expression on my face like it was all a joke.

When I sat the juice in front of Graeme he lifted it to his nose and then his mouth. A frown followed. "It tastes...," his tongue worked around inside his mouth. "almost of apples."

I laughed. "Almost? This is what we call apple juice in our world."

He grinned. "When we have an abundance of fruit our chatelaine makes jams from the overripe. Then what's left we mill into cider. What isn't consumed turns to vinegar but a good deal of it into wine." He held the glass up for inspection. "There's no," his fingers fluttered in the air, "pulp. How dae ye ken it was made from apples?"

I considered his question. "I don't know that it was, come to think of it. I'm an environmental scientist and I ken there are animal...products used to make certain flavors...stronger than they are in their natural state. Tha' way the makers can call them natural flavors and not be lying." I held the glass up to the light. "You're right." I poured both glasses of liquid down the drain.

He laughed for the second time to my hearing. It was a happy sound. There's too little laughter in my life.

When he lifted the tub of butter-like substance from my refrigerator, I knew what was coming. I placed my hand over his and shook my head. "We must eat something. This is what we have. I have no cows to milk, no churn for butter. I buy food in a market."

He grinned for a moment then looked at my mouth, stood, leaned over the bar, and kissed me. His lips felt like they fit mine, not too hard, not too soft. His hand held my neck gently. The tip of his tongue traced the part of my lips. He sat back on his stool, opened the tub, and spread yellow goo on his bread.

It took me a few seconds to recover. Then I dipped my knife in the goo, and covered my toasted bread as well.

When my voice could be trusted, I spoke. "The lab has supplies we'll need. I'm going there first, then to see my mother. Shan't linger, just pop in on her. She's particularly restless mid-morning. It seems to be her worst time for pain."

He dipped his head once. "Dae what ye must, Lizbeth. I appreciate ye helpin' me."

"What ruse do you have planned to explain my presence to your family?" I leaned on the bar.

"Been considering that. Will ye marry me?" His dark eyes appeared guileless, his expression sober. He watched me closely.

"What happens when you don't need me anymore?" I flushed, locking eyes with him.

He took a moment. His voice was thoughtful. "Why dae ye believe I won't need ye?"

"I mean when we're finished. When you solve the mystery of premature deaths in your kingdom, then what?"

He shrugged. "Then ye stay and be my wife if it's wha' ye want. Tha's what marriage is, man," he pointed to his chest, "woman," he pointed at me, "together until one of us dies. At least in my world it's tha' way."

"Would you like more coffee?" My hands quivered like leaves caught in a gale.

"I would at that." He grinned, dazzling white. There was an abundance of phosphorus in the well water he drank.

The phone rang. "Hullo?" I swallowed the bite of toasted English muffin in my mouth.

"Have you finished with your *business* yet?" My brother's hateful manners frustrate me. He's a vicar. He should be kind, at least sometimes.

"Nay, we haven't concluded, Aaron. I told you I'd call you and I will. Goodbye." I heard him yelling before the phone was cradled.

Graeme studied me. "Angry lover?"

"My brother. He and his wife live in Mom's house and he wants me to sign over the deed to him." I studied the yellow spread, mostly unmelted on my bread. "I won't. She's still alive and even though she'll never go home again...." I choked back a sob.

Graeme covered my hand, resting on the countertop, with his own. "I ken yer problem, but must he be so mean?"

His beautiful hand, large and square, sparse black hair lying flat against his dark skin, clean square nails, held my gaze.

"Aaron's different. I don't recall what happened to make him like he is, but he's very unhappy. I don't like to add to his troubles; however, I can't let the property go until Mom— passes." I looked up into his black eyes, so dark the pupils and irises fused.

Graeme squeezed, then loosed my hand and sat back.

I poured coffee, refilling both our cups. "I wrote down the lab and care home numbers by the phone if you need me. Bran said you ken the phone." I placed his cup on the bar, trying not to slosh over the rim in my quaking.

He sipped and smiled. "I won't."

I nodded.

He watched me, studying every move. "Bran set up a place to keep money. He put yer name on everythin', as I requested." He sighed and removed a checkbook from his back pocket.

"A bank account?" I frowned.

"Aye, tha's what he calls it. He sold coins and put money aside fer ye. Whate'er ye need, lass, use tha'. I daen't want ye dipping into yer own funds, ken? He said ye'd be good to almost one million pounds fer now. Daes tha' make sense to ye?"

I nodded, picked up the checkbook, and opened it to the balance, £10,000. I closed it and glanced up at him. He eagerly awaited my answer.

"Aye, thank you kindly, sir. It's more than adequate."

"If ye need anythin', Bran will sell more coins. Ye'll jes' need to tell him before the sum gets low."

£10,000 was equivalent to four month wages for me. It was certainly adequate.

****

30

Returning from my errands, I found Graeme just coming in from the loch. He smiled and offered his hand for the box I carried in from the lab.

"How long until we leave for the place we go to enter your kingdom?" I slipped out of my jacket and hung it in the foyer.

"We have a little time yet." He waited for me, placing the box on the bar. We made our way to the sofa.

The way he switched between Gaelic and English must have been challenging for him, yet he was determined I understand his meaning.

"If we're betrothed I must know something about your family."

"Are ye havin' second thoughts abou' this?" He sent a sidelong glance my way as he settled into the soft cushions. "Ye say it as though there's another option, Lizbeth."

"It was a turn of phrase. I'm nervous, Graeme, about to do something I've never done with a man—who is foreign to me." I pondered where my steps were leading, into an unknown but historied existence of the clan I married into the first time. "So, tell me who lives in your castle." I sat against the arm of the sofa, tucking my legs beneath me.

He laid his thick arm along the back and considered me. "Tomas and Ruane live below stairs. A cart overturned and pinned my eldest brother beneath, crushing his legs. That was ten summers ago. Their son, Rodney, is the only child left to them. They lost both daughters to the plague. My youngest brother, Niall married Cora. They have a bairn, William. Our mither lives with us." He squirmed. "Ye'll meet them when we arrive. We'll marry on the morrow and…." He waved his hand through the air.

"All that." I nodded.

He grinned. "Then we begin the quest for the plague. We can't travel abou' unmarried, Lizbeth, unless we take a chaperone, which would be inconvenient. I'll tell them yer family allowed ye to come wi' me because we married in their kirk before we left. Our mither will insist we marry in our kirk so she can be certain I've taken a bride."

"I see." I smiled. "Are ye a bit of a rogue, then, Macpherson?"

31

He paled. "Nay! She's been looking fer a wife fer me three summers now." He blushed and grinned. "A rogue, indeed." He reached for my hand, compared it to his. "Ye need to mind ye daen't talk to anyone but me abou' the plague. They need to believe ye hale from a near clan. Ye're a Walker?"

"Aye."

"Tha's good. Walkers are more than a day's ride away. It explains why I come back with ye."

"I need to return to run the tests on the samples we collect. It'll take several days. Then my mother's illness...."

"Aye, that'll keep ye gone. When it's over, ye'll come home to me straightaway."

He made it all sound so easy. I smiled. "Do you think your brothers will speak with me?"

He shook his head. "Tomas, mayhap in time, Niall, nay."

Venturing into unknown territory, I felt I'd choke with jealousy. "Have you ever been married?"

"Nay, but once betrothed. Our parents arranged the marriage. Their clan joined ours fer protection." His dark gaze latched onto a small flame lapping a log in the fireplace. He cleared his throat. "Her brothers were bringin' her to me but they were attacked on the journey and she died." He turned back to me. "Not long after, I begin to have strange dreams...."

I stopped breathing and whispered, "Abou' wha'?"

He smiled. "Lizbeth, we daen't need to say everythin' right now, dae we? We have a lifetime to talk."

"Nay. Have you a woman?" I looked away from his piercing eyes.

"Why?" His voice was gruff.

"Do you keep a woman? If we're to marry, I have a right to know."

"To be assured, ye *daen't* even have the right to ask such a question." His attempt to gentle his tone failed.

"If tha's the case, we shan't marry." I turned to rise, trying to smile. "Why should I care what your people think of me, traveling with you without being married? I'll return to

32

my life here when all is done. Bran can do the running to save you embarrassment."

He seized me, pulling me onto his lap. No small feat, that, at 5'10 I'm a big girl.

"Tell me why ye think I keep a woman." His voice sounded amused, his strong hands gently caressed my back.

He was doing his best to make light of an awkward situation. It wouldn't occur to him that he was taking liberties. We were alone in my home and I *had* joined him in his bed during the night.

I could barely swallow, much less talk. I managed to squeeze out a few words. "I didn't say you did. I only asked. Please tell me, aye or nay."

"Nay. Dae a few summers ago in a village far from our own. I've had no one since. Lizbeth, I promise to be…faithful to ye."

A moan escaped from me, as I closed my eyes and sighed.

He tilted my chin to fit his mouth and kissed me again. I fell into it, like slippin' in the muddy edge of the loch on a rainy day. Complete immersion followed.

Chapter Five

Dressed in one of my best medieval costumes, I packed two more in a tapestry bag that would pass inspection from a distance. I crammed the flannel wrapped vials, chemicals, and tools into a leather pouch that looked old to me because it belonged to my great-grandfather. Graeme propped on the door frame, changed from jeans into his kilt and leine, knee high leather brogues laced up on his legs, the size of young tree trunks.

He shifted and reached for my bags. "I'll leave garments since we'll be wed when we return."

"Aye." I croaked, struggling to swallow again.

He hefted both bags and carried the lot to the front entry to set them down. I followed.

"Lizbeth, ye daen't have to be afraid." He reached for me.

"I'm not." Blood rushed to my face at the lie.

"Aye, ye are. I won't allow anythin' bad to happen to ye." He caught my face in his hand and growled, "Look at me, lass. I'll guard ye wi' my own life. I'm about to be yer husband and yer laird."

Our eyes met. "I trust you, Graeme." The words didn't come out as robustly as I wished.

He nodded doubtfully. "Ye will in time. I've never broken an oath. I'm already responsible fer ye." He smiled and bent to kiss me again.

I held his arm with both my hands, feeling as though I drifted in one of the dreams where we meet. I expected to find myself alone in bed, disappointed again upon waking. My eyes opened to find the most beautiful man I've ever encountered smiling down at me.

"I love the look on yer face when I kiss ye, Lizbeth." He smiled and hefted luggage again and we left my home behind.

****

A taxi dropped us out front of the replica of a medieval village. Gaslit torches flared up and down the narrow, rocky paths, all the way to the edge of the present day shops and byways.

We used my security badge from the festival to get past guards. There was a gathering of workers and minstrels for the supper hour in the outdoor cafe. A friend waved and blew me a kiss as he munched a burrito. Another turned and called out hullo.

"Let me use modern facilities one more time before we go through." I tugged my hand away from Graeme and handed over the leather pouch I carried.

"Aye, go on then, lass."

I scurried past colleagues shouting to me. I waved and kept moving but ran into a girlfriend who chatted for a moment until she realized she kept me from the loo.

Drying my hands on paper towel, I reentered the arena.

Nearby musicians dressed in period attire, struck up a woeful melody. The violin wept in the hands of a master, Matt Gordon. The lute wailed, piercing hearts and ears. A lovely soprano sang a somber tune.

No turnin' back, once you choose to go.
No place to laugh, all abide in woe.
You're steppin' out from everythin' ye know,
no goin' back, no goin' back.

"I'm ready, sire." I grasped Graeme's arm.

He glanced down at me frowning, his mouth open slightly. "Ye're sure o' this?"

"What?" I asked, noting his uneasiness.

A mallet struck the bass drum, sending a chill through me.

"Nothin'," he shook his head. "Nothin', lass. This way."

We left the area for the back of the castle, but the haunting lyrics shadowed our leaving.

Ye're pressing on 'gainst an awful foe.
Ye have to reap every seed you strew.

35

Fate's die was cast very long ago.
No goin' back, no goin' back.

We passed around the rear of the castle ending our third and final trip. Graeme checked with me again before he pushed the stone. "Ye're sure, Lizbeth?"

"Aye, I pledged my support, sire." An eerie stillness shrouded my pleasant mood.

He reached for the edge of the portal and pulled it open. "It'll be time." We stepped through. He struck a match, scored from Bran, on the stone, and laid it to the torch by the door, lighting our way. He hoisted the flaming stick and proceeded.

Shivering, I wrapped my arms around myself. "It's cold."

"Aye and damp. Walk this way. Stay with me." He reached his hand out to me.

"Don't worry about losing me, won't happen." I grasped his belt with my right hand and followed on his heels.

We carefully traversed the stone corridor, slick with moisture. In a flash, brilliant light loomed through the broken wall at the end of the curved tunnel. The dazzling, whirling gleam forced me to close my eyes.

"*Tha's* wha' we're looking fer." Relief strengthened his resolve.

****

"Are ye well?" Graeme turned to me in the intense light. He lifted my chin.

I held onto him, feeling dizzy. Passing through the curtain of static electricity caused my skin to feel prickly and ache.

"It throws ye off kilter at first. After ye make the crossing a few times, yer body gets accustomed to the change."

"If you say so." I swallowed nausea, brought on by the passing or perhaps the fear gnawing my gut.

"I dae, Lizbeth. Come, let's get ye home to meet our family and we'll settle down fer a bit." He entwined his arm with mine and led me through the blinding light, free of ozone depleting smog.

When we arrived, he opened the front door of the castle I was familiar with, from dreams and the festivals I participated in each year. I stopped in the foyer to get my bearings and let my eyes adjust to the dimness of pre-electrical lighting. Graeme took my bags to hand off to a servant mumbling instructions about where I was to lodge and to announce our arrival.

He gripped my shoulders and turned me into a room off the entrance. Hide covered manuscripts, paintings, a few books and collectibles lined shelves on the perimeter, reaching ten feet up the walls. Lamps glowed, throwing the corners of the library into shadows.

There was a good desk, backed to the window for best light. I inhaled the fragrance of peat fire and old things. A fine wool rug covered the stone floor. The chairs and settee were tapestry covered. It was a pleasant room.

"I'll give ye a moment to get yer bearings before meetin' our family." He kept his hands somewhere on my body, gently touching.

I wondered if he was concerned I'd dart away if left to myself. There was nowhere for me to go, but he probably wouldn't consider that. I smiled and tried to calm my racing heart.

When he felt I was ready, he pulled me round to face him. "We'll go into the parlor fer tea, Mither's tradition. The family gathers there. They expect us." He smiled, the gap in his teeth so endearing. "Are ye ready?"

"Aye, we may proceed." I tried to feel confident.

"Good." He bent and kissed me. "Stay beside me."

"Aye, sire." I followed him to the massive oak door I'd failed to notice upon entering and passed through ahead of him. I turned back to wait for him to take my hand, securing it in the bend of his arm.

We made the trek across a large corridor hung with paintings. Displayed around the room were armor and weapons. An overlapping row of shields lined the top of the wall.

Graeme stopped to explain. "Each shield represents a Macpherson fallen in battle. They're tributes to our ancestors and heritage."

Watching pride animate his features, I nodded assent. *I'll never tire of you or the stories of your people. I'll always look forward to hearing your voice.* I felt pleased with his legacy.

We continued across the galleria to another large oak door with iron hinges. He glanced down at me and whispered. "They're in here."

I held his consideration a moment, swallowed my fear, and readied myself.

He opened the door to a room full of people, all in various stages of getting tea. We stood inside until they stilled.

He spoke Gaelic. "This is my wife, Lizbeth." He looked at me. "Our family, mo a `stor."

His brothers nodded as he introduced them, but Ruane and Cora immediately came along each side of me.

Ruane took my hand then hugged me. "We're so happy to have ye here, Lizbeth." Cora nodded agreement and slipped a kiss on my cheek.

My eyes teared. I couldn't remember a time I'd felt more welcome or that I belonged to so many people. My mother was all I had for more than fifteen years. Aaron was always more a trial than a friend, even though he was blood kin.

I swiped my cheeks as an elegantly beautiful dark-haired woman approached. The ladies parted to make a spot for her in front of me.

She kissed both my cheeks and whispered, "Welcome, Lizbeth. I am Graeme's mither and now, yours." She pulled me into a warm embrace and sighed. "Ah, another daughter."

Graeme kept me tucked closely to his side. He poured my tea and handed me a china plate embossed with a red rose. It held a delicate teacake with a sturdy biscuit alongside.

Every glance we traded lingered.

At one point, Tomas, a large ginger-haired man in a wheeled chair, laughed at something Niall said just under his breath. Graeme glared and silence reigned in their corner of the room.

Niall favored Tomas in coloring but Graeme in stature. They all had the mark of the gap between their front teeth, I assumed inherited from their father.

Tomas finally spoke directly to me as he raised a cloudy green glass half full of dark liquid. His deep voice resonated in the room. "Welcome to our clan, Lizbeth. We're pleased ye've made a family man of our brother."

Niall raised his glass and concurred. "At long last. Here's to a new era."

Graeme smiled and raised his teacup, but his attitude was sharp at his brothers' delight. "Ta, lads."

Ruane braved male domination and spoke up. "As ye're finished wi' tea, may I shew ye to yer chamber, Lizbeth?"

She stood as she spoke, so I responded by standing. "Aye, it would be well."

I glanced back at Graeme for direction. A curt nod was all I received.

"Thank ye kindly, Ruane." I followed her from the room, but not before I heard Tomas' voice again.

"She's a beauty, Graeme, but is she blind? I can't see the likes of ye with her. Trickery, mayhap? Will she wake from a spell only to find herself married to the Macpherson ogre?"

Graeme answered. His words were lost to me as we crossed the gallery.

Ruane led me to the chamber beside Graeme's. She informed me, as we passed where each family member lodged.

"Tomas and I have an apartment below stairs. We...our daughters were but bairns and stayed with us there. Now only...us." She paled.

My heart tightened for that kind woman's loss. I wanted to assure her we would find out what caused their deaths. I stayed silent and squeezed her hand.

"Our son, Rodney is old enough for an upper room. Our mither lives in an apartment down the hallway. Her maid's name is Nellie and she's fiercely loyal. She began with Mither when she was first in service at a tender age. When our mither sends fer ye, it'll be Nellie comin' to fetch ye."

We reached my chamber. Ruane opened the door and preceded me into the room. I followed to find it simply furnished with dark furniture, the bed covered with a white embroidered quilt. It was as though they'd visited my bedroom at home to check my taste. A fresh fire burned in the hearth in the heavily chilled room.

"Graeme will be in to ye shortly, I imagine. He'll see to the parson after tea. Ye'll need to marry, for Mither, in our kirk. Have ye a dress in mind fer the ceremony? We're near enough in size, I can loan ye one if need be."

Reaching for my bag, I began to unpack. "I brought few gowns as I must return home at once. My mam is dyin'. I want to be with her 'til the end. Graeme was most insistent we come to his home and marry here now." I pulled out a soft, sage green, silk empire waist gown trimmed with ecru lace. I snapped it once to shake out wrinkles. "I'm sure as it hangs the wrinkles will relax."

Ruane watched me with interest then touched my shoulder. "We're sisters now, Lizbeth. We share everythin'. Daen't fail to ask fer whate'er ye need. Cora and I are well provided, as ye will be as the wife of The Macpherson. But until ye're settled, we can supply ye with more than necessary."

"Thank you, Ruane."

She smiled and hugged me. "I'll be off then and see ye on the morrow."

"Aye, thank you, again." I followed her to the door and closed it behind her. The bed looked inviting and I had nothing else to do until Graeme showed up so I pulled back the quilt, lay down, curled into a ball, and slept in complete silence.

Chapter Six

I swatted at a fly teasing my ear. Abruptly, I woke and sat up to find Graeme hovering. He sat on the side of the bed and massaged my outstretched leg.

"Ye were asleep. I got tired of waitin' fer ye to wake." His mouth constantly threatened to smile. His merry black eyes held secrets I ached to know.

"The bed's comfortable." I scooted over to allow room for him to lie down.

He slid into place. "Aye, 'tis. Well, is this where ye want to consummate our marriage or will ye come to my chamber?"

Whispering, I questioned him, "When do we marry?" No telling who was at the keyhole. I lay beside him, not touching him, yet every fiber aware of his proximity.

"On the morrow, after Matins. We'll go to the chapel. Mither, Ruane, and Niall will be witnesses."

He propped on one elbow and gave me a studious look. His gaze dropped to the lacing on my dress. He plucked the bow and began loosening the cord. Then he stopped and lay back, staring at the ceiling. "We're already married so it would seem strange if we daen't sleep together."

The same thought flitted through my mind before I napped. "Well, we were together last night." I gulped and wished I hadn't spoken. The memory of his fine removal to the bath that morning scorched my face.

"Aye, true that." He rolled to his side, checked the progress he made on my lacing and moistened his lips. His face lowered to my ear. He whispered heated words, "Must I wait for the morrow or may I seduce ye now?" He drew back and studied my reaction.

We were on his turf and he was sure of himself. It wasn't like I'd resisted him earlier in the day. He had every right to ask.

"Why did you not seduce me last night?"

41

He smiled shyly before answering. "Um—ye weren't ready, lass."

"What do you think is best?" I sent the ball back to his court.

He sighed and dropped onto the pillow. "I feared ye'd say that." He studied the ceiling for a few minutes. "I'm a patient man. I can wait to have ye if I must, but I will have ye, woman. We're sharin' a bed tonight. So, here or in my chamber?"

"Whatever suits milord." I looked away and bit my lip to keep from laughing.

****

The parson performed the ceremony quickly, but I have to say it was beautiful. Particularly the part when we promised to worship each other's bodies. I'd read about that, so I wasn't surprised, but the emotional and physical attachments we committed in front of his family almost overwhelmed me. I wanted to sit on one of the hand-carved benches and cry, try to come to terms with the meaning of it all.

There was no time for nostalgia. My husband was anxious.

Graeme held me gently and kissed me passionately. He whispered in my ear. "I promise to take the worshipping part seriously, Lady Macpherson."

I smiled and he kissed me again.

We left Mither and Ruane in chapel. Niall followed us out, and with a wave, left us at the barmekin to go to the fields.

Graeme held my hand as we hurried to his chamber. I giggled, trotting to keep up with him. Once inside he closed and latched the door.

The same dark wood fixtures in my room furnished his chamber. Sheep skins stitched together covered his bed. A maid or page had been in to fold back the covering.

"Now, may I undress ye? Are ye willin'?" His touch was gentle as he turned me to face him.

I waited for him to begin the dance; after all I now belonged to him.

"Lizbeth, I hope ye wan' me as desperately as I wan' you." He smiled.

"Aye, milord." I bobbed my head once, giving him permission.

He began on the lacing of my dress.

I removed the brooch pinned to his shoulder, unbuckled his belt and leaned back to watch his kilt fall to the floor.

He lifted me as though I weighed very little and laid me across the bed. He climbed in with me. His kisses were just as unhurried as before, but his hands explored. He'd left my cotton shift on me, so little separated us.

I had a thought and whispered, "Husband, what abou' the sheet?"

He murmured, "There's a page waiting fer it." He gazed into my eyes. "It's no' a problem. Mither gave me a bottle of color to use. I told her we'd already been together, more than once."

"Do you tell her everything?" I frowned.

He grinned. "Nay, tha's Niall." He mussed my hair with his face. "She said how like my parents we are. They required assistance on their wedding day as well. Her confession conjured images *I* could have lived without."

As he worked his way down my neck to the top of the shift, I sighed.

Smiling, he glanced up. "Wife, may I remove the remainder of yer wardrobe?"

"Aye, sire." I sat up and allowed him to slip the thin shift over my head.

He shed his long tailed leine and joined me. I gloried in our exploration of each other's bodies. His strokes and kisses were tender.

He pulled my hand to him, his expression serious. "Touch me, my love. I ken this might be a challenge." His face nestled in my hair beside my ear, sending shock waves through my frame.

I grasped him and understood his concern. He was large.

"Nay, just...go slowly, sire." I opened myself to him as he rolled over me, tracing a path on his way across my burning flesh. I wanted him. My body screamed for him. He lingered, perhaps as recompense for resisting the night before.

After what felt like an hour he tested my reception. I gasped as he pulled back and pressed further a few times before we joined completely. He paused to allow me time to become accustomed to the intrusion.

I moved first to assure him we were united in more than a physical sense. He smiled as he watched me. I was intrigued with his attention to my delight and achieved ecstasy too soon the first time.

He groaned, shuddered, gasped, and lowered himself to tease my skin with his mouth.

He growled into my ear. "Woman!" He slid his arm under my hips and rolled to his back. He brushed hair from my face, holding it back and peered into my eyes.

"Aye, sire?" I met his gaze.

"Lizbeth, I should've tol' ye before."

I whispered, "What?"

His hand softly kneaded my flesh, up my bottom to my back. "I daen't ken...."

I murmured again, "What, husband?"

"Love could be like this."

I felt him throb inside me again. He shuttered and sighed.

It occurred to me that he had never been with a woman he loved. I wondered if he'd recall telling me, later.

He disengaged himself reluctantly, and we separated. I scooted to the other side of the bed and helped him remove the sheet. He dumped a little dark red liquid into a puddle of our bodies' fluids.

He folded the sheet inward and opened the door to pass it through. "Ta, Quinn."

We slept for an hour and made love for an hour alternately through the day, maids delivering our meals. In between sleeping and loving, we talked. He was unguarded and revealing. We kept our voices low and intimate.

"We're taking a hamper with us to the field. If we need to stay overnight, I'll kill or catch our supper, if it suits ye."

"Where will we sleep?" I lay in his arms, my fingers raking through the thick dark hair on his chest down to his taut belly.

"Shall I pack a bed as well, then?" He hadn't stopped smiling since we said our vows.

That pleased me, as most everything about him did, even if it was only for these few days. "I guess we needn't worry about sleep."

He laughed. "Oh, mo chroi, we may need a nap. I ken a few places fer shelter on our land. There's a cairn near the woodcutter's house I want a look a', while we're about, not for napping, but perhaps fer crossing."

His hand drifted to my thigh, then lower. I detected a pattern to his arousal. I'll never forget the thrill of his hands gliding over my skin, the depth of his kisses, or the pain of separation.

Changing forever that day, I became completely reliant upon my husband.

Chapter Seven

A page brought our horses from the stable in the barmekin. Graeme tied on the lead of a shaggy gray donkey laden with a woven hamper and blankets. My tools were safely packed away from curious eyes.

Ahead, the moor was a vast sea of grasses and vibrant wildflowers swaying in a gentle breeze. The glaring sunlight throbbed in my eyes and I longed for my sunglasses. I borrowed a hat from Ruane and pulled it low on my brow to cut the brilliance. Praying for rain would have been an abomination on such a perfect day.

Milord set our course. "We'll begin in the northern fields. We'll follow the burn as it winds through all the grazing land in this section. We canna visit every one unless ye've a sennight or two. Another time I'll take ye throughout our lands."

Smiling at his plans that assumed I'd comply, "I'll look forward to that, sir."

He watched me, his brow furrowed. "We'll stop at the woodcutter's bothy coming home. The cairn I want to explore is in back of his place."

"Aye, lover." I nodded.

We passed a cluster of crofter's cottages soon after leaving the castle.

"Most of their bairns have passed." Graeme studied the village. "The well in the center of the square is deep, like our own."

"Might I collect a sample of the well water?"

He glanced my way. "I think no'. Too many curious eyes, mo chroi."

Nodding, I pulled Daisy's reins to the right to continue our northwards journey. My husband stayed alongside me, though he looked back several times, a concerned frown in

46

place. We soon put enough distance between us and the poor villagers that the laird's attention could be redirected.

About noon, according to the position of the sun in the sky, we stopped. While Graeme unloaded the hamper, I took my leave to the burn. I dipped a vial in the cold clear water, wiped off the outside, wrote on an adhesive label, and stuck it on the glass. A small soil sample suited me, after taking a good sniff. The odor was clean dirt.

We had a pleasant dinner of cold meat, white cheese, and apples. The flavors of the food were more intense than at my home. I savored each bite. Graeme untied a square of snowy linen and held a rectangle of biscuit to my mouth. I bit into wild honey and thyme infused pastry. He grinned, watching my reaction.

Leaning across the few inches separating us, I kissed him. He responded as though he was starved for my attention.

Out in the wild, enclosed by natural surroundings, my husband's hot-blooded disposition became even more evident. Watching his brothers and their wives during communal gatherings led me to believe mine was not the only passionate son of our mither.

We left the site of our picnic and lovemaking to wander farther north, entering the fields where Niall's sheep and goats grazed.

A lone shepherd watched over about five hundred of the animals. Two herding dogs accompanied the young man. He waved from a hilltop. Graeme waved back, a signal to let him know who was there. The dogs paid careful attention to our progress.

"May we alight here for samples?" I indicated an area where the burn ran into a shallow pool, widened for the animals to drink.

"Aye." He turned and slid off the saddle.

He reached for me and I slipped down into his arms. There was no fast escape. He had a dismounting ritual that involved kisses and teasing. It could take days to fill a few test tubes at his pace.

As quickly as he released me, I hurried to the burn with my case. I kept my back to the young shepherd to avoid his sharp eyes picking out my odd actions. I gathered the fullness of my skirt above my knees and tied it into a knot. I was about to straighten when I felt Graeme's strong hands on my hips. I leaned back into his grasp and turned my face to him.

"You're a hindrance, sire." I plucked at the raven black hair above his shoulder.

"Ye're an enchantress, my darlin'." He dipped to my lips for another kiss. "I'll leave ye be so ye can get yer work done." He released me and I felt undone, like a lamp with no hope of ever being lit again.

I bent to the task and took water and soil samples in the clear flowing stream and closer to the bank. I lifted the soil sample to my nose and sniffed. *As I suspected, dung.*

In moments I rejoined my husband who lifted me to the saddle and mounted his horse. We proceeded to the farthest point for that day where I gathered another sample. We directed the horses homeward and picked up the pace.

There was a cairn to inspect and I imagined we needed to be there at a specific time. We rode at a gallop to the woodcutter's bothy and Graeme dismounted. I waited while he spoke to the man's wife. He came back for me and I glided into his arms. He led me to the short porch of the small cottage.

"Agnes, this is Lady Macpherson, my bride. Mo 'stor, this is Agnes, our healer."

Turning his hand he indicated the middle aged woman before us.

Her back was bent, her eyes faded and her scrutiny of the new Lady Macpherson felt scorching.

I curtsied. "Agnes, 'tis a pleasure to meet you."

Her strange icy blue eyes saw through me.

She curtsied and bowed low. Her voice was deep and gravelly. "Milady." Standing upright, she reached out her worn hand to me. I extended mine. She turned my palm up and ran her fingertips over it while studying intently. "Mmm...." She looked up at me, her eerie eyes blazing through any secrets I may have hidden. Her mouth worked as she chewed on what she saw. She patted her hand over my abdomen and smiled. "Ye carry a son."

"We only just married," I argued.

"Seed's planted to grow a son." She dropped my hand, turned and walked inside the bothy.

I stepped back, feeling a shadow fall over me. *How could she know that? We've only been together a day and a half. We've made love only three times today. How can she ken a child already?* I glanced at Graeme. He appeared somber.

"What?" I felt comforted by his sudden embrace.

"Are ye well, Lizbeth? Ye look as though ye're frightened."

"Nay, I'm fine. She shocked me, that's all, love."

The door opened and the woman reappeared. She pressed a small bundle of cloth into my hand. "This is fer yer belly. Ye'll feel sick in a moneth and thank me fer it. Steep two leaves in yer tea twice a day. It'll keep ye settled 'til the worst passes." She met my eyes again, backing away, haunted. Her voice dropped, her tone sorrowful. "I cain't dae a thang fer the tempest."

"The tempest?" I asked.

"Ye'll 'ave ta choose—life or death. Fer ye and yer child." She turned to Graeme and her voice took on a whimpering note. "I beg forgiveness, sire. I daen all I can." She flipped her aparan over her head and wept.

Graeme looked confounded and sighed. "Agnes! Stop, woman!" He held me with one hand. "Stop! I'm takin' my wife now. We'll speak another time."

He turned back to me and we mounted our horses, riding a short way to the cairn. The emotional atmosphere was thick and charged with darkness. The sun was about to set. Graeme studied me for a moment before leaving his horse.

He pointed at me. "Stay there. This'll take only a moment." Sunwise, he strode round the cairn, a rock hut nearly the size of my bedroom at home. Three times he made the cycle and disappeared inside when he bowed through a small opening.

It seemed he tarried an hour, but it was surely less than half.

The eerie encounter with Agnes had shaken me. I wondered if my mother died while I was away. Anxious to return to her, I knew the trip would have to wait for morning.

I resolved to leave my horse if The Macpherson failed to appear before I counted to one hundred. At ninety-eight he ducked out and grinned. He raked his hands through his hair, having caught cobwebs and such from the abandoned chamber.

"We've a second place to explore next time we cross."

"I have to leave on the morrow," I reminded him, though I needn't. He would always honor his word.

"We'll ride here before dawn. I daen't ken where it'll take us, but we'll deal wi' that when we arrive." He climbed onto his horse. "Let's be off to the castle and on time fer a late supper before bed." He turned his horse and mine followed the donkey in tow.

We arrived at the castle before light was completely gone. We rode into the barmekin and left our horses and the gray donkey at the stable. Graeme grasped my arm as we entered the castle. We hied to our separate chambers to clean and dress for supper.

He entered my room without knocking and caught me in mid-dress. "Where's yer girl?"

"I sent her away." I answered in a whisper and took a few steps closer to him. I turned my back. "Will ye button me, please?"

He complied, mumbling about small buttons and large hands, but he stopped to lay a kiss between my shoulders several times.

Whirling back to him, I whispered into his ear. "I'm not sure if my clothing would pass close inspection, even that of a servant. That's why I sent Ann off. Was I wrong?"

His arms encompassed me. "Nay. I daen't think of it. Are ye well, after the words Agnes spoke?" His hands swept up and down my back.

How have I lived without this in my life before now? "Aye, she scared me, that's all. Does she prophesy often?"

He shrugged. "Sometimes. I daen't put stock in seer's words 'til they come to pass." He laid a broad hand over my abdomen with a grin. "But a son? I'll pray her prediction is righteous." He kissed me gently at first, then with mounting passion. He pulled back, cleared his throat, and sighed. "Our dinner and family await, milady." He opened my chamber door and we passed through.

50

Chapter Eight

We rode through the darkness of predawn hours to the cairn. I prayed Agnes would still be abed when we left our horses with the woodcutter.

He asked no questions when he and Graeme traded words on the stoop. I waited in the yard, bags in hand, my cloak's hood pulled low over my face. I studied the layout and watched my husband approach.

My husband. The words were no small comfort as we made our way down the path leading to the cairn.

Graeme carried both bags and held my arm. "Be cautious ye daen't turn yer ankle on this rough lane, lass." He chuckled. "I'm sorry. Wife. I like the sound of it on my tongue almost as much as I like the taste of ye."

I blushed in the dark and smiled to myself. "Every word you speak, laird, is a blessing fallen on my ears. I'll miss yer voice, but mostly your hands, and the rest of you as well."

He chuckled and tightened his grip.

Thick fog lying atop the grass on the glen swirled round our legs as we shuffled through. The waning light of a full moon reflected off the moisture, illuminating the low cloud, making it glow. The sky in the east began to redden.

"I'll stay 'til ye have an answer fer me to bring home. Then I'll return and take care of matters here. Afterwards, when the row dies down, I'll come to ye. If ye need me before, if your mam...send Bran."

"Aye, sir, I will." I inhaled the deep, clean, crisp morning air and ducked my head to enter the cairn.

Graeme circled the stone hut sunwise three times, before joining me just as a bright flash of light shot through the inner darkness. I was almost disappointed it worked.

He held my skirt as we passed into a lower chamber, heads bent. I stumbled on the way and landed in a pile of leaves. My

51

husband helped me stand. We looked round and brushed ourselves off. We stood inside a cavern on the side of a low mound of earth. We stepped through. Fog shrouded the area ahead of us, though not as thickly as on the glen.

"Ye ken where we are?" Graeme glared at the unfamiliar area.

"'Tis a park. Let's walk to a light and see if we find a sign of some sort." I set the pace, more familiar with the lay of the land here. We passed jungle gyms and horseshoe sandpits.

At the paved entrance we found a sign, Bendarroch Public Park.

"We're only about three miles from my house. If we walk south we can take a bus as far as Gare Loch."

We set out and found a bus stop less than a quarter mile away. I plopped on the bench and inhaled the polluted soup we call air, on a good day. Graeme sat next to me. His awareness was keen and I noticed he was uneasy.

"What's wrong, Graeme?" I lay my hand on his knee.

He barely whispered, "Shh, we've been trailed. There're a coupla lads hiding in bushes behind us. They think we daen't ken they're there." He leaned back and watched the road to our left, a ploy to keep his head turned and his ears tuned to the noises he heard.

I failed to detect a peep until they were upon us. Two young men grabbed Graeme on each side, while a third seized my arms from behind. Graeme let them believe they had hold of him for almost thirty seconds before he jerked his arms forward, catching the backs of their heads in his hands. He stood, lads dangling from his hands and arms and threw them forward into the street.

The lad behind me squealed and tried to loose me, but Graeme had his shirt in hand and launched him over the bench. He flung the young man into the pile with his friends. All three stood there in a pool of dim light from the street lamp and studied him in awe, before sprinting for the wood across the way.

Graeme rejoined me on the bench. "This is a hell of a place to live, wife. I'll be glad when it's over and ye'll be home wi' me where it's safe to sit outside of a mornin', when there's no' a war on. Wha' dae they think they're daen'? Are they robbers?"

"I imagine they're gang members, which is like a clan of thieves. The wood's alive with evil, sir. I can think of places where that cairn could've led that would suit me better. But at least we didn't have to dodge security here, like we do at the castle."

"Ye daen't come here alone. Have Bran come wi' ye if ye need to cross or send 'im fer me, ken?"

"Aye, sir." I kissed his mouth and heard the rumble of a city bus braking to pick us up.

****

I unlocked the front door and stepped in ahead of Graeme. I hurried to the answering machine to check messages, deleting those beginning with the sound of Aaron's voice. Three were from him, two from Bran, and one from the nurse caring for my mother.

"Lizbeth, this is Molly, your mother's nurse. I'm calling to tell you she's had two good days, yesterday and today. Come by when you have time. She says to tell you she loves you. Bye, now." The dial tone followed. The time stamp indicated she called the night before. So the tempest Agnes spoke of wasn't Mom dying whilst I lingered in heaven with my husband.

I turned to Graeme. "How about breakfast? I haven't bannock and homemade jam, but I can scramble eggs as well as any chef."

He grinned. "That'd be fine. After, go to yer mam and whatever chores need seein' to." He followed me the short distance to the kitchen and watched from the bar as I made coffee and prepped breakfast.

I worked for a few minutes acutely aware his gaze followed every move I made. I glanced up from cracking eggs. "What?"

"Ye're incredible, Lady Macpherson."

"Because I can break eggs?"

"Because ye're mine. Might I...well, go along to see to yer mother?" He was uncomfortable asking and quickly slid his attention out the picture window to the loch.

"You'd do that?"

"Wha'? I married her daughter. It could be the only chance we have to meet."

I nodded. "True, that. You're more than welcome to accompany me anytime, sire." I heated a bit of Spanish olive oil in a skillet and scrambled the eggs while English muffins toasted in the countertop oven. "I want to get to the lab to run tests, but I'm thinkin' it'd be wiser to wait for the end of the day, when most everyone's gone home. There are three I want to culture. One from the well, one from the pool in the burn, and one from the sheep pasture. That takes seventy-two hours. Can you stay four nights or would it be too much time away?"

He grinned. "I would love to be wi' ye four more nights and days."

"Yes, and days." I smiled and plated eggs.

****

Mom dozed when we arrived at the nursing facility. Molly sat nearby, reading. She stood when we entered the room.

"Molly, this is my husband, Graeme." I turned to him. "Molly's Mom's nurse."

Graeme nodded her way but didn't speak. Molly nodded back.

"If you wanna break, we'll be here for a little while." I checked Mom's hook-ups. She was on an IV and catheter.

"Aye, tha'd be nice, then." She kept her eyes on my husband, a half smile on her face.

The proximity of a handsome man holds charm, no matter a woman's age or taste. Molly passed by, still scrutinizing him. He's pleasing from the back as well.

Mom opened her eyes, heavy from morphine for the pain. "Lizzie?"

"Aye, Mom, I'm here. I brought someone to meet you." I motioned Graeme forwards a few steps and held out my hand to him. "Graeme and I married day before yesterday. It's been a whirlwind romance. But that's the only kind I have time for, you know."

He grasped my hand.

"Wha's 'is?" She smiled up at my husband. "Welcome to our sorry, depleting family, Graeme." She fought to lift her hand.

He leaned forward to take it and bent to kiss her fingertips. "It's my pleasure, Maggie." He smiled as though he wasn't charming a near corpse. "Ye raised a fine daughter. I'm proud to have her as my wife."

"Thank you, son." She studied him a moment through flaccid eyes and her smile softened. "We've met before....I can't think where. Do you recall?"

He thought for a second that he clearly didn't need. I'd seen the answer in his merry eyes. "Was it by the burn?" He cast a quick glance my way.

"Aye, that was it!" I hadn't heard her voice so excited in months. She lifted her hand for emphasis, almost six inches off the bed. "We talked about land management, I think."

"Aye, we did, though we call it different words, and then took dinner by the loch. Lizbeth joined us there. Ye dae remember. I feared ye would not." He grinned with satisfaction. "'Twas a lovely day." His voice sounded wistful. "I caught salmon and we roasted 'em over a fire on a spit fer our supper tha' evening. Then ye two ladies stayed at the castle fer the night."

Mom smiled and blushed. Her words slurred, tripping over each other to run together, "It seems like a dream now. Somehow the...memory fades. I'm glad you wed my daughter." Her voice weakened. "She's an excellent lass and deserves an exceptional man. You'll live in your castle, then?" She struggled to keep her eyes open.

"Aye, in a little while. There's no hurry yet." Graeme checked with me as Mom's eyes closed.

She snored softly.

Molly stepped in.

We slipped away.

When we were back in the car I turned to him. "Thank you for playin' along with her."

He sobered. "I wasn't playing, Lizbeth. Wha' she remembers *is* a dream." He studied the car park around us. "Verra like meeting ye in dreams, fer three summers now." He sighed and paled.

"Aye, three summers, sire." I watched this man, who said he loved me, closely.

"Ye as well?" He smiled.

"Aye, the nightly visits began a few weeks after Bran's brother died in the car crash." My eyes teared.

He reached for my hand. "The first time was at the pool in the burn, where we stopped fer a swim?"

"And lay in the sun for almost an hour to dry. You picked flowers from the heather and wove them into a garland for my hair."

He chuckled. "Aye that was a good day."

"It was, Graeme. I hope for many more…real ones, not dreams."

He nodded. "Aye, my treasure. I daen't ken wha' it all means but…."

"I know; me either."

Chapter Nine

Crossing my fingers, I studied the culture under the microscope.

It was still there. Hateful little bacteria exploded into new cells before my eyes. I entered my findings on a tablet beside me and turned to the second culture with the same results. I sighed, hoping the third was on par with the other two. It made it easier to pinpoint the culprit. I placed the glass slide under the scope and said a quick prayer. My hope was founded. The bacteria in the final sample matched the two previous.

Niall's sheep project came with a price—contaminated water. I celebrated for a moment. Knowing what caused the problem was just the first step. Graeme must return and figure out how to tell his brother. That was the larger mountain to scale than finding these lethal germs thriving in the burn.

I headed home to see my husband for one more night before he left me. While in part, the news gratified me, my heart was heavy for the task before him, and the emptiness of life without him after he left.

When I opened the door, I smelled something delicious cooking in my kitchen. That was an odd occasion at my house.

"Hullo!" I called out from the foyer, hanging my jacket on a hook.

Our communication was evolving into mostly English, or a Scottish version of English, with occasional Gaelic words thrown in when English failed my husband.

"Hullo, mo `stor." He leaned in the doorway with a tea towel over one broad shoulder.

I stretched on tiptoes for a kiss. "What on earth are you cooking, milord?"

"I caught fish today from yer loch. They're roasting now, in yer oven. I had help to figure how to work this…." He gestured at the stove.

57

"The stove. Who helped?"

"Yer neighbor, Harold. He's retired?" He winced. "He brought line and we fished fer supper."

My stomach growled. "You're remarkable and you cook."

He pulled me into his arms. The clock was ticking on our last hours together. He kissed me, drawing me into his hard body with our passionate connection. It left me breathless when he finally released me, holding on for a moment to steady my frame, left weak by his attentions.

I opened a bottle of good white wine to accompany the feast of six roasted trout. I put a salad together as Graeme watched from the bar.

"What're those leaves ye're using?"

"It's called lettuce or cos."

"We use kale at home."

"Aye, and it's very good. It's harder to get kale at the market sometimes so we use cos when kale's scarce."

We sat together at the breakfast nook and devoured our sumptuous feast. With our fingers, we picked the bones clean of fish.

I dreaded telling him the results of the tests.

He finished, wiping his hands and mouth on the tea towel and leaned back. "What news have ye fer me?"

"I hate to tell you. On the other hand if you can remedy the situation, your people will stop dying from the plague."

I hoisted my wine glass and sipped the crisp, cold liquid. "The problem is the sheep droppings near the burn. The dung mixes into the water and bacteria floats downstream. Bacteria can be good or bad, like poison." I paused and patted his hand. "It's also infected your well. There must be a channel from the burn to the well. It might be installed to protect water supply during drought, or in case the underground spring that feeds it goes dry or changes course."

His arms crossed and his eyes left mine to peruse the loch through the picture window. His voice was soft, as though he talked to himself rather than me. "I wonder if the channel feeds from the bottom of the great pool in the burn. It makes sense that's the case; it's the deepest point."

"Aye, most likely. There are chemicals now days that could clean up the water but we can't do that. Another solution that will work is to pasture the sheep somewhere they can't contaminate the burn or loch. A large spring fed waterhole would suffice for them."

He looked back at me. "How dae I tell Niall this and make sense?"

I smiled sadly. "I'm sorry. I don't know what to say to him without revealing the source unless you have Tomas talk to him and suggest moving the sheep, as a trial to see if it helps. Then you have to find the channel that's contaminating your well. Only drink water boiled for at least ten minutes. That'll kill the bacteria until the burn recycles itself. Also, if you dig out the area of the burn where the sheep water, it will hasten the process. You can use that soil for fertilizer after it ages a summer. Even with that, it may take a year or more before it's safe to drink the water."

He listened while his mind whirred. "Aye, unless we flood it out from the loch. Would that not help to clear the dung?"

"Mayhap, unless in the flooding the water washes over more infected soil, it may even contaminate the loch."

He nodded. "A year or more?"

"Aye."

"Ye canna stay here fer a year or more waiting to test our water again. Can ye bring over wha' ye need? There're a thousand hiding places in the castle."

"Aye, I can do that, send a little at a time over with you when you return. I'll have to purchase a field microscope. A quicker solution may be to dig another well far from the present one and hope the spring and burn waters don't flow in that direction. Once dug, I can check the water source for bacteria."

"That'll do then. We'll need to find a dowser."

"Um, there are lots of springs there. Historically speaking I can provide as many as two hundred sources."

"How dae ye ken that?"

"From current maps. I can get the information and know where to dig for your water."

He checked the sunset, too late to go home tonight. He grinned when he turned back to me. "Looks like I have to wait 'til mornin' to leave."

Pleased, I smiled. "On the morrow, sire."

****

We spent our evening united, literally. Savoring the moments of quiet, we celebrated our passion for each other. It might be weeks before we'd be together again. Long, lonely weeks…at least for me. Graeme had his family at home. I'd come back to a houseful of emptiness, made more so for his absence.

Morning arrived too soon. I switched off the alarm though neither of us slept. We rolled out of bed wordlessly and dressed. I gathered vials and slides to send over with him. I needed time to buy a field microscope and all the incidentals and chemicals I'd need.

Graeme sat at the bar and drank a mug of coffee while he stared at me. He smiled. His eyes never left me.

I covered his hand with mine and sighed.

"Aye, I feel the same, mo chroi." He lifted my hand to kiss my fingertips.

"I pray that all will go well with Niall and finding the water channel to the well. Don't forget to tell your cooks to boil the water at least ten minutes before they use it. To be safe, have them boil the bathwater as well."

"I hate leavin' ye in this place. Are ye sure ye canna cross wi' me?"

"But for Mom, I would. I'll go back to work and try to pretend nothing's changed in my life. The past two weeks have been incredible. Classes begin again next week at university and I'll have a full schedule. There's no telling what I'll learn that can help us through the years."

"I daen't give a tinker's damn fer more knowledge. I want my wife with me."

I smiled and rounded the bar for another hands on kiss. "We'd better go."

"Ye come across with Bran in a fortnight. We'll use him as a dowser. He's yer cousin, eh?"

"I'm sure he'll be delighted to return to your land."

He nodded, but the smile he usually wore faded. "Send Bran if Maggie passes before then. I'll come to ye straight away. Promise me."

"Aye, sir, I promise. I wonder if Mom will remember your visit."

He smiled and kissed my neck.

"I have an idea how to break the news to your brothers."

"Wha's tha', darling?"

"You met my great-uncle when you brought me home. He shared a story he'd heard from a friend, about sheep droppings poisoning the water upstream from his friend's land. When he found the landowners above the sheep were not experiencing illness, he went beyond his property to find those below stream. There were a great number of dead and more ill. It almost wiped out the entire village. " I watched his response as he pulled on a cloak and removed my ruana from a hook.

He nodded. "I like it. It'll serve well." He pulled my cape over my shoulders and kissed me.

****

The car park nearest the cavern was empty. Graeme took my hand. "Ye go now."

"I'll wait 'til sunrise. I need to know you're safely across— just in case."

"Then ye go home." He tried being stern with me without success. We were both too sad at parting.

"As soon as the sun's up, I will." I leaned into his kiss. "Now go. Hurry." My hand still rested on his back as he left the seat.

He dashed across the grass and loped past the east side, made a round, then another. He moved like a cat, long graceful strides consuming the distance. My last sight of him was at a full run down the east side before he rounded the south end to the entrance.

The sun began its climb, splintering the steely indigo sky with violent red carnelian, amethyst, and amber. As the red orange ball crested I felt a jolt, like an electrical shock, and knew Graeme was gone. I watched for a moment longer and cranked the BMW, turning towards home.

I will not cry.

I will not lament my loneliness.

I will not lose heart.

Chapter Ten

The two weeks until Bran and I could cross over dragged past relentlessly. Long hours wore my patience thin. I began to experience nausea in the morning and knew Agnes read me right. I'd know for sure in a few days. My cycle was due and I was always regular.

To be sure we were still on for the crossing, I phoned Bran.

"Explain again how I ken where to find the water."

"You'll use a divining or dowsing rod. The forked willow limb I packed works great. I'll give you coordinates from the map we use at the office. Granted, it's more than three hundred years advanced but we should be able to get close enough to be impressive."

"And this will save the children and everybody else from bacteria-laden water?" A smile seasoned his voice.

"Aye." I knew where the questions led.

Bran needs to be the hero of every story. It's hard for him to see his broker job as anything but fun. He should have been a fireman or policeman, but then again that requires too much common sense and he has none.

He chuckled. "I ken, Lizzie. It's just I can't get over *you* wanting *me* to go in and take all the credit for saving the Macpherson clan and changing history."

"Somebody has to, Bran. It might as well be you. It can't be me." I grinned at his delight.

"I'll be there around five?" He counted down the hours, almost as avidly as I did.

"Aye, I'm packed and ready to go. Be sure you're armed. We have to go through the cavern in the park. Horses will be waiting for us at the woodcutter's cottage."

"Aye, lass, I'll be armed. See you in a few hours, then."

We rang off and I glanced around the busy lab from my desk. Coworkers went about their chores like hamsters on running-wheels. My hope was to be able to give notice soon. I could leave anytime. Graeme provided an adequate income, but the lab gave me something to do to make the desolate hours pass quicker.

****

When Bran pulled into the drive I dashed out with my leather satchel and tapestry valise. We both wore our medieval costumes again. I opened the garage door and he pulled his expensive silver-blue Mercedes inside.

He hopped out and grinned from ear-to-ear. "Lizzie, we'll have a great time."

"Aye, we will. Remember to mind your manners with the ladies, though." We climbed into my ancient BMW and let it idle for a moment to warm the engine.

"I'll be the height of discretion, the epitome of virtue." He used his best actor voice.

"I'm serious, Bran."

He sobered. "As am I, lass. They're a tad more sensitive about rakes in Graeme's kingdom and dead *is* forever."

We parked under a streetlight on the boulevard fronting the park, along with a few other vehicles. Then we made the trek through the park arriving at the cavern early. No one was about, it seemed. We ambled through the woods until the sun's light dimmed.

Bran pushed up his right sleeve and looked at his watch. "I checked the time of sunset before I left. We have about three minutes. Let's get to it."

"You need to pocket your watch."

"Och! I hadn't thought of it, sis, thanks." He slipped off the watch and dropped it into his sporran.

We walked the path Graeme trod a fortnight earlier, sunwise round the magical mound of earth and stone. We entered the cavern.

There were four natives inside, smoking hashish.

Bran loudly surprised the gang and grinned. "Ah, cheerio, mates."

Stopping just short of the portal, I observed the drama. I'd determined to make the trip to my husband tonight regardless of what lay in my path. I studied the four lads, all high.

The biggest of them was not as tall as Bran. Between us, I thought we could send them packing.

The tallest one left the rock he leaned on and stretched out his hand to push Bran's shoulder. He seemed to move in slow motion.

Bran shifted his bag and laid out the young man with a crisp clip to his sparsely haired chin. The lad dropped in front of him.

"Right then, anyone else?" He checked with the three left standing, his grin still in place.

They looked at each other, then at me, in the near dark. They left their rocks and eased past, out the cavern mouth, nodding deference. "Ma'am."

"Good lads." I threw in a compliment to let them know they'd made an intelligent decision.

A flash lit the dark space with waves of blinding light. Wind howled and lightning split the sky ahead of us. A rumble of thunder or an earthquake beckoned. We rushed through a blaze and eerie whistling screams into the midst of a severe thunderstorm.

Graeme waited nearby wrapped in a wool cape. He held his horse, another, and mine. He swept over the distance and captured me in his arms.

"Come! Ye'll ride wi' me." He handed over the reins of my horse to Bran and lifted me onto his saddle.

He joined me, opening the poncho to wrap me beneath its protection. His body heat was welcome as I was already drenched. I snuggled into his embrace and felt elated for the first time since he left me a fortnight ago.

"We'll be in time to change fer supper," He spoke near my ear.

Lightning, from cloud to earth, brightened the sky and thunder roared. The ground vibrated with the shock of nature's attack on civilization.

I looked up and called back. "Good, I'm starved and I missed you terribly."

He chuckled. I couldn't hear his voice but felt the rumble in his chest. "And I ye, wife. My heart and body long fer ye. I thought of missing supper, but I daen't want Bran on his own."

"That's wise, sire," I assured him as I wiped a stream of water from my face.

We made the castle in good time. A lad from the stables dashed out for the horses. We hurried through the torrent for the main entrance. Quinn waited to take our wet outerwear and hang it on hooks away from the dry cloaks.

No one blocked our way up the stairs.

Graeme sent Bran into the room he stayed in on his first visit. We proceeded to the master's chamber, slipped inside and locked ourselves into a warm embrace. We undressed each other and deposited our wet clothes in the copper tub of the privy.

I pulled on dry undergarments and a shift. Graeme dressed in a fresh leine and trews to avoid the time it would take to don a kilt. I donned a frock Cora made for me from Ruane's wonderful woven fabric. Ecru lace edged the dark green linen and antler buttons adorned the front placket and buttoned the back.

"Hae daes Maggie fare?" My husband buttoned the front of his saffron leine.

"Touch and go...I mean there's been no change. She sleeps a great deal. When awake, she's in tremendous pain." I turned my back to him, so he could button my dress.

After, I faced him. "I've news for you."

"Mmm, aye?"

"I'm with child." I tried to keep the joy from my voice until I could assess his response. "There's a test I used to find out early."

He sighed, a smile teasing his full lips. "I'm pleased, but feel greater urgency to bring ye home."

I nodded. "I feel greater urgency to be here, sir."

He wrapped me in his arms again and kissed the top of my damp hair.

"My hair needs to dry a bit, so I'll sit beside the fire for a few moments."

He pulled a chair near the peat fire for me. I combed my hair out with my fingers before tackling it with a wide toothed comb made from bone.

"Tell me of yer plans fer the morrow." His gaze ravished me.

I kept my voice low. "I packed a witching rod. I have the coordinates written down for Bran and he's going through them, so I'm sure he'll have them memorized. He's really good at that."

Graeme smiled and brushed his fingers across my jawline. "I've missed ye something fierce, wife."

"My life is empty without you, milord." I closed my eyes and kissed his palm.

He sighed heavily. "Tomas handled Niall. They've moved the sheep to an upper pasture and enlarged a watering hole already there. The pool, in the burn they used to water, is dug down to fresh dirt. I smelt it. Quinn, Rodney, and I dove to find the channel, from the burn to the well, figuring it to be the most direct route. We plugged it, fer now. Cooks are complaining, nonetheless, they're boiling the water."

"This rain will make it hard to dig. The witching rod will find water everywhere."

"Aye, I thought o' that too. We'll see what the morrow brings. Mayhap the day after." He shrugged. "There's nothing else to do but...." He scratched his chin and eyed the bed with a grin.

"That's an excellent idea. What'll we do with Bran?"

"Tomas remembers him from his last visit. I wasn't sure he would with all the grief over losing…his daughter." He wiped his hand over his mouth. "So, he can move around with freedom as long as he daen't try to mount everything in a frock."

I laughed, giggled really. He was frustrated with Bran, yet we wouldn't be where we were, but for my randy brother-in-law.

"A word from you will curb his eagerness, I'm sure."

He grinned. "I'll make it a point then. Are ye dry enough fer supper? I'm starving fer food and my bride. The quicker we get supper finished, the sooner I'll sate my appetite fer ye."

We left his chamber for the supper table and family.

Bran joined us on the way down. "Ah, it's good to be back, sire."

We all relished the fragrance of fresh barley bread and the best efforts of Mary, the chatelaine.

"Man, tha' smells good." Bran expressed our sentiments.

We entered the dining room to find the family just coming together from the parlor and pre-dinner aperitifs.

Ruane and Cora left their husbands to welcome me home, with hugs.

"Thank you both for the lovely dress." I raked one hand down the front of the skirt. "We need to speak on the morrow. I'll need larger clothes soon." I smiled and Ruane picked up immediately.

"Ye may use mine. I'll hem them fer ye. Cora's too tiny to share; but ye and I are about the same size." She looped her arm round me and we set off for supper.

Our husbands and Bran followed.

Ruane lowered her voice. "Our mither is not at table. She had a tray in her room. We spoke, at tea. She said to tell ye that ye're sorely missed and she'll feel brighter on the morrow. Rain tends to make her joints ache. She uses heated stones and herbs fer the pain, but fares best not climbing the stairs."

"I ken that. Rain makes my mother fret over her aches and pains as well."

"Hae's she faring?" Ruane took the seat beside me at table.

"Nearing the end." My eyes teared.

"I'm sorry, sister. I bring ye sadness when we should be celebrating new life." She smiled and patted my hand.

"Thank ye kindly. I've never felt more at home than I do when I'm here. Soon it will be mine as well." I glanced at my husband. "We both want to hasten the day, but it's in the hands of our Lord."

"Aye, wisely said. We must learn to trust." Ruane became uncomfortable.

I thought of her tiny girls, the pain she must have endured when they'd just stopped nursing. The separation alone would have its issues, but then to lose them to death within a month of weaning them. That agony would take years to overcome.

I squeezed her arm. "I ken, Ruane, though this is my first child that I carry. My heart bleeds with yours, sister." She grasped my hand and lifted it to her cheek.

Tomas watched us closely from across the wide table. He sat at the head sometimes, as the task of being The Macpherson was shared between himself and Graeme. No one occupied the seat that night. Tomas chose to sit across from us and focus on his wife. Surely her sadness broke his usually jovial heart.

She glanced up and met his somber gaze. A tear slipped his eye and he wiped it away hurriedly, sniffed, and took a long draught of wine.

Tomas' deep voice was low. "Lizbeth, our soul sorely aches. It's two years past since our first loss this day. Les..." his chin trembled, "was our bright one; she was, eh, mo chroi?" He watched his wife as he spoke.

"Aye, sir, most certainly." Ruane let her tears wash freely over her creamy complexion. "We've spent this day grieving our daughters. It's a heavy day fer sure, my love." She patted her belly. "But we'll celebrate anew soon, wi' the grace of our Lord."

I took that to mean they were trying to have another child. She wouldn't be loaning me dresses had she been pregnant.

Graeme reached for my hand on the other side. I glanced his direction. He smiled to let me know he was pleased I was there. For the moment we were a family. His knee found my leg and he pressed against me. I pressed back.

Niall and Bran were intent with each other, though Niall didn't forget Cora was at hand. He included her in some of his remarks. Bran was the life of the party at that end of the table. Cora giggled and blushed beautifully.

****

To be polite, we stayed at table as long as necessary; but my husband tapped his foot in impatience to be away to his chambers.

69

I lay my hand on his knee several times and raised a brow. He sighed and stilled.

The roast venison was delectable, trimmed with potatoes and onions. The kale was steamed to perfection, and the coarse bread, excellent, served with freshly churned butter.

Finally desert came, a flan with thick caramel served with a side of fresh wild berries. Mary had outdone herself. The custard was smooth as velvet on the tongue. The caramel, clinging to the top and sides, lent a sweet, buttery edge to contrast the tartness of the berries. It was a perfect finish.

Tomas signaled one of the serving girls. "Ask Mary to come in, please."

Mary appeared in the doorway immediately, locking eyes with Tomas.

He raised a glass to her. "Ye, madam, are a goddess in the kitchen. Here, here!"

"Pshaw, ye've too much liquor, milord." She answered soberly, but blushed and drew her aparan into her hands, looking away.

We all raised a glass to honor her incredible skill, sitting in the middle of the Highlands, in a castle built by the grandsire of three brothers in residence in the seventeenth century.

I felt blessed, loved, and honored to be part of this clan. On the morrow I would visit with our mither.

My husband turned his ear to the clock chiming in the gallery. He sighed and looked around. "It's late and I need my bride. Goodnight, all."

My face warmed at his bluntness.

We rose. He captured my hand and headed to the stairs.

We went directly to his chambers. There was a fire in the hearth. The room was cozy. We undressed slowly, desire heightened by the excellent port that topped off desert. It was wonderful just to be and then….

He touched me.

Closing my eyes, I took a deep breath, relishing his scent. His body felt like a sensuous extension of my being. He took my hand and led me to the bed, the room dimly lit by the fire.

I watched every supple move he made, determined to commit it to memory for the long lonely nights ahead.

He kissed me, then ran his tongue down my neck to my breasts and everywhere else. I melted into his body, ecstasy sweeping over me. And that was just the beginning.

****

The next morning, Nellie knocked at our chamber door. I dressed, with Ann's help, in a lovely scarlet dress from Ruane's closet.

Ruane, waiting impatiently, opened the door to our mither's maid. "Aye, Nellie?"

"Madam sends fer Lady Lizbeth. Ye come along, if ye will. Cora will join us after she feeds William."

"Thank ye kindly. I'll bring Lizbeth up as soon as she's dressed." She closed the door and leant against it. "I kenned Mither would send fer ye this morn. It's a lovely day, full of sunlight. She'll feel much better."

I brushed my hands down the skirt of the dress under Ruane's critical eye. "I could've taken off another half inch or so."

"It's beautiful." I interrupted her perfect sewing lesson. "Thank you for thinking so sweetly of me, Ruane. Mayhap you'll need it back soon."

"I hope to be a month or so behind ye is all. Dae ye think diggin' a new wellspring will fix our problems?" She gazed out the window to survey the area where Bran, Graeme, and Niall scouted for a spring. "I have no desire to bury more bairns, Lizbeth. My heart canna bear the anguish."

"From what I ken, it makes sense. I listened to Bran and Graeme discuss the possibilities the plague was waterborne. It could be. When Graeme took me home, my great uncle joined us for supper. He told a tale he'd heard about sheep causing problems with water, some years ago. We'll pray 'tis the answer and there'll be no more death due to the sickness. Eh?" I pressed my arm round her waist.

She squeezed me and nodded. "Let's hie to our mither. She may have scones prepared to break our fast. It's her favorite."

71

We left our chamber behind, passed by my bedroom, that Graeme promised to never allow me to sleep in alone, and down the hallway to Mither's quarters.

Nellie opened the door to us and bowed us into Mither's presence.

Mither sat, elegantly attired in a burgundy silk dress trimmed with black lace. She wore rubies at her throat, ears and on her wrist. She waved her hand to the seats we were to occupy and smiled at me.

"I understand you are with child, Lizbeth?" Her brows arched, a smile on her lips. "My son woke me with news this morning."

"Aye, Mither." I self-consciously placed a hand over my small belly. "Not evident yet except in my habits...and the nausea, but Agnes gave me an herb for relief."

"Good, have ye plenty?" She poured tea and I thought about the coffee she loved too passionately to indulge herself.

"I believe so, thank you." I stirred sugar into my pale China cup with a tiny silver spoon.

Mither uncovered the scones, warm from the oven, with churned butter in a bowl beside them. My mouth watered. My stomach flipped.

We served ourselves and nibbled at the buttered scones slathered with a spiced apple jam that Mary made each fall. It was blissful to break our fast with such luscious repast.

"Tell me how yer mother fares, my dear." Mither took a delicate bite of scone from a silver fork.

"She lingers in such a state of pain I pray for an end to it soon. But the Lord kens best and I'm in no haste to lose her. Though I do long to be home with my husband." The tears were uncontrollable. I dabbed my eyes quickly and took a deep breath. It's part of my wonder of pregnancy, to cry over every little thing.

Mither's smile was tempered. "Aye, we mourn the loss of two years ago, losing our precious. We have not been able to say her name yet." She wiped a tear away.

A tap sounded on her door. Nellie opened it to Cora. She swept in, a petite blond with the complexion of Scandinavia.

Dark lashes lined her clear blue eyes. She resembled a porcelain doll.

Ruane tapped her knee. "Wha' secret, sister? I ken ye."

She smiled around at each of us and wiggled into her seat. "My sister writes to say she's coming fer a visit. She'll be married soon and wants help with her trousseau. She chose to bless me with the making of her wedding clothes."

"That is good news." I glanced down at the dress I wore, exhibiting her fine handiwork. "She's in for a treat, that."

Cora beamed.

After tea Mither dismissed my sisters to speak with me alone.

"Now, ye may disrobe and lie on my bed. Nellie will assist ye. I made a salve fer yer belly. I'll show ye how to apply it to help the bairn grow without hurting yer skin." She held a brown glass jar with a cork stopper.

I rose and followed Nellie to the bedroom. She took my dress to hang on a hook nearby.

"Ye may leave on yer shift, Lady Lizbeth. We'll hike it up over yer stays."

Feeling awkward, I followed orders, glad all my underthings were period costume. I rolled up the shift. "Like this?"

"Aye, tha's it. Now lie down close to the edge so Madam can reach ye."

I obeyed, stretching out under the rose and cream canopy over the ecru quilted bed. I glanced around at the fine, elaborately carved antiques. Surely they were her family pieces from Spain.

Nellie covered my legs and upper torso with shawls.

Mither joined us, an aparan over her satin dress, sleeves rolled away from her knobby arthritic fingers. She slathered the cream on her hands.

"I perform this ritual with Ruane and Cora during their pregnancies. Their skin is lovely. We must labor to keep our skin moist, Lizbeth, to retain our youth...and our husband's interest." She smeared the warm, slick cream over my non-existent belly. "Ye have wide hips, that'll make birthin' easier, plenty of room for the babe to grow."

She loaded her hands again and coated my belly and hips. Her hands were strong. "I do hope ye return home frequently. I love doing this for my girls. It allows me to be part of your lives while we wait for our little ones." She finished massaging in the lovely fragrant balm. A fusion of lavender, rosemary, and roses permeated the warm air.

My eyes grew heavy. I dozed in the quiet. Sometime later I woke, covered with a blanket. I fought to wake, in the cocoon-like bed surrounded by love. Mither and Nellie were in the drawing room speaking softly. I rose, stretched, and dressed myself.

Chapter Eleven

Well-digging had begun. During dinner break Bran snagged a vial of the water, running clear and cold from the ley tapped into by the crude instruments used on the hole. He passed it off to me and I tucked it safely away in my leather satchel.

We return home day after the morrow. I'll test the fresh water and wait for Graeme to fetch the results, or Bran to return without me.

I hoped to go with him, but it all depends on Mom and work and...if my heart can bear the separation from my husband.

Graeme, Bran, and Niall bathed and changed, for the largest family gathering of the day, prior to coming down. I was at aperitifs with Tomas, Ruane, Cora, and our mither.

Graeme blew through the portal of the parlor like fresh wind. He scanned the room until his eyes landed on mine. A look of relief washed over him. He smiled and calmly approached. I patted the seat on the settee beside me. Graeme eased onto the red velvet divan and took my hand. He kissed my fingers. I felt warmed through at his appearance. His thigh pressed against mine and he smiled as he kept my regard.

Tomas had just begun telling a story of an ancient battle. "Twas winter, November, I ken, of 1542 when more than a hundred of our noble men lost their lives to the marshes near River Esk." He leaned back and studied the tall ceiling, blackened by the peat fires in the hearth.

"England's Henry VIII broke off with the Roman Catholic Church, expecting James V, King of the Scots, to do the same because he ordered it so.

"James was Henry's nephew, by the by. The Scottish King not only refused, but ignored Henry's request to meet him in York. Well then, Henry took offense and ordered troops sent into Scotland.

75

"King James commissioned Lord Robert Maxwell, Warden of West March, to raise an army. He was able to gather between 15,000 and 18,000 men who proceeded to invade England. Because James failed to officially *name* Maxwell the commander of the army, Oliver Sinclair took it upon himself, being one of James' favorites, to declare *he* was the supreme leader. That mistake resulted in a large number of nobles and their men walking away, leavin' chaos in their wake.

"Maxwell intervened and fought with the remaining Scots. Forced to leave their mounts on the bank of the River Esk, they advanced on foot into England, meeting Thomas Wharton with merely 3,000 men.

"King Henry's commander, Wharton, was the appointed sheriff of the order shires to keep us in line. It was rumored later that he proposed to invade and take James hostage at Lochmaben. Tha' man had no love fer us atall and only quelled his hatred by having free reign to cross over and burn our villages and murder our tenants.

"The Scots encountered the English near Solway Moss, with no definite leader and very little organization. But hey, we love a fight. A hundred or more men lost their lives in the marshes by drowning, but it's said that the remainder fought well until they were overrun. They surrendered their ten field guns to English Cavalry.

"I do believe we may have been fascinated by our own superiors, thinking they could carry the day. It's often the case, when a leader comes along that men will follow him to the death. No matter that it makes no sense, a warrior's always looking fer a battle—to prove he's able."

A touch of sarcasm tinted his voice. "The good King James, grieving the loss of his friend, Sinclair, died a fortnight later. He was barely thirty summers old, leavin' behind his wife and Scotland's precious Mary, but six days old." Tomas scratched his grizzled chin. "The mayhem that followed her da's death was far more than we bargained fer. But, tha's another story. So ends the Battle of Solway Moss, family."

Mither presided and led a prayer of blessing for the food and over our child and Ruane's womb. My eyes teared, while my heart soared with joy at the love and acceptance of this precious clan.

Mary put out another fine spread for supper. Chicken pie with wild mushrooms followed kale and barley soup simmered in ox tail broth. A salad of herbs and wild greens was dressed with apple cider vinegar and wild honey. Desert was berry cobbler with fresh honey-sweetened cream. There was mead and a fine apple wine to drink, followed by more of the port we'd enjoyed the night before.

Tomas called Mary out of the kitchen again to drink a toast to her abilities. Something passed between them that almost escaped my notice, but I was so engrossed with my husband that the thought was shelved for later.

Graeme and I retired to our chamber after an acceptable amount of conversation. He was not the least embarrassed to take my hand and inform the family we were going upstairs to enjoy each other. My face burned again, but I was pleased with his declarations of affection.

The door hardly closed before he swept me into his arms. His tongue explored my mouth; he tasted my skin. I would have swooned if the constant barrage on my senses hadn't abated. I caught my breath as he undressed me and felt his urgency press me.

"The thought o' ye being so bloody close all day and I couldn't have ye was almost too much to bear, mo chroi." He tossed my dress at a line of hooks on the wall.

It caught.

He ran his hands over my back, thighs, and bottom, lifting me with one arm to hip level. I clenched my knees around his waist, holding fast to his shoulders, through the ecstasy that followed. Spent, he carried me to our bed and lowered me to the mattress.

We stayed entwined as the hours ticked past, making love three more times slowly, deliberately tantalizing every nerve sensor until we fell exhausted into slumber. I slept curled against my husband; the crook of his arm, my pillow.

At sunrise Graeme stirred, waking me with kisses. "Ye're beautiful, Lady Macpherson. Look at me, a stor." He stroked my cheek with the back of his fingertips. "Yer eyes are the color of the loch on a stormy day. I stare into its depths, longing to gaze into my beloved's eyes."

I stirred against him, feeling his renewed passion, unrelenting. "Mm, milord, what have you left to give me?"

He chuckled and kissed the top of my head. "All of me, if ye'll have it."

I opened my eyes and watched him shift, pushing me back against the mattress. He took succor at my breasts and probed my eager wetness. I met him before he lowered himself to complete our coupling. A wave of nausea swept over me, but that rare moment was too precious to lose.

Later, cold mornings alone brought that beautiful sunrise to mind more than a few times. I could close my eyes and revel in the smell of his skin, the touch of his hands, the sweetness of his kisses.

Chapter Twelve

I spent the day with my sisters. Ruane and Cora took great pains to explain the process of weaving, wauking, and stretching the fabric they were so proud to render into beautiful frocks, capes, shirts, and cloaks.

I sat in the room at the top of the tower while Ruane's nimble hands wove lisle through the loom. She showed me how to vary the color of a piece, adding stripes and how to blend the colors for breacan. She worked on a piece of wool for a cape.

"When Graeme met us, the night Bran and I came, it poured rain. He wore a wool breacan cape but it shed water. How is that?"

"Lamb's wool is rich in oil, Lizbeth. After Cora finishes the cape I treat it again by rubbing oil into the fabric. It seals well and even sloughs off mud." Ruane smiled with the deference a teacher has with her student.

"It was wonderfully warm as well." I recalled the heat of my husband's body as he encased me in the cloak and his arms. I felt my cheeks tingle at my wandering mind and turned back to Ruane. "Will you teach me how to make one when I come home to stay?"

She grinned. "Aye, 'twill be my pleasure, Lizbeth." Her fingers fluttered about their task as she worked the loom's foot pedal in a soothing rhythm.

I studied Cora, as she cut and stitched her design into a garment. She worked on her sister's wedding clothes that morning. A piece of fragile gossamer cloth became a stunning headdress. Cora modeled it for us and we applauded her efforts. She swept her lithe form into a curtsy worthy of any stage actress.

****

Dinner that evening was uneventful. Tomas drank heavily and Ruane watched him with a stern eye. The meal was as good as the previous evenings but Tomas made no attempt to call Mary from the kitchen. He kept his gaze directed at the dark liquid in his glass, swirling it and sipping the fiery brew.

Graeme and I left the family as soon as we could. We both hankered for the last of our loving time. We spent the night entangled and slept little.

Bran and I left before daybreak. Graeme led my horse, but I rode to the cairn in his arms, astride his black gelding.

His whispered words sent a shiver through me. "My love, I must come to ye in a sennight fer a few days. I canna be without ye."

Mist thickened along the edges of the burn and swirled about the horses' taut legs. The moon had set so there was little light, but the approaching sun.

I lay my hand on his cheek. "You're welcome, sire. My heart and body will be starved for your touch." I pushed my face into the opening at the neckline of his leine, inhaled his familiar scent, then gazed heavenward.

The stars and planets glittered like fine gems against slate blue satin.

"Ye sorely tempt me to cross wi' ye this day." He kissed the top of my head.

I regarded his handsome features and drank in every nuance. The memory had to sustain me. "Whate'er suits you, milord."

He pulled up at the cairn and dismounted, lowered me to the ground and wrapped his arms round me. "I rarely choose to satisfy myself, mo chroi, except with ye." He leaned his forehead against mine and sighed.

Bran rounded the cairn three times sunwise while we said our goodbyes. He pulled his watch from his sporran and slipped it over his wrist. He looked my way and tapped the crystal.

I reluctantly joined him at the mouth of the cairn. I raised a hand to my husband.

Graeme glanced away, taking in a bushel of air. "Farewell, my heart."

I barely heard the words from his mouth as I ducked inside, after a last peek at his fine stature astride the tall strength of the gelding.

Clamoring welcomed us at the entrance to our world. Bran grasped my hand and pulled me through into a den of illegal drug users.

Our entrance was anything but subtle.

Bran loosed my arm and yelled at the top of his best acting voice, "Run, lads, hurry! There're banshees behind us!" He pushed his way towards the opening, but the lads were right enough to get there first and scattered.

He looked about with a grin and took my arm in hand. "Well, then, sis, we're almost home."

We ducked out the entrance and found ourselves alone in the wood.

Leaving my husband in the wee hours that morning, felt as though I'd lost an arm and a leg. It was difficult to move about, like being drunk from the merry-go-round at the park. I had to stumble along through life until we were together again.

Chapter Thirteen

Work at the lab was interesting enough. Classes began at university, but I decided to postpone my education. I had to be ready to cross to my husband and be available when he crossed to me.

Mom fared well, even rallying for three days. We had lunch and supper together and she kept the wee bit of food she was able to swallow.

Aaron called multiple times each day, alternating between threats and appeals to my better nature, which had worn thin. I never saw him with Mom, and he rarely asked after her. I supposed he had his hands full with Margot. At that time, I had no idea what he endured at home. I would soon be privy to far more than I wanted to know.

At the appointed time, I prepared to meet my husband. I waited in my car, near the park entrance. Graeme would meet me here if he made it through the cairn in time. It was late. I'd decided to leave when I spied movement in the shadows and remembered the drug users we'd encountered on our trip a sennight ago.

I cranked the BMW, doors locked, and waited for the shadows to coalesce. A familiar shape materialized...my husband.

He carried a walking stick, propped on his shoulder, and kept a wary eye on his surroundings. He wore a breacan cloak and boineid set at a jaunty angle, the black band tied in back.

I pulled out of the parking space and crept forward. He stopped and studied the car a moment before realizing it was me. He leaned to open the door.

"What'd I tell ye about comin' here alone, woman?" He climbed in and across the seat to kiss me on the mouth. He tasted like heaven.

"I couldn't wait for you to get to the house, so I came here to fetch you." I held his face in my hands and loved the look of him.

"Ye'll get caught by some of the brigands who haunt these woods. I canna bear anythin' bad should happen to ye, Lizbeth." His tone was gentle but earnest.

"I'll give you a key and bus fare then. I was anxious to see you, milord."

"As I am ye, mo 'stor." He sat back and I drove us to the house beside the loch that used to be my home.

I opened the door and preceded him inside. He closed and locked it behind us.

"I bring ye well wishes from our family, wife. Mither and Ruane miss yer company. Cora's sister arrived to be fitted fer her wedding finery. I wondered at all the fuss and was told she's marrying an English lord." He hung up my coat and his cloak. "I fail to ken why there's so much worry over the blessing of the contract when the best of the event is after the ceremony, but then, I'm not a lass." He chuckled and grasped my waist.

"I miss you as well, milord."

He kissed me thoroughly and led me to the bedroom. We spent the evening inside.

We lay together watching the shadows of cloud to ground lightning dance over the ceiling.

"You didn't ask, but I must tell you the water in the new well is very good, 99% pure. You cannot do much better than tha', sir."

He chuckled. "It flew my mind when I saw ye." He turned and faced me. "Everything leaves my mind when I see ye, woman." He kissed me and drew back to comb his hand through my hair. "My beauty, mo chroi."

We gazed at each other in silence for a while, cherishing the moment alone.

"My lord, I'm curious about Tomas. Is he usually given to bouts of grief or is it remembering the loss of his daughters that has him so low?"

He studied me a moment before he answered. "Tomas is like our da in tha'. He grieves life." Graeme shook his head. "No one can lament more fiercely than my brother or laugh more heartily than he, on a good day. Why?"

"I noticed something passes between him and Mary and...."

He sighed. "I hoped ye would not see tha'."

"What is it? Ruane seems to ken. I see it in her eyes. It breaks her heart."

"A dark secret held close fer too long." He pushed himself up and leaned against the headboard. I joined him as he pondered words. His speech alternated between Scots English and Gael. "When Da was a young man he took a widow as mistress. She was a bit older than he. All the better, we think, because a woman would be skilled in the art of love, mayhap. Mary and Agnes are both Da's daughters." He scratched his upper arm, rippling with muscles.

"Oh!" I was shocked, having seen no resemblance between them.

"There's more. When Tomas lost use of his legs he drank heavily to help kill the pain. Ruane was away. Mary was straightening the bedroom one day. Tomas...well, he set about seducing her, in a drunken stupor. She could not resist 'im, he's laird." He spit the last words as though they left a bad taste in his mouth. "It was after tha' she told hi' she was our da's daughter."

"Oh, my!" I caught my breath, saddened at the pain Tomas must feel every time he looked at the sister he raped.

"It daen't end there. Ruane was young and had no expertise in love. She daen't ken what to dae with her husband now he was no longer the lover he once ha' been. She confided in Mary." Graeme took in a bushel of air. "Mary took her to Tomas. He ha' to tell Ruane of his sin. Mary, always practical, took Ruane in hand to teach her how to take care of his needs. Her shame was redeemed, but Tomas was just beginning to feel guilt over wha' he'd done to his family."

"We can't live deceitful lives and avoid the snares." I offered the little wisdom I possess on such matters.

"Aye, well said." He turned to eye me with a sidelong glare. "Please daen't view my brother as untrustworthy. Had he been himself, it would not have happened."

I smiled in the dark and brushed my hand over his arm. "I won't. I promise."

We slept soundly for a few hours then welcomed the sunrise making slow deliberate love. Graeme moved in such a relaxed pace as to send me reeling. He watched me in the dawning light, amused or pleased at the effect he had on my body. After I exhausted my supply of joy, he filled me with his own, moaning my name until he collapsed beside me.

I left him sleeping and drove to the nursing care facility to see Mom. She slept soundly and I left after a peck on her cheek and a note to Molly to call me when she came in for the day.

A stop at the market to stock the pantry was last on my list before I headed back to the house by the loch. I'd begun to think of it that way. No longer my home, it's where I'd stay a little longer. Then *home* with my husband, this wild, beautiful man who had spun my world askew.

The BMW came to a halt in front of the garage. I sat listening to the neighborhood come alive around me.

It struck me like a brick, this odd realization that Graeme was from another time, more than three hundred years difference in our ages. I looked down at my swelling belly and wondered if the reason I felt so estranged to this place grew inside me.

I carried in groceries. He walked from the bedroom. One glance and I knew I didn't care if he was a thousand years older and I had all his babies on this side of the rift. I loved the man, was totally in awe of everything about him. He smiled and stretched, then came to take the grocery box from my arms.

His tone and speech were lazy with sleep. "What's 'is then?" His black hair fell over his eye when he yawned. He raked a hand through it, carrying the box in one hand as though it weighed nothing.

"Breakfast, lunch, dinner; you ken food?" I smiled at his reaction.

One dark brow rose over a sardonic look. "I prefer ye to everything else." He tabled the box and turned to lift me off my feet and spin in the middle of the floor in the living space.

I held up one hand. "Not wise, milord. Don't make me dizzy. I do that without help."

He stood me on my feet and held me gently. "Oh, mo chroi, I daen't ken these things." He mussed my hair with his face and kissed my neck. "I pray our child will look just like his mother."

"What if he's a girl?" I peered into his dark gaze.

"Then she'd best look like her mother. I daen't want a daughter who has to shave every day. She'd be hard pressed fer a suitor."

I laughed and fell into his arms.

We loved the day away, taking breaks for nourishment. Too soon, he had to leave again. There were war councils. The English beat the drums of invasion. I knew it was imminent; I'm a history buff.

As we parted, at the park near the entrance, I prayed for his safety as I watched him lope up the hill and around the cairn. I felt the tremble of earth and the vibration of the air and knew he'd crossed. Leaving me behind was difficult for my lover. Staying behind was nearly impossible for me.

Chapter Fourteen

I felt our baby move. At least I think that's what happened. I'd lived through the queasiness Agnes promised would be my constant companion. That was past two and a half months ago. My doctor said we were well. I'll birth a strong child. In two weeks we have a sonogram and may determine whether we'll have a boy or girl.

I was so excited I had to tell someone, so I told Mom. She smiled and gripped my hand with more vigor than usual. I told a friend at work, Mindy. I hope to tell my husband soon.

Graeme's due to come over in a few days, barring trouble.

****

Molly, Mom's nurse, called at three in the morning. It was time.

I called Bran's home to leave a message. "Hullo, Bran. I need you to go across. The care facility just called. I'm going to sit with Mom...."

"Lizzie?" He picked up the phone, his voice fuzzy with sleep.

"Aye, 'tis me." I wiped my face free of tears and sniffed. "Will you fetch Graeme, please?"

"Aye, I'll cross this mornin'. Are you alright, sis?"

"I'm fine. We've had so many last moments with Mom it'll almost be a relief. Her kidneys shut down last night. It's the end for sure."

"I'll bring 'im to you. Should I try the house first?"

"Aye, I'll be here unless I'm not. You have a key. I'll try to call you if I miss you after dusk. Thanks so much."

"You're verra welcome."

We disconnected and I dressed for the long day ahead.

****

87

Aaron was on premises when I arrived. He immediately scolded me. "Where've you been?"

"Home, asleep, it's almost four in the morning. When did you get here?"

He shrugged. "A few minutes ago. I thought you'd stay with her since her organs were failing."

I faced him full on, held his eyes with mine, and snapped. "Stop this right now. If you're going to be an ass, do it somewhere else." I held onto the stern expression, though I'd rather have cried. "I won't deal with you, Aaron. If you can't be calm and civil, be gone."

I turned to check on Mom. Her mouth dropped open, but she was breathing. A touch of her skin left a damp film on my fingertips. Her pores released the fluids her kidneys could no longer process. I sat beside her bed and watched the woman who gave me life slipping away to the other side...to perfection.

Once, when I was ten, she surprised me with a birthday party. I had piano lessons after school and came home to a dozen friends who jumped from hiding places screaming *surprise*. She made a green and pink maxi dress for me and bought me a Barbie doll in Highland clothes.

We had buried my father two weeks earlier. She tried so hard to make life normal again, though it had completely altered. We lost the house, the car, and private school.

A month after my birthday I no longer had the same friends. We'd moved to an estate in a poor region of Glasgow. Mom waited tables and scrimped to get us through. After six months the restaurant owner promoted her to assistant manager and she took night classes to be the best in her field. She retired a regional manager of a national chain of fine restaurants.

She never remarried or even dated, but devoted herself to raising Aaron and me and making a home we returned to frequently over the years. She was a good mom.

I heard her gasp and looked up to see her lips curl into a smile as she exhaled this foul earthly air for the last time. I kissed her hand and laid it across her midsection.

"Well, *that's* finally over."

I'd forgotten Aaron was still in the room.

"You may go now." I eyed him with defiance. "I'll call you with funeral arrangements."

"I guess I could stay and...."

"No!" I barked. "Please go."

He watched me, hands in his pockets. "You can sign the house...."

"Get out!" I left the chair, longing to get my hands around his throat and choke the life from his body.

"I'm going." He turned and swung the door open, sliding through it with grace.

Molly stood and pressed her hand on my shoulder. "Do you want to be alone, lass?"

"No, ma'am. I'm going to finalize arrangements. Will you tend to what's left to do on this end?"

"I will. Call me if you need me." She squeezed my shoulder and I left.

****

I waited for the vicar in the sanctuary of the church. Sitting on the front pew, I studied the Stations of the Cross in stained glass windows. The sunlight behind them lent tender beauty to each one. I closed my eyes and took a deep breath of incense fragranced air.

My heart felt calm. I would miss my mother terribly, but God gave me a reprieve these last nine months to prepare for her passing. Watching her daily struggle through the pain was difficult to the point of feeling relieved that she finally attained permanent rest.

Soft footsteps echoed on the ancient wood floor behind me. I stood as Father Anthony reached me and extended his frail hand.

"Lizbeth, my dear, how are ye?" He kissed my cheek, a lock of snow white hair slipping across his brow.

"I'm fine, sir. Mom…."

"I ken, Rosemary told me ye'd called. When do ye want the service? I have Thursday open at 1:00 if it works fer ye." He grasped his hands in front and wore a studied frown.

"That's fine then. Rosemary completed the order of service months ago. I just felt that I needed to come by as I haven't actually been here in a while."

"That's understandable, dear, with Aaron in service nearby. I'd expect you to prefer his younger congregation." He smiled, teeth yellowed from years of tobacco use.

"Ah, well. That's all I needed, sir. Thank you for takin' a moment to speak with me. I'll be goin' now."

I walked down the same center aisle I'd walked, as a young bride. Could it only have been five years instead of a lifetime ago? As I rounded the corner I caught a glimpse of the bride's room, where I'd dressed. A woman inside arranged a bridal gown on a stand. There'd be a wedding in a day or so.

God, please bless that marriage.

I climbed into my old BMW and warmed the engine for a moment at this site that had such impact on my growing up years. My father's funeral had been held here, I was married here, and Aaron was ordained in this sacred place. It was right that Mom's last visit to a church would be this one.

I headed to the house by the loch. In a little while, perhaps my husband would arrive. At least we'd have a few days together. Hopefully the solicitor would have the legalities worked out so I could return home with Graeme.

I walked inside the house as the phone rang. I listened to the machine as it answered. Finally the familiar, nagging voice began to record. "This is Aaron, *again*, Lizbeth. I ken you're there. Pick up the phone!"

I wouldn't give him the satisfaction of really knowing where I was. I punched delete at the first opportunity. The light blinked. He'd called four times since he left me at sunrise. I knew what he wanted and why, but he'd have to wait.

I ran a hot bath and climbed in without turning on a light in my bathroom. One small, high window provided enough to see. I relaxed, letting the warm water soak away the tension and loss. I felt renewed enough for a nap when I finally pulled the drain. I dried and used our mither's balm on my round belly and my breasts. The fragrance of rosemary, lavender, and roses filled my senses and fed the longing to go home.

I slipped into a white gown and stretched out on my bed, pulling the quilt over me. The wind picked up, blowing clouds into rain. The gentle patter of drops pelting the windows was like a lullaby. I slept.

His breath, blowing softly across my face, woke me. Opening my eyes, I rolled to my back to find my husband poised over me with his beautiful smile.

"I watched ye fer a bit, but got tired o' waitin' fer ye to wake." He nuzzled my neck, his face chilled from the coolness of the rainy evening.

Wrapping my arms around his neck, I began to cry. He held me. His strong embrace was a comforting place to be, regardless of the reason. He gathered me in his grasp and sighed, kissing my hair and forehead.

"Graeme, I miss you so much. I want to go home wi' you this time. I must be finished here to go." I sniffed and wiped my face.

"I ken, mo chroi. This is the last time we'll cross. Bran left; said he'll return in a bit with provisions."

"He's gone for Chinese take away." I smiled and wiped tears. I studied my husband's face. "You look tired, milord."

"Aye, a bit." He ran his hand through his hair and frowned. "Tomas is ill, beloved. He has troubled breath, um...." He searched for words.

"Hacking cough, cold and hot at the same time?"

"Aye, all tha'. The healer's been to 'im twice and a physician called in to check him. They say he's dyin'. I daen't ken." He looked away.

"How's Ruane handling it?" I sat up and kept my hands on his arms. He felt wonderful.

91

"She's fair. Ruane's buried two children, if she loses Tomas...?" He shook his head.

"I ken, sir." A thump into my rib cage made me smile. I reached for Graeme's hand and pressed it to the top of my belly. "Our bairn's awake."

A grin slowly spread over him. His head tilted to one side, he closed his eyes. "Ah, there ye are little one. Yer da's anxious to have yer mam home so we can dae this ever' day." He leaned over my belly and kissed the spot where our baby moved. The little one kicked him. He guffawed. "Tha's a Macpherson fer ye, lass. We're strong limbed."

The front door opened and closed. "Hullo?" Sacks rustled.

"That'd be Bran. I'll get up and dress."

Graeme helped me off the bed and pulled me into his arms. "Ye're the most beautiful thing my eyes have landed on since the last time I left ye."

"I love you, Graeme." I kissed him gently.

"And I ye, cuisle mo chroi."

Pulse of my heart—I had no idea how many times I'd replay his words when all hope of ever seeing him again eked away.

Bran cleaned up the take away containers, chattering about one of the ladies he met while waiting to come back with Graeme. "What's her name?" He looked at my husband who shook his head.

"I daen't ken. Her brother's name is Fergus, though, big lad, none too bright. He's the smithy in the barmekin."

Bran's face went blank. "Wha' do you mean?"

"I'm just saying, ye ken, be careful who ye get...well, caught up with, tha's all. Ye may be able to walk away from a lass here after ye've," The Macpherson's hand waved back and forth. "been with her, but tha' won't be the case if ye tamper with a lass who has a brother in tow. Ye'll find yerself married, ye will."

Bran grinned, dimples and the cleft chin so alluring to unsuspecting victims. "I ken, sire. I had no intention of takin' advantage. Perhaps, I'm thinkin' of lookin' for my own lass?"

"You, married?" I laughed. "Good luck to the bride."

"I know you have trouble believing me, Lizzie, but I'm thinkin' hard about settlin' down." He nodded and crossed his arms. "Aye, been thinkin' it for a while now. I want a family, little ones to look after and such." He studied the ceiling. "Could be just the thing. Sire, do you think I could make a life in your land?"

Graeme deliberated an answer as he watched his lustful friend. "Well, mayhap so." He grinned. "The right woman might turn more than yer head though, lad." He reached for my leg and rested his hand on my thigh.

Glancing down, I did a double-take. I brushed the top of his hand with my fingertips. It was different. Recalling the day, more than six months earlier, that I first touched his hand at the kitchen bar, sparse black hair lay flat against beautiful skin. His skin had aged more than ten years; white hair replaced more than half the black. Maybe I was mistaken. I looked up to find him watching me.

I smiled and rubbed his arm. *What's going on that he's aging more rapidly? It could be the pollutants here or the stress of the electrical field in the crossings, maybe both.*

Bran began talking coin sales with Graeme. Suddenly, they both turned to me.

"Pardon?" I hadn't been listening to them.

"Dae ye need more money here, lass? Bran will buy back coins if we're ready to go home after laying Maggie to rest." His brow furrowed.

"No, I don't. There's more than nine thousand pounds left in the checking account. Sure, buy the coins back." I checked my husband. There were silver streaks in his raven black hair that had not been there a fortnight ago. I swear.

"There then is yer answer. Take what you need as payment fer yer trouble." Graeme leaned back and scrutinized the neighbors at the loch, walking, jogging, and pushing a pram on the sidewalk. Crow's feet on each side of his eyes were new.

"Well, thank you, sire. I'll get out of your way and see you Thursday then. I can be here by 10:00, sis, if it works for you."

"Aye, Bran, tha's fine."

We stood and Bran reached to hug me.

"I don't believe I've ever seen you more lovely, Lizzie." He squeezed my shoulders, released me, and headed for the door. Bran too, looked suddenly older. Why haven't I noticed?

Graeme sat in silence for more than an hour, meditating. He didn't see the people milling about at the loch where his gaze fixed. I wondered if his mind was home, with his brother.

I watched him for a while and then left to find an appropriate outfit for Mom's funeral. I clawed through my limited number of loose frocks hanging in my closet, finally coming out with a simple black sheath belted for a svelte look. No need for a belt these days. I lifted my gown over my head and pulled the sheath on after securing my new larger bra. The dress was a snug fit over my midriff but might pass muster. I found a long, loose eggplant purple jacket that worked as camouflage for the belly.

When I turned, my husband filled the doorway, lounging on the jamb with a pleased look on his face.

"Ye have nice legs, lass. Are ye sure ye wanna show 'em off like tha'?"

I glanced down at the dress hem striking below my knees. "Sir, the dress is long in this realm. If you'd rather I not wear it, I may find something else in my closet." I grimaced. "Perhaps trousers?"

"Nay, wife, if it's custom here, then it's fine wi' me. But if I catch a man leering, I'll have to kill 'im." He smiled but somehow I knew he meant the threat, as stated.

"I doubt that'll be a problem. You'll be with me so I don't think a man would be inclined to ogle this shapely bod." I turned sideways and slipped off the jacket.

He was already beside me, passing his hand over my enlarged belly to the base of the nest where his child grew strong. He smiled and kissed my neck. "To bed, lass. I'm starved fer ye."

He began the process of disrobing me. He's methodical in a sensual way, with his lips on all he can reach. He chuckled when he felt our bairn began to kick.

"How dae ye stand all the commotion?" He led me to bed with a smile.

"I enjoy it, knowing he's well." I sat on the side of the bed while he lowered himself in front of me and wrapped his arms around me.

He nestled his face between my breasts and moaned. "Mmm."

The situation improved from there.

Chapter Fifteen

Graeme and Bran stood a little apart from my family and the few friends of Margaret Campbell Walker who braved the icy November afternoon. We grieved by her graveside, our last connection with the shroud that had been her body. Father Anthony murmured words of comfort as he clasped each of our hands. I scooped a handful of dirt and tossed it onto Mom's coffin.

"Ashes to ashes, dear, sweet one." I whispered, swiping at my wet cheeks.

I felt a stern grip on my upper arm, hauling me to my feet.

Aaron demanded my undivided attention. "Now this wretched circus is past us, we can get on with more pressing matters." He nodded in Graeme's direction. "What's *he* doing here?"

"He arrived last night. His name is Graeme, and *he*'s my husband." I snatched back against his grasp. It tightened. His nails dug into my flesh.

"Well, send him back. We have family business to discuss and it has nothing to do with him." He pulled my arm, turning me away from our mother's grave.

I tried to break his hold again. I gritted my teeth and whispered, "Stop, Aaron!"

"Shut up!" he growled. "Don't make a scene or I'll expose everything right here. All the world can know you whore to a dead man. Oh yes, I know who he *was*."

Graeme approached us at a brisk pace. "Wha's this then?" He glared at Aaron and reached for my arm.

Aaron released me to my husband and smiled. "She felt weak for a moment. I was supporting her. This has been such an ordeal for all of us. Dear Mommy took more than a year to die, wasting away to nearly nothing. She suffered so much

96

and poor Lizzie was always right there by her side." He turned a cow-eyed glance towards me.

I straightened. "Graeme, we have some family issues to finish." I looked back at Aaron. "We can meet at the solicitor's office. Our appointment is at half two. He was to have paperwork ready this morning, but his assistant was out."

"That'll be fine, then, sister. You get a rest and I'll see you at two-thirty." He offered his hand to Graeme, his vicar smile in place. "It's good to see you again, Graeme."

The Macpherson shook my brother's hand. "Mmm." He glanced at me, keeping a wary eye on Aaron and Margot as they left.

"Lizbeth, wha'?" he demanded.

I looked up and tried to smile. "Nothin', milord. Let's go to the house by the loch and I'll find us a bite to eat." I looped my arm through his and we started for the car with Bran trailing. "Remind me to give you something for Tomas when we get back. I found medication in the box Molly put Mom's last things into. It may help him get well."

Graeme kept his eyes on me as we walked. "Aye, 'twill be appreciated. Ye may pack it in yer things as ye're comin' wi' me."

I looked up and smiled. "Aye, I don't want to miss crossing today, but let's be sure to pack it in your bag, just in case things go badly at the solicitor."

Bran parked behind my old car. He waited for us to stop talking and hugged me. "I'll get outta your way." He glanced up at Graeme. "I'll see you in a few hours, sir."

My husband opened my door and closed it behind me. He nodded. "Aye, Bran, 'til then."

****

"I ken he's yer brother, but he's an eerie fella. Has he always been so?"

"Aye, I often thought something in his mind didn't form right. He's cruel at times." I stirred the pan of tinned condensed soup for our late lunch and caressed the bruised arm from my encounter with Aaron, graveside.

97

Graeme stood at the bar watching. "Lizbeth, ye'll have to be quick about yer business if we're to cross at dusk."

"I ken." I glanced back at him and felt my knees go weak. "I'll meet you there if I'm late. Bran can drive you to the cavern and I'll follow as soon as I can get away."

He untied the thong that held his hair back, and propped on the bar his head tilted to one side. His wavy salt and pepper mane fell to cover his ears. "Lizbeth, somethin's no' right."

I laid my hand over his arm. "Graeme, we have to stop crossing...." I glanced down at his hand and brushed my fingers over his wrinkled brown skin. "It's too dangerous. There's cellular damage to your system. I'm afraid for the bairn and...you." I bent to kiss the back of his hand. His skin felt like crepe paper against my lips.

Chapter Sixteen

Graeme paced the front of the cavern. Bran waited in the car, expecting a call from Lizbeth, any moment, if she didn't appear.

The Macpherson sighed with relief when he spotted Bran lifting the receiver to his ear. He looked back at Graeme with a frown and then hung the phone back in its cradle. Bran took his time getting out of the car and walked round back with his hands stuffed into his pockets. They met in the middle of the lawn.

"That was Lizbeth. She said to go on without her." Bran braced for Graeme's reaction.

"Wha's happening that she can't come home wi' me?"

Bran glanced away. "I don't know, sir. She says there was still business to attend concerning her mother's death."

"Bran, look a' me. Tell me wha' she told ye—exactly."

"She said, 'Tell Graeme I'll join him as soon as possible. Tell him *not* to come back. Have you got it?' I said, 'He won't like the message.' She said 'There's nothing I can do to change what must be.' That's everything."

For a moment Graeme pondered what the conversation meant.

Bran spoke up. "Graeme, I don't know if this makes sense and I'm not saying Lizbeth's like this but...there was a woman once." He turned away.

"Finish yer story, Bran." Graeme checked the sky.

"She's the only woman I would have married. Anyway, she found out she was pregnant, uh, with child. She finished with me. I begged her to marry me. She continued to refuse. Finally, she laughed and said she got all she wanted from me.

"She wanted the child, not a father, or a husband. She used me and tossed me aside." Bran scuffed the toe of his leather shoe on the path. "I have a son growing up somewhere in London. A mutual friend told me when he was born. I've never seen him."

Graeme shook his head. "I can't fathom Lizbeth...."

99

"And I'm not sayin' that's what's goin' on. It's just...a lot like what happened wi' me." Bran started to leave, then whirled back. "You ken, forget it. I'll bring her to you as soon as she's ready." He took two steps away and turned back again. "Don't pay any attention to what I just told you. I'm sorry, really." He hurried to his car and hopped off the curb.

Graeme called after him before he made the car door. "Tell her a fortnight, not a moment longer!" He stormed past the park patrol who was leaving and picked up the pace. He made haste to reach the cavern.

****

Mom's solicitor left Aaron, Margot, and me alone in his office for an urgent call in his conference room. We'd concluded our business.

I looked into my brother's cold hazel eyes. The sneer he wears most of the time is infuriating. He serves a tiny church on the edge of a small town nearby. It suited his wife, Margot, to live in Mom's house. It was free, quite spacious, and close to the church. She and Aaron are very good to act the part of the pious vicar and his supportive wife. They have one problem they can't overcome—Aaron's impotent and sterile. Margot wants a child.

Margot's voice sounded cajoling. "I ken this fake marriage business, Lizbeth. Maggie told me you were expecting. That's no way to raise a child. We want to adopt him when he's born. You can stay here and have him, then go to...well, that other place to your man."

I know her better than to believe she means well.

I turned my glare from my brother to his wife. "There's no fake marriage, Margot. Graeme and I took our vows *in a kirk*, with his family as witnesses. I don't need to provide any kind of proof to satisfy you." I gathered my coat and purse and looked back. "We're finished, the three of us. You have the deed to the house now. You have no more need of a relationship with me." I headed to the door. Neither made a move to stop me.

The drive home gave me time to reflect on our conversation. Aaron followed Graeme and saw him cross over. He held that over my head as the threat to make me miss tonight's deadline. It was almost eight o'clock.

If authorities caught my husband on this side, with no papers or identity, he'd rot in jail. They couldn't even deport him as they do European, Middle Eastern and Asian immigrants, who stow away or cross in boats, running drugs and whatnot. There's no place he belongs, but Scotland, no time but his own.

I pulled into my driveway, parked, turned off the car, and sat listening to the tick of the engine cooling.

What to do? Go to bed, get up early and make the crossing at dawn. I still had my security pass from the festival. I should be able to enter the castle grounds without detection. If a guard appeared I'd flash my badge and go girlie on him until he succumbed to my charms. Hah!

Fumbling for the front door key, I got out of the car. I unlocked the door and prayed Graeme changed his mind. As I opened the door, my hope vanished. It was dark, cool, and empty. He hadn't returned. He went home without me. Tomas' illness concerned him and he could use the antibiotic from Mom's box to keep him alive.

Glancing down at my growing belly, I hung up my coat. Esperenza, Graeme's mither, will have missed three full months of my pregnancy. She dotes on all her daughters, enjoying the pregnancies with us. I long for her almost as much as Mom.

This used to be my home, my sanctuary. Since the day Graeme stepped into the space, it revolved around him. I turned to the living room and flipped on a light. It was cold, impersonal, and lonely. I wanted to go home *to him*.

The phone rang. It was Bran. "Hey! How'd things go? Did you finish your business?"

A smile crept over me. His voice was upbeat and happy.

"Aye, it is complete. Do you have all you need to sell this house?"

"I do, are you goin' over?" His tone was hopeful.

"At dawn. I'll pass through the castle. Will you remember where the cavern is in the park?"

"I will." The line went quiet for a moment. "Lizzie, I wish I was coming with you. You want me to take you on the morrow? I can sleep over tonight."

I shook my head and chose a tin of soup. "No need, I'll take a taxi. You can always visit, just not often. I've noticed cellular damage on you and Graeme. Both of you have more lines in your faces, and your hair is grayer than six months ago. Did Himself get off alright?"

"Aye, he was angry though. He yelled 'a fortnight and not a moment longer'. He'll be fine when you get there. You ken he loves you, lass?"

"Aye, and I love him with all my heart, Bran. I really didn't know what it meant before. I did your brother a terrible disservice, marrying him. Well, we'll say goodnight. I'm going to bed. Thank you for all you've done."

His voice softened. "You're welcome, sis."

"Bye!" I grinned.

I hung up and wiped a tear away.

Being pregnant is fascinating, but it's an emotional roller coaster ride. I warmed soup and sat at the bar, watching the loch out the window. A few gulls and ernes fished for supper. A neighbor jogged past with his Golden Retriever. A family from next door strolled by with their children. It felt odd to be here. I didn't belong anymore.

Most of my personal items were packed for charity. What the house buyer didn't want of my furnishings would go as well.

A quick wash up took care of my dishes. I'd set the clock in time to cook scrambled eggs and drink the last of the juice in the fridge. I poured and drank a glass of milk, resolving to remember to dump the remainder down the drain. Bran would spend the following night there to be sure everything was ready for the house agent.

I carried a glass of water to my bedroom and sat it on the nightstand. I turned down the white embroidered quilt my mother made when I was a teen and gave to me, as a new bride.

Even brushing my teeth reminded me of home. We use birch and sweet gum twigs at the castle, after each meal. Acid in the wood destroys bacteria in the mouth and the frayed ends clean below gum lines and between teeth. The water's chocked full of minerals and no chlorine. My children will have healthy teeth.

My clothes were laid out to cross over. When I came back, I'd worn a dress that Ruane let me borrow. She made the cloth and Cora made the dress. It was a coral linen high-waisted dress trimmed in hand tatted lace and buttons made from ram's horn. I felt very pretty in it and it was fine fabric. Ruane takes pride in her weaving and wauking. She'll teach me how, when I return…home.

There, I made the final commitment in my heart. I sat on the side of the bed and whispered prayers of solace for Graeme, health for our child, and a safe crossing on the morrow. I slid out of my slippers and wiggled my toes in the deep pile carpet.

The doorbell rang.

Thinking perhaps Bran decided to come spend the night after all, I pulled on my robe, ran to the front entrance, and flung the door open.

I don't know why.

I'd never done that before.

I just knew it was Bran.

Margot grabbed my arm and propelled me back into the foyer. I saw Aaron behind her with something white in his hand.

The odor was familiar.

Ether.

Chapter Seventeen

Coming to, in the dark cold basement of my mother's house, I discovered a nylon cord lashed my hands, another tied around my waist and the stairs tread behind me. I shook my head to clear it and took a moment to figure out how I got here.

Yes, the ether Aaron held over my nose while Margot clutched my face, nails dug in. At least they didn't dump me down the stairs to the cold concrete floor.

Passing my face over my bound hands, I felt dried blood near my left eye.

Wiggling round to get an idea where everything was, I struggled to reach upwards. On the underside of the handrail was a light switch.

Years ago, Mom slipped on the steps. It frightened her so much she wouldn't go down unless I was there with her. I installed a light underneath the hand rail to brighten the way. There were treads but no risers to keep a person from slipping through.

Once the light was on I untie the nylon cord with my teeth. When I was free, I tried the door. Locked from the outside. I stepped down, with care, and surveyed the premises.

The arrangement looked prepared for a guest. A cot sat against one wall with a pillow and a blanket. The single light above was a bare bulb. There's a toilet and sink in the corner. I tiptoed to them to check for running water. I adjusted the water line below each. After a spit and sputter of air in the lines, rusty fluid shot out the faucets and splashed my gown.

I formed a mental image of what the abduction meant. They could keep me down here until my child came then do away with me. It was a grim thought, but I knew Margot and Aaron well enough to believe them capable. No one would miss me. I lived between dimensions in time.

I lay down on the cot and covered myself with the coarse wool blanket and cried.

Why not? It was what felt natural at that moment. I'd conjure a way out later, I thought.

****

The door to the cellar scraped open. The lights were off. I sat in complete darkness. Aaron took the steps down slowly. He carried something on a tray. He hit the light switch at the bottom of the steps and glanced around.

"There you are!"

"Worried I was gone?" Sarcasm was my best tool.

"I brought you breakfast. Be grateful. Margot wants to leave you down here on your own. I think we need to feed you occasionally. If nothing else the child needs nourishment." He sat the tray, with toast and juice, on the end of the cot.

"How kind you are, brother. What do you plan to do with me?" My knees were pulled up, my arms wrapped round them for warmth.

"You've mysteriously disappeared, Lizbeth. We'll take your child. Margot will finally be happy and, after a suitable amount of time, we can have you declared dead and take over your assets. We just want to be able to provide our child with what it needs." He had it all worked out in his own evil way.

"You won't get my assets. Bran has power of attorney. He's in the process of selling my house now." I reached for the toast and nibbled.

"Well, we can change that. We have paperwork declaring you mentally incompetent." He grinned with self-satisfaction.

"Ah, Margot's brother, the solicitor! How clever you both have been and all this time I've assumed you were just greedy fools. The job she had filing for him paid off, eh?" I finished the toast and sipped the juice. I needed strength.

Aaron smirked and turned to leave. "I'll be down in a bit to pray for you. I'll teach you to pray, Lizbeth, as I've learned. I'll teach you of our Lord and Savior before your death. It's the least I can do." He took one step up.

"You've always been one to do the least, Aaron." I smiled without humor. "No thank you, I know how to pray."

He scaled the wood steps and slammed the door. I listened to the lock and decided he'd put a latch with a padlock on it. The key to the handle had been lost for years. It would be harder to break the door down to escape with the new fastener.

My feet were cold. I had no shoes on and no other clothes, but my gown and robe. I decided to explore the cellar and see what was stored that might be useful in my escape.

Pulling dusty boxes from under the stairs I began to sort through them. Memories abounded at the cards and letters, keepsakes and mementos. No shoes. No clothes. I pressed on, checking case after case until I got lucky. That's a matter of opinion, but I was trying my best to keep my attitude positive.

One parcel contained fabric scraps. I pulled out a partial quilt top. I stood, shook it out, and hung it on a nail behind the stairs. I continued rifling through the pieces of fabric. There was an incomplete corduroy skirt. It lacked finish work on the waist and hem. I set it aside. I found a pair of mules.

My mother made slippers of various fabrics and sewed vinyl soles on them. She made very fancy ones to match dresses or robes for costumes in plays. These were plain denim and too short for my long foot by an inch, but welcome anyway. I pulled them on and kept digging. There were a few more partially made garments that I might be able to use.

At least I wouldn't be bored trying to survive in the cold damp cellar. Until I could escape, that is.

By the afternoon, a handy pile of possible tools and clothes was collected. I also found jars of pickles, applesauce, and beans that my mother canned a few years ago, before her illness. I figured I had about a week's supply of nutrients should Margot decide to stop feeding me. I cached my treasure and checked the iron bars over the two windows, both secured in the concrete wall. The windows swung to the inside, or used to. Now they were nailed and painted closed.

I sat on the cot and pondered my dilemma. A key scraped in the padlock. I lay down and pulled the blanket over my chilly frame.

Aaron returned to teach me to pray for my mortal soul.

"Well, you're doin' fine, then. Get up! We're going to work on prayer as a way of life, Lizbeth." He carried a cat-o'-nine-tails in one hand. Embedded glass and sharpened metal adorned the leather lashes.

I got the idea before he explained.

"This," he wielded the whip, "will teach you humility, Lizzie." He appeared convinced.

"Don't call me Lizzie. It implies we're chummy. I'm Lizbeth or Mrs. Macpherson to you." I continued to curl under the blanket.

He reached for my wrap and snatched it away, swinging at the same time. He caught my shin. When he snatched the whip back it ripped flesh.

I screamed.

Aaron froze, the whip poised for another strike. He stared at the blood spurting from my torn shin. I had nothing to press on the flow unless I revealed my stash. It would have to wait.

I tried to inhale, but failed to get my breath.

He had a strange look on his face. My first thought was bloodlust. If he swung the whip again I had to launch into him and take it away. I studied him watching me bleed. I pushed myself further away to the head of the cot, dragging my injured leg.

He turned, lowered the whip, and beat a hasty retreat up the stairs. A few moments later he dropped a roll of paper towel over the handrail. The door slammed and he locked it again.

I crept to the bottom of the steps and brought the towels to my cot. I tore off a few sheets and tossed them aside. I folded two more and applied the compress to my bleeding shin. I didn't have the stomach to check the wound for depth. I salvaged a long strip from the fabric remnants and tied the paper towel over my shin, went to the toilet and threw up the little I'd eaten earlier.

Day one proved eventful. I now knew what they planned to do with me after the child was born. In the meantime it appeared I'd be tortured. Aaron's lack of fervor, beyond the first blow, might soon be remedied by his wife's dissatisfaction.

I left my leg free of the blanket, feeling there was a better chance of the blood clotting if I was cold. Somehow I slept. Hopelessness hovered in the shadowed corners of the cellar waiting for an opportune moment to pounce.

My leg throbbed. I woke in the darkness, reminding me where I was and what was at stake. I gently turned to my back, getting a glimpse of the unfinished ceiling above. I had to find tools and weapons. I had to tear or fight my way out of the cellar. I hobbled to the light switch and studied the dim bulb. Broken it could serve as a weapon. I felt better about the situation.

I crawled under the steps and checked along the concrete wall. Sometimes I laid box cutters or dykes down after I used them. The shelf along the wall was a catchall in my basement. I found a wrench and hefted it in my hand. Not heavy and no sharp edges. I added it to my small pile and proceeded. My left foot hit a metal box, stubbing a toe.

Cursing, I tried to rub another pain away. At least it eased the ache in the shin on my right leg. After I regained some sense, I reached for the box. It had a metal handle on top and looked like a military issued container. A small padlock held the clasp shut.

I hauled it to my cot and collapsed. After I got my wind back, I used the wrench to pry the clasp off the box. The thin metal guards gave way easier than the padlock would have done. I eased the lid open, concerned about it squeaking. I didn't want company.

Inside was an army knife. The blade was not long enough to do mortal damage but it might protect me. I wanted to dance. A few old medals and a small can of spray lubricant finished the list. I tested the sprayer and it worked. Not great but better than nothing. I thought about the lubricant and realized there was more to the box.

A false bottom, pried out with the army knife, revealed a few more items. A whetstone to sharpen the knife lay on top of an oily flannel. Wrapped in the flannel was Da's army issue pistol.

I wanted to check for ammo, but that would have to wait.

The people upstairs began to stir. I rewrapped the pistol in the flannel and tucked it back inside the box. I hid the knife and whetstone under the thin mattress on the cot. I doused the light and lay down, pulling the rough blanket over my chilled body and curled into a ball.

I needed a plan.

Chapter Eighteen
One month later

Graeme tapped on the woodcutter's cottage door. The healer answered.

"Sire, me man's no' here or dae ye come to see 'bout Lady Macpherson?"

Graeme nodded. "The latter, Agnes. Wha' news of my wife?" He propped his hands on his hips and stepped to the back of the small stoop.

Agnes cleared the door and wrung her hands in her aparan. "'Tis no' good, but 'tis no' me fault." She looked him straight in the eye and waited.

"Aye, woman, just tell me!" He sighed heavily.

She cocked her head to one side and studied him, eyes squinting. "She be in a dark place. She be hurt, bleedin', wi' fever."

"Wha' kind of place?" Graeme straightened.

"I daen't ken." She closed her eyes. "It be like a room in de groun' wif no light… a dungeon." She opened her eyes. "Bu' salvation cometh by a unlikely path." She left him, slamming the door closed.

Graeme turned to find the woodcutter waiting for him in the yard. "Sire, she been havin' fits o' the fae o' late. Her sleep is sorely troubled. She cries out wi' pain." He sighed. "But I ain't tellin' ye yer business."

The Macpherson mounted his horse and cantered away. A mile down the road he whipped the gelding on with urgency. He had time to slip over tonight. He'd use the cairn and call Bran from Lizbeth's home.

****

110

Tomas rolled his chair nearer Graeme. "Tell me wha's happening wi' ye, runt." He laid a broad hand over his brother's arm.

"I canna," Graeme grimaced. "Truth is a difficult master these days."

"Ye can trust me." Tomas plied his stubborn sibling.

Graeme looked away. "Remember the trip we took through the tunnel as wee lads?"

"Aye." Tomas chuckled. "I snuck back a few times."

Graeme glanced up. "Ye did? Ye shoulda told me. I did too."

"I figured if Mither found out we'd get a good hiding. Besides, takin' Niall woulda made it a surety. He tells her everythin'."

"I ken. Well, I went back after Bran's visit and met Lizbeth. Tha's where my wife's from, the other side."

"Ruane kenned that the first time we saw her. Said the fabric of her garments was different from any she'd ever seen. The texture was loose, she said, not nearly as strong as her own weavin'."

"Lizbeth stayed behind after I went over fer her mam's funeral. She's carrying my child, brother, and refused to come home wi' me."

"Is tha' why ye've blocked the tunnel?"

"Aye. I went to the seer today. She tells me my wife's in a dungeon."

Tomas leaned back in his chair. "Did Lizbeth say she'd come back to ye?"

"Aye, but she daen't. I gave her a fortnight and that's passed."

"Mayhap she canna. Are ye going to see to her?" Tomas pressed his brother.

"She tol' me not to return."

"There's a reason, Graeme. Tha' woman's smitten wi' ye. I swear there're times ye're blind, bro. Go find wha's keeping her from home."

Graeme scrubbed his chin with a knuckle. "Ye're right. There's a way over, a cairn behind the woodcutter's bothy."

111

"Use it. See to yer wife. It's sin to leave her alone in tha' world and it's no place to raise a child. It's filthy; ye can barely breathe the air, man."

"True that. But if she found trouble, she'd send Bran fer me."

"He may not ken."

Graeme nodded slowly. "Ye're right. I made the decision to close the tunnel in haste."

Tomas slapped Graeme's arm. "If it weren't fer these," he poked his wasted legs, "I'd hie wi' ye. Go, I'll handle things here. Daen't let on to Niall. We'll just say ye have to see to your wife's family. Now, go!"

He left his brother's chambers for the stables.

****

Graeme entered Lizbeth's house with the key she gave him. He turned on a light and went to the phone. There, on a pad, were numbers for Bran, as she'd left them months earlier when she went out for errands. He picked up the strange instrument and put it to his ear. It buzzed. He held it away from his face. He touched the lit buttons on the phone and listened to it ring.

"Hello? You've reached Bran Macpherson. I'm not available at the moment but leave a message at the beep and I'll call you back….beep."

"It's Graeme. I'm at Lizbeth's. Get here, please." He hung up the phone and repeated the process with another number to reach Bran.

"Hello?" Bran sounded puzzled.

"'Tis Graeme. I'm looking fer Lizbeth. Dae ye ken where she is?"

"Where are *you*?"

"At her house by the loch. No one's here. I'll wait fer ye." He cradled the phone. He searched the rooms. There was little in the refrigerator, nothing in the larder. He went to her bedroom. He paused in the door, switched on a light and peered inside. He looked into her privy. Everything was very

112

neat except there was a frock lying on one side of her bed and the bed linens were turned down.

He heard a key in the front door. *Let it be my wife.* He stood in her bedroom doorway and waited.

Bran popped through. "Hey, man, I was just a few miles away. Lizbeth went over to you more than a month ago. I talked to her the night before she left."

"Nay, I've no' seen her. Where was she crossing?"

"The castle." Bran pocketed the key and looked around. "I spoke to her on the phone the night you left. She was prepared to go over. I thought she had. I just went by the house agent's office and dropped off a key. I should've looked in on her."

Graeme sighed. He'd closed the castle tunnel too soon. "Ye ken her habits here better than I dae. Has she been gone a while?"

Bran opened the refrigerator and found a carton of milk soured. He grimaced and closed it. "This is *not* like Lizzie. She hates coming home to a mess. She's one to always empty the milk down the drain if she's to be away." He checked the egg carton. "Even the eggs are out of date. No, not like her at all. Hey, I ken where to look." Bran made a dash to the foyer. He snatched up Lizbeth's purse and opened it. "Everything's here. She wouldn't leave her purse. Even if she goes for a walk, she takes her keys." He held up the key fob.

They went back to the living area. Bran scanned the room for more clues.

Graeme entered her bedroom again, after steeling himself for the emotional roil. "Looks like she was interrupted on her way to bed."

Bran followed, lounging behind him in the doorway. "Aye, it does that. There's even a glass of water there on her nightstand." He picked it up, holding it to the light. "There's a layer of dust on the surface and around the glass on the table."

"Hae ye spoken to her brother?"

"The right Reverend Aaron Walker? Nay, he's got no pleasant words for this filthy sinner. He said that to me once."

Graeme's brow rose. "Really?"

"Aye, said I disgusted him. I said that was fine, didn't care much for him either." Bran straightened. "I'll find her address book and get a number for him."

Graeme nodded, then paused with his hand up. "Wait! Let's surprise 'im instead."

Bran parked a quarter mile away from the preacher's house. "I don't want to give our presence away. We'll walk from here."

He and Graeme left his car and strode up the darker side of the road.

They passed the house and doubled back, entering the property in shadows. The front porch lamp glowed in the haze.

Graeme stood to one side of the doorway while Bran used the knocker.

Bran whispered, "I hear someone comin'."

Graeme nodded, hands clenched into fist at his sides. *What a hateful place this is. The air's like breathin' damp soot.*

The door swung inside. Aaron smiled, obviously expecting someone other than Bran. "You! What do you want?" He demanded rudely.

Bran cleared his throat. "Just wondering if you or your wife has any idea to the whereabouts of your sister. We've been to her house. I was concerned because I've tried to…."

"No! She said she was going to be out of town for an indefinite period of time. That's all I know." Aaron put force behind closing the door when it struck Graeme's large boot.

"Ye're lyin'." Graeme pushed his weight into the door and shoved the pastor back against the wall in the foyer.

Bran followed him in after a covert glance around at the sparsely populated neighborhood.

"Check everywhere ye could hide her," The Macpherson ordered Bran, turning to Aaron, firmly pinned to the wall by his stout arm.

Aaron paled with fright. "I'll call the police! You have no right to enter my home!" He shook with ire.

Graeme glared and growled, "I think ye shan't be allowed that privilege. Ye'll tell me what ye ken 'bout Lizbeth."

"I don't have to tell you anythin'…." His feet cleared the floor when Graeme forced his thin frame up the wall with one hand on his chest.

"Ye daen't ken the urgency of the situation ye're in, preacher. My wife's missing and I'll have everything ye know."

Aaron pressed his thin lips together and shook with rage.

Bran walked back into the foyer. "No sign of her, but there's a locked door I think leads to the cellar."

"Where's the key?" Graeme asked Aaron in a pleasant tone.

"My wife has it." Aaron spit through snarling lips.

"Bran, look fer the key. We got all night." Graeme kept the preacher pinned to the wall, the toes of his shoes barely touching the floor.

Five minutes passed. Bran reappeared. "Nothing."

"Ye hold the parson here and I'll look. Around this corner, ye say?"

"Aye." Bran grinned into Aaron's distraught face as he restrained the preacher against the wall.

A curse followed the crunch of wood. "Damn! Bran, bring him and come." Graeme's footsteps pounded the wooden stairs inside the cellar.

Bran soon joined him, pushing Aaron ahead, down the steps.

"Wha's this?" Graeme glared at a cot with a blanket and pillow, a toilet and sink in the corner and a bare light bulb dangling from the ceiling. He picked up a soiled gown, lifting the neckline to his nose. "This is Lizbeth's."

"Is that blood?" Bran paled.

"Aye." Still gripping the gown, Graeme turned to Aaron. He roared, "I'll have ye tell me where my wife is now."

The preacher wept. "The hospital—my wife took her to hospital."

"What'll we do with him?" Bran's grip bit into Aaron's upper arm.

"Kill 'im." Graeme glanced around for any other sign of Lizbeth.

"Um, tha's against the law."

"You fetch yer car. I'll kill 'im." Graeme reached for Aaron.

"Sire, I canna be a party to that. I ken he's done something awful with your wife but we have people who deal with that sort of thing."

Himself studied his companion for a moment. "If I daen't kill 'im now, I'll have it to dae another time."

Bran released Aaron and climbed the steps back up from the basement. Aaron followed, Graeme on his heels.

Bran led the way out the door. The Macpherson stopped at the entry and looked back at his wife's brother. "Ye have a brief reprieve. Use it wisely. If I lay eyes on ye again, ye're a dead man. If ye lay a hand on my wife, ye'll have sealed yer fate."

Aaron trembled, keeping his eyes cast down towards the floor.

"Dae ye ken what I'm saying, preacher?"

"Aye, I understand." Aaron kept his eyes lowered.

Graeme cleared the door, meeting Bran outside. He growled at his friend, "I hope we daen't live to regret tha' decision."

"Aye, sire, I hope we made the right choice, for Lizzie's sake."

Chapter Nineteen

Shocked at the sight of Graeme in the hospital room I snapped, "Get out! Hurry!"

"Ye're my wife, having my child. I'll no' leave ye." My husband crossed his arms and met my eyes with a chilling gaze.

I glanced away, then back at my husband's pallor. "I don't want you here, Macpherson. Go!" I looked past him at Bran. "Please, get him out of here."

Sweat beading on my brow, I whispered, "Margot will be right back. Graeme, *you must go*. Bran, please."

"He canna make me dae anythin', Lizbeth. I'll be staying here with ye." Graeme insisted, pulling a chair round to sit.

Bran shook his head. "Sir, I think we need to heed her wishes." He looked back at the hospital room's door.

It opened slowly. Margot entered with a cup of coffee in one hand. "Wha's this? Who're you to be in here with my sister?"

Bran spoke confidently. "She's my sister, too, Margot."

"And who is this man you're draggin' round wi' ye?" Sneering, she examined Graeme with a critical eye.

"I'm her husband, woman. This is my child she carries and ye'll kindly leave the room."

An evil grin slid over Margot's narrow face. "Is not your child she's bearing; he's mine. She's givin' him to me." Her head bobbed side-to-side as she spoke, a smug expression in place.

Graeme turned to me, watching my eyes.

Tears joined the perspiration slipping down my face. "Tha's true, my love. The child will be taken by my brother and his wife." I met his eyes. "Aaron helped me see we're not properly wed, you and I. He's helpin' me see that the best thing for our baby is to have a proper Christian home and upbringin'."

"If ye daen't want the child, I'll take him. Ye daen't need to find someone else. He has a da. He has a family." Graeme pleaded, not grasping the situation or the strange turn of events.

117

I had to get him to go away.

"No," I shook my head. "It's better that he grows up with Aaron and Margot." My voice faltered at the end. I closed my eyes. Tears choked me.

Graeme laid his hand over mine. My fingers snaked around his and clasped them.

He waited.

I adjusted the pillows behind me with the other hand. He rose and kissed my forehead, wiping the beads of moisture off and onto his leine. He whispered, so only I would hear. "My heart, I daen't ken wha' ye're doin' or why. I'll go, as ye ask, if I must. I'll not cause ye more pain."

He released me and turned away. I refused to open my eyes.

I could not watch him leave.

****

Bran touched Graeme's arm, once in the hallway. "Sire, let's duck into the coffee shop and talk this over." He led the way.

They drew coffee from urns and sat at a corner table.

"I don't ken what's happened with Aaron and Margot, but obviously they hold Lizbeth against her will."

"Aye, did ye see the lashes on her arms? I fear to ken what's under the bindin' on her leg." Himself sipped the coffee and winced.

"Might I suggest a ruse? Why don't you wait in my car? I'll go back up and talk to Lizbeth when Margot steps out again. I'll catch her alone and find out what's happenin'." Bran glanced around the small shop. "Could they know who you really are?"

Graeme scrubbed his chin. "Mayhap we were followed. I daen't ken." He sighed.

"Come on." Bran rose and they hied to his silver-blue Mercedes. He unlocked the doors and they slid inside. "I may be awhile. Do you want me to take you back to Lizbeth's house or will you be alright?"

"I'll wait here." Graeme propped his elbow on the doorframe and rested his head in his hand. "Go on, then. I'll no' leave the car unless I see ye runnin' out the door with her in hand."

Bran chuckled. "Aye, sire. If this doesn't work we'll make a new plan. At least we ken she's here. I'm sorry. I should've gone by her house like I said I would." Bran opened the door and loped back to the hospital and the room where Lizbeth awaited treatment.

He loitered in the corridor until a nurse approached him. He flashed a darling smile. "My wife's waitin' for treatment from an injury." He nodded to the door in front of him. The door to Lizbeth's room opened and a doctor emerged. "Ah, I'm at the wrong door." He rolled his eyes.

Hurrying after the doctor, Bran called out, "Excuse me, sir, did you treat Lizbeth Macpherson just now?"

The doctor turned. "I'm tryin'! The wound on her leg has gone septic. The woman with her insists I release her, but I cannot let her go."

"Nay! You're right. She's my wife. I apologize, I'm Bran Macpherson." He offered his hand. "Margot brought Lizzie to the hospital while I've been out of town. I'll sign whatever you need to keep her here."

"That'd be fantastic. The witch with her is wearin' me down. Go on to her room then and I'll send up paperwork." The doctor turned away and made hasty steps to the nursing station. "Let's get Mrs. Macpherson admitted. Her husband's here now." He looked back at Bran, pointing. "That's him there."

Bran threw his hand up and flashed a smile. He headed to Lizbeth's room. He tapped and opened the heavy door.

****

"You again?" Margot demanded.

"And why should I not be here? I'm her husband." He turned to Lizbeth. "Darlin', I just spoke to the doctor. Someone will be in shortly with paperwork to sign. He wants to admit you and I gave him permission."

Margot shrieked. "You canna do that!"

119

Bran grinned. "We have the same last name and I say we're married. You have no authority over her."

Margot opened her purse with a fiendish glare and produced a legal document. "I have complete control of her. She's been declared mentally unfit." She waved the official looking paper in Bran's face.

I said nothing, surprised at Bran's bravado. I watched the two of them go at it. Bran was far more intelligent than Margot, but she was a hellcat.

Bran glanced back at me. "Lizzie, do you want me to stay with you?"

I looked away. Bran needed to get Graeme back to the cavern. "Where's Graeme?"

He considered me a moment. "Nearby."

"Get him home, Bran. After the paperwork comes, make sure he leaves. He cannot be caught on this side."

"Ha!" Margot propped her hands on her hips.

I turned to face her. "I'm not leavin' hospital. If I don't have treatment there's a good chance I'll lose my leg or even die, *before the child is born*. I won't try to escape. Just let Bran get Graeme out and I'll be a good girl and not run away."

I shifted my eyes to Bran. "Get me something to write on and I'll pen a note so he'll go without an argument."

Bran handed me a pad from the bedside drawer. I wrote a few words to Graeme. As I folded it I spoke to Margot. "Step out a moment. I need to tell Bran what to say to my husband to get him to leave." I held up the paper. "This won't be enough."

She eyed me with mistrust and slithered her thick torso through the door to wait on the other side.

I lowered my voice and motioned Bran to the bed. "Go by my house and get clothes and shoes for me to cross. Have them ready in your car. I don't know when I'll get free of Aaron and Margot, but it *will* happen. I have to be here until my leg heals, Bran. Be sure Graeme understands that I can't cross over with this infection. It's a tick away from being gangrenous."

He nodded. "I'll come back and check on you. This paper she has...?"

"It's something she lifted from her brother's office and forged signatures and seals. It won't hold up in court, but...."

The door swung inward. Margot sneered at Bran, her narrow lips pursed. She snapped at us, "Time's up!"

"Go, Bran." I tried to assure him with a look.

He strolled towards the door to prove Margot didn't intimidate him. "I'll come by later and check on you." He blew me a kiss when he opened the door.

I smiled and shook my head. He's always the actor.

Two days after rushing to emergency I was well enough to leave. Aaron joined Margot in the hospital room, a concerned and caring brother. The nurses smiled as he assured them I was well cared for and sorely missed at home. All but one; Carol Ann Myers watched my family through narrowed eyes. I don't know what she was thinking, but I would have bet money that she and Bran were acquaintances.

I left without protest and held a box of pads and medicine to change the dressing. I had no illusions about my place in the household. It was back to the cold damp cellar with me.

I removed the shapeless dress Margot loaned me and tugged on my robe. I found a box under the stairs with Mom's old muumuus and scored one. The laundry detergent, lavender scented, was captured in the cloth. I lay back on the cot, covering myself with the rough army issue wool blanket and quilt top and sighed. My leg throbbed and I couldn't take serious pain relievers because of the bairn. A cold pack would have helped, but I had none and no place to chill it anyway.

After an hour's nap, the door opened and my brother descended. "Margot and I discussed your return and we think you should be helping more to keep the house. So, we're assigning chores that you'll be responsible to complete each day. You'll spend several hours upstairs, under constant guard, of course. You have the freedom to move around a bit more and even get a breath of fresh air occasionally. Any questions?"

"No."

"Good, today you begin by scrubbing floors. So, up the stairs with you." He stepped back and motioned me upwards.

I slipped my feet in the short denim mules and lowered myself on the stairs to scoot up backwards. My injured leg was not strong enough to climb.

Aaron rolled his eyes but didn't say anything. At the top I stood, with help from the newel post, and padded into the hallway and through to the kitchen.

Margot waited with a scrub brush and a bucket of soapy water. She tossed the brush in the middle of the floor and placed the bucket beside it. "Get with it, then."

I bent double and lowered myself to the floor, keeping my leg straight beside me. I dipped the brush into the hot soapy water and scrubbed the filthy tile. "I need a towel or two to dry where I scrub."

Margot studied her nails and barked. "Use your clothes, stupid!"

"Then I'll be naked. Do you really want a naked woman cleanin' your floor?" I kept my voice low and smiled to prove there was no malice intended.

"Then we'll use your precious mother's clothes." She left for a guestroom and returned with an armload of Mom's finest suits and dresses. She tossed them into a pile beside me.

I picked up a silk blouse and folded it, laying it to one side. A silk dress followed. I reached for another that would not absorb water.

That was the first time Margot kicked me. She caught me square in the ribs with her pointed toe flats.

It hurt.

I pretended to feel like a rib cracked, but that didn't hinder her from continuing to kick me. She grabbed my hair and pulled as hard as she could manage until I felt it release from my scalp.

My head burned with the pain but also with fury.

I grasped her ankle when she closed in on me again and snatched her to the floor. She clawed and pummeled me with both fists, but I didn't allow her to rise. She spun on the floor, trying to get her feet under herself. Aaron jumped to the rescue and hauled her up.

She turned on him.

He tried to cover his face with both hands as she beat him with her fists and tried to rip his hair out. He cried but would not retaliate.

I watched the scene unfold in awe. I knew they were dysfunctional but had no idea the extent of damage she could do. She flung herself into beating him with all she had. She cursed him and called him filthy names.

"If it wasn't for you, you poor excuse of a man, I'd have a baby by now. But no, we have to get some second class kid off your whore sister. How am I supposed to hold my head up with pride in this community with a bastard for a bairn? Huh?" She kicked his shin and aimed for his crotch but couldn't raise her fat leg that high. "Answer me, you fool!"

For a moment, I considered helping him then decided against it. He brought her rage on himself. I studied her moves for future reference. I knew she hadn't finished with me. The quiet I'd experienced the few weeks prior had worn her abusive nerves thin. She needed action to release her anger at life.

By the end of the day I'd cleaned the kitchen floor and watched helplessly as Margot ripped Mom's lovely clothes to pieces and tossed them in the trash. Aaron sat in a dining room chair and wept. His mouth swelled into his nose; both bled freely.

After the floor was clean, I dragged myself up and limped to the cellar door. I saw where it had been split and mended and wondered if my husband had a turn at the prison.

Margo still spewed and screamed. I lowered myself down the stairs one at a time.

I had to find ammo for the pistol, tonight at the latest. I wanted to be ready the next time I went upstairs.

Chapter Twenty

Late night brought quiet if not peace. I lay on the tiny cot and stared at the ceiling. When there was no sound evident, I crept to the storage area under the stairs to retrieve the metal box. I gripped the tread in front of me to steady myself. The feeling of rough wood had me curious. I ran my fingers over what felt like carving. I replaced worn oak treads for Mom with pine, soft enough to carve into. I couldn't make out the letters and had no light to luminate the area.

Grasping the metal box, I carried it to the cot and gently raised the lid. The tray came out next and my hand wrapped around the firearm, still wrapped in flannel.

I searched the box for bullets. There were none. I checked the clip. It was empty. When I looked into the chamber I saw my salvation. One bullet would have to do.

The corduroy skirt, found on the first night I spent in the cellar, wrapped neatly around the gun. I felt the need to have weapons close. I was not sure I could shoot to kill a person, but my emerging belly made it necessary to try.

Searching further through the boxes would have to wait. I was too tired. My leg throbbed. After fighting off Margot, it began to seep blood again. I changed the dressing and lay down to fall into exhausted slumber.

My husband haunted my dreams. *He lay on my bed at the castle, weeping. He dozed only to wake startled and glanced around the room as though he were lost. He turned to my pillow, burying his face in the down and sobbed.*

I woke and studied the bare light bulb, sculpted by a full moon casting filtered light into the cellar through a gray, grimy window.

I wondered how Tomas fared. A chill swept over me when I realized the advantage of Tomas' death. If Graeme were free he could marry Ruane and seal his descendants as laird of the Macpherson's. *No, please, no.*

Graeme wouldn't think of it, but Niall and his mither would. The clan always came first.

Crying stirred me. I listened closely to Aaron's heartbreak and wondered if I really knew my brother at all.

****

Almost a week passed without Margot pitching a fit. She was sarcastic and pushy, but not violent. Over the months I had discovered a pattern to her behavior, interesting and terrifying.

I wanted to escape before my son was born. It would be easier to run once my leg healed. With a plan in place, I lay on the hard cot and dreamed of crossing the tunnels of time and dimensions back to my husband and family.

Sometimes, in my dreams, Graeme's reception was cool, other times warm and loving. I prayed for him and our son throughout the day, every day.

It was all that kept me going.

I lost heart on an hourly basis.

Aaron could no longer make eye contact with me.

Margot never left us alone. He silently brought me a little food once a day while she waited at the top of the stairs. He came to pick up the tray and loudly prayed for me, so she could hear each word he said. I considered passing him a note but felt it too risky.

They left the house for Sunday morning worship. It was the only time they were both away. While alone, I used the short bladed knife to scrap paint from the screws holding the bars over the windows. Once loosed from paint, I could use the screwdriver blade to remove the screws.

I was there for six weeks before Margot went with Aaron the first time. I took care not to be hasty about carrying out my plan. She was savvy enough to set traps for me. I wanted her to be comfortable leaving me alone. Sooner or later she'd make a mistake.

Then I'd be free!

****

Before dawn one morning, a Monday I think, Margot shocked me awake. She appeared in the cellar, switching on the bare bulb over my cot after she lurched down the wood steps with a torch in hand. I sat up and watched her warily. She rounded the hand rail and stood at the end of the cot glaring.

"You stupid cow! Do you think I don't know what you've been doing down here?" She snatched the blanket and quilt off me and tossed it behind her.

I sprang off the cot and backed away. The pistol was wrapped in the skirt under the cot. Damn!

She turned the cot over and rifled through the few things I'd collected from storage boxes. She snatched the skirt. The flannel swathed pistol tumbled to the floor. She slowly lifted the bundle and removed the weapon, a maniacal glint in her eyes.

Her voice became syrupy sweet. "Wha's this then, pet?" She held the pistol like it was a toy, turning it one way then another to examine the chamber. I didn't believe she realized the clip was missing.

I didn't answer.

"Wha' did ye have in mind, whore? Did you think you'd kill me with this toy?" She walked towards me pointing the gun my direction. She shrieked and shook the weapon in my face. "Answer me!" She was four feet away and far too cognizant for me to take her.

I whispered instructions. "If you're going to kill me, go ahead." I pointed to her discovery. "There's a bullet in the chamber, Margot. Just pull the trigger." I smiled and nodded, hoping against hope she'd take the bait.

Her arm dropped to her side. "No, you'd like that, wouldn't you, stupid?" She smiled with her mouth. Her eyes appeared dead. "Then you'd escape. I'll just take your toy wi' me. Wait 'til I tell your brother about this. No rations for you this week!" She grinned and took the steps spryly.

She closed the cellar door. The lock clicked shut. I was alone again. Still alive and disappointed by the fact.

I checked the stash of canned foods and chose a jar of pickles. I've never liked them, but hopefully they retained at least some potassium. It would be a long week with no rations. Aaron had been delivering an egg and a slice of bread every day.

The sink in the corner produced rusty water. I made filters from the fabric scraps and drank sparingly.

After the sun rose, Aaron came down the steps with the cat-of-nine-tails minus the shards of glass and metal spikes imbedded in the tips of the leather straps. "What did you think you were going to do with that gun, Lizbeth?" Holding the leather strips, he tapped the handle against his leg.

I sat up on the cot and slipped my feet into the denim mules. Half my heels hung over the ends.

"I found it. It was Da's. Just something belonging to Da, Aaron." I looked away.

"I see. Well Margot's convinced you were going to kill her."

"Would you hate that?" I met his eyes.

"She's my wife, Lizbeth, and my responsibility." He glanced down at the whip and hefted it in his hand. "Bare your back. You must be chastised. Then you can repent with a clear conscience and your plea will be heard by God." His lips pursed, his chin rose and he looked as smug he does when standing in his pulpit.

Mom's muumuu slipped off my shoulders easily. I turned my back to him. I really didn't care anymore. I wanted to die.

He drew back and struck me.

God, it stung!

The second lash sent sharp needles shooting through every nerve in my upper body. I bit my lower lip, doing my best to be brave and not cry out.

"I hate to have to do this, Lizbeth. It pains me, really it does, but you must learn respect for authority. This way you can pass to God in peace."

He drew back the cat-o'-nine-tails and hit me again.

He began to cry as he raised the scourge high and slung it at my bare, bleeding flesh again.

****

Eight tense, hate-filled weeks passed after Margot's last two day long violent outbreak. We were overdue for a venomous storm.

I scrubbed the bathroom floor tile when she intruded.

"What are you doin', *stupid*?" She parked her fists on her broad hips.

I tried to keep my face passive, my voice without inflection. "Cleaning the bathroom for you, Margot." My gaze remained lowered, but I caught her movement peripherally.

She leaned over me, bared her teeth like a mad dog, and screeched. "I hate you!" She drew back her hand and slapped me.

I didn't react, kept my eyes down and continued to scrub the tile with a toothbrush.

She wasn't satisfied. "Say somethin', *stupid*!" She drew the other hand and slapped me again.

"Lovely day, eh?" I didn't look up for fear she'd see the fury in my eyes.

She grabbed my hair.

I clutched her wrist.

I roared, "Stop!"

She'd hauled me to my feet. Though my boy still grew, I had lost more than thirty pounds.

She slapped me with her free hand. She aimed for my shoulder, with her teeth, to bite me. That spot had just scabbed over from the last time she bit me, a few weeks earlier. I slammed her wrist into the door jamb with my head.

Something cracked.

She screamed.

Aaron ran to the hallway and caught her in his arms. "Margot, what's wrong?"

She pointed a finger at me with her good hand and cried. "That stupid whore broke my arm."

I was back in the floor scrubbing tile with my toothbrush and shook my head. "She slipped into the doorway when she tried to pull my hair out." I didn't look up.

"Shut up!" He screeched. "I didn't speak to you. You may not speak unless we give you permission!"

I glanced back at his swollen, red face and thought he might resemble a baboon if his coloring was darker.

Mind games saved me the torture of their demeaning words. Deconstructing the periodic table of elements was my saving grace...and knowing the screws were working out of the bar over the window in the corner of my prison.

Aaron squawked, trying to amend Margot's pain. "I'll deal with you when I return! You get down those steps—now!" He half carried and half dragged Margot to the front of the house.

She went along like a weak, whimpering, fat Raggedy Ann.

I eased up from the floor and quietly padded towards the cellar. After locking the front door, Aaron took Margot out to their car. I sat on the top step, listening to the doors close.

The car cranked. They backed out of the driveway. I was not locked in the cellar.

For a moment he forgot about me.

I ran to the phone and called Bran's number. The answering machine responded. "Bran, please, please pick up! It's Lizzie. I'm alone for a moment and have to escape. Please, please pick up!" I hung up and tried to recall his home number. After a moment I dialed uncertainly. It rang. He answered.

"Hullo?" He was asleep.

I had no idea what time of day it was, only daylight. They kept the clocks covered when I was upstairs and I hadn't seen a calendar in weeks.

"Bran, Lizzie. I'm trying to escape. Meet me two blocks south of Aaron's house within the hour...at the wood. They left without locking me in. Please, hurry!" I hung up the phone and ran to Margot's closet for a shift and shoes.

Slipping the shift over Mom's old, dirty muumuu, I must have looked a sight. I pulled on a pair of oversized athletic shoes, tying them on in the kitchen.

The front door burst open.

Aaron took furious, long strides towards me. "You little minx, you thought you could run out on us after all we've done for you!"

I grabbed a chef's knife from a wood block and held it securely. My voice was soft. "Let me go or I'll kill you."

"Hah! You wouldn't dare. You want to go back to your man, don't you? As soon as you drop our son, you can be gone. Out of our lives forever." He crept closer.

Once he was in range I swiped the knife at his face. He ducked back, quicker on his feet for the years spent with a crazy woman. He grabbed at my arm but I kicked his shin.

He stopped, and in a flash transformed into the cow-eyed pastor. "Now, Lizzie, would Mommy want you to act like this when all we're doing is our best to tend to you? It's our Christian duty to try and teach you the right way."

He took a step and so did I—into him. I thrust the knife into his abdomen up to the hilt. I jerked the knife free and backed away.

His eyes widened, he gasped. He couldn't believe I'd stabbed him.

He staggered forwards and took a moment to fall, all the time staring into my eyes. He landed on his back clutching his abdomen.

Margot met me at the kitchen door to the deck. She stepped back when she saw the knife in my hand. She cast a glance around for a weapon and started for a nearby brick. I followed.

When she bent sideways for the brick I pushed her down and dashed for the steps to the backyard.

I snagged the toe of the loose shoe on a tree root, at the bottom and tripped.

Scrambling to my feet, I glanced back.

She yelled and lunged for me.

I whirled, holding the knife point straight up, with both hands, and walked into her as she landed on top of me. We hit the ground together.

One push and I rolled out from under her, leaving the blade imbedded, and ran, with all my strength, to the wood.

The nearest neighbor was a quarter mile from Mom's house. A drawback that kept me captive for months was now an asset. Margot could yell her lungs out. It would be a while before anyone responded.

Maybe, just maybe, Bran would be waiting for me. I loped along, watching my footfalls to avoid tripping hazards.

I supported my son with a firm hand under my belly. I stayed out of view of the road to keep well-meaning neighbors from spotting me. After five minutes I made the wood just in time to see Bran—driving away. Dust boiled into the air from the road behind his fine silver-blue Mercedes.

Chapter Twenty-one

There's no way I'd been more than fifteen, maybe twenty minutes. He had to come back. I waited off the gravel road and prepared myself to walk if he didn't return soon. I heard a vehicle in the distance and stepped back into the underbrush.

Bran topped the hill and slowly made his way down the road in my direction. I ran out to meet him, waving my arms. He saw me and stopped.

His mouth dropped open and he tore off his sunglasses, as I climbed in the passenger side of the car.

He was clearly shocked at my appearance. "Lizzie?"

"Aye, 'tis me. Let's go, Bran. Hurry!" I broke into tears. "I think I killed Aaron, maybe Margot too. They came back before I could clear out of the house." I dropped my head into my hands and sobbed.

He goosed the gas pedal and we flew off in the opposite direction of Mom's house. I felt his hand on my arm. "Darlin', I won't let anything else happen to you, hear me?"

I nodded, but couldn't stop crying.

"Let's get you to my place and you can shower before we go over. Lizzie, you're a mess."

"Not your apartment. That's the first place police will look, and maybe my house."

"Not your house anymore. It sold a month ago, luv." He still had his hand on me, patting solace.

"Okay, a motel?" I began to shake.

"Aye, that'll do, then. You stay down when I find one, so it'll look like I'm checking in alone."

Ten miles down the highway Bran parked beside a motel entrance and bailed out to pay for a room. He was back in less than five minutes. "Got a double room in case you wanna nap after your shower. We'll have to wait, Lizzie, four hours at least, before we can cross. I picked up some crackers and a

132

bottle of water." He handed me the clean, clear water and packets of crackers spread with powdery cheese.

They were divine.

"Where will you park?" My teeth chattered. I kept busy trying to chew and swallow.

"The room is in back. I'll park between vehicles, or I could drop you and park a few blocks away. They may decide I'm helpin' you and look for my car. I hadn't thought of that earlier. I should have driven your car."

He stopped and let me into the room before going back for the clothes he'd packed in his boot for me months ago. He returned, talking while I showered in warm water. I still quaked and shivered.

I'll take a breath and tell you that shower was the most wonderful of my whole life. Though the hot water scalded the open wounds on my back and arms, I was able to wash with soap. It smelled heavenly. I was sore in a lot of spots that hadn't felt running water since I left the hospital two and half or three months earlier. My leg still oozed occasionally so I scrubbed around that wound and soaked it well with a hot compress.

When I emerged in a towel Bran caught his breath. "Lizzie, what's wi' the bruises and cuts on ye?" He stood, walking towards me. "Lass, you've been beaten! You're skin and bones!"

I met his eyes. "Aye, it's no picnic at my brother's house, Bran. This is my first attempt to escape. I had to wait 'til my leg healed. It hasn't. I ran outta bandages and the only water in the cellar is rusty. If they weren't watchin', I'd sneak a damp cloth to bathe it and once I found peroxide when I scrubbed the tile in the bathroom and used that." I went back in the bathroom trying to pull on period correct underwear.

Tonight I'll see my husband. Please, God, stop my body from shaking. I need to function.

Bran loitered outside the door. "I'll run to apothecary and fetch what you need for your leg." He paced and talked to himself. I couldn't make out all his words.

I tried to get the stays on. I couldn't fasten them so I left it off. I stepped back into the room. "Bran, what's the date?"

"February 21st, Lizzie, why?"

I sat down on the side of the bed. My balance felt off. I was wobbly. "My baby was due a few days ago." I looked up at him and clenched my hands together to try to stop shaking.

"Don't you think you better birth 'im on this side? After all you've been through, wouldn't it be safer? He may need medical attention." He leaned his hands on his knees to lower himself to eye level.

I lay back on the bed. Bran caught and swung my feet up to the mattress. "I'm afraid if I try a hospital, they'll find me. The police will be after me, Bran."

"Aye, but what if I give a friend a call? She's a nurse. Maybe she can help us." He pulled a comforter over me. "Calm yourself, lass. It's okay. You're safe now."

I appreciated the way he included himself in my troubles. I nodded. "Please be sure she doesn't tell anyone." I lay under the warmth of real covers and closed my eyes.

"She won't. We can trust her."

****

Carol Ann Myers stood over me and peered down into my face. "Lady Macpherson?" Her voice carried the calming melody of an American Southern accent.

I opened my eyes and recognized the nurse hovering. "You're from the hospital where I stayed before." My voice didn't sound like my own.

"I am. Bran tells me you need help getting your baby delivered. Well, I'm your gal. I've been in maternity for ten years in the U.S. and two here. I need to check to see if you're well-hydrated."

"No. They haven't given me anything to drink for weeks. The sink in the cellar has rusty water that I filtered through fabric scraps. I was afraid to drink too much of it for fear of lead poisoning."

She pinched the loose skin on top of my hand. It stood for her ten second count. Her slow Southern drawl was comforting. "This *will not* do. Okay, I'm calling a pal who works an emergency shelter to see if we can get an I.V. or three. The baby will need to be hydrated, too." She whipped out her pager and checked a phone number, sat on the bed opposite and dialed. After a moment she spoke. "Denise, Carol Ann. I'm in a pickle, hon. I need four I.V. bags of glucose and a preemie kit...."

Bran watched me studying the savior he'd brought to rescue me and the child I carried. When I glanced up at him he winked and grinned.

I wept.

****

"Why's an American nursing in Scotland?" I smiled as I struggled to sit up on the bed. My body felt very heavy and still vibrated from the aftershock of the adrenaline rush.

"Well, long story short, my husband came over to work for the oil company in Aberdeen a few years ago. I came too, got certified in the U.K., and found a job. We divorced, but I love it here and it's home now." She surveyed the room, hands on her hips. "You know, I am not liking this place as a delivery room. We're gonna move to my house." She passed a look between me and Bran.

He nodded. "That suits me fine. I need to leave my car at my apartment, if you don't mind. Or do you even need me?" He glanced my way.

"You'll be no more than a phone call away?" My lower lip trembled, tears springing to my eyes.

"Aye, I have appointments here in Glasgow day after tomorrow. I need to call the office and have my secretary reschedule a few things in Edinburgh." He rubbed his hands together and gave me that grin that always made me smile. "Let's get you moved and I'll beat it. Maybe the police will call me in and grill me. I've always wanted to do that. And while out, I'll round up take away."

"I'll ask you to go by the clinic and pick up the supplies I ordered and maybe a few personal items for Lizbeth." Carol Ann was already gathering the few items we'd brought. Her eyes landed on the filthy muumuu and shapeless shift in the corner of the room. She pointed them out to Bran. "You may want to burn those."

"Can't leave evidence behind." He snared the clothes and dropped them beside the door.

"I need to go to the loo and I'll be ready. Oh, shoes! Bran, did you bring them?" I trembled all over.

He hefted my bag. "Everything's inside, darlin'." He grinned at Carol Ann.

The nurse's hands held my hips from behind as I wobbled to the loo and closed the door. When I sat on the toilet, an awful weight pressed down between my legs, compelling me to push. My water broke. I yelped at the contraction that gripped me.

Carol Ann was nearby. "Lizbeth, are you alright?"

"Water broke. I'm experiencing a spasm now." I panted through the pain.

"I can't get to you. Can you make it off the toilet after the contraction passes or do you need help?" She said something to Bran that I didn't understand.

"Let me try." I gripped the handicap bar on the wall and the sink to pull myself up as soon as possible. "Okay."

Carol Ann pushed the door open and grabbed two towels. "All righty then, we'll get you to *my* delivery room."

She grasped my elbows while I held her forearms. Bran slipped my soft brown mules on my feet, in passing, as she led me out to her car. "I know you're probably starving, but hang on a little while. I'll feed you as soon as we birth this young'un."

Everything in me tensed when we cleared the door. Images of police cars surrounding the motel, guns drawn, filled my mind. I shivered. Too much telly.

Once on the road I kept an eye on the side-view mirror in case a police car followed us. I was a fugitive from justice on my way to a new friend's apartment to have my first child by a man in another dimension of time who lived more than three hundred years ago. My world and existence were no longer my own.

A year ago I considered my life boring.

Chapter Twenty-two

Carol Ann drove well for a Yank. We parked in front of a brick townhouse in an older part of the city. Warmly decorated on the front stoop, it beckoned us inside.

I studied her view to the community commons while leaning on a chair panting through a contraction. She had a small patio with pots full of herbs and lettuces. She's a resourceful woman. I hoped Bran had sense enough to marry her.

"How 'bout you come this way?" She led me to her guest room, filled with comfortable clutter. She lowered my bag to the floor. "I'm goin' to get everything ready to deliver the baby. How are we doin' this?"

"You mean lying down or squatting?"

"Yeah, that."

"I suppose you don't keep a birthing stool handy?"

She laughed. The full rich sound of a happy woman. "Not on the premises, but I could run to the hospital and borrow one."

"That's a lot o' trouble. How about a small hassock?"

"I'm thinkin' of my footstool. We can set up here." She indicated a spot at the foot of the bed. "I'll take the shower curtain down and cover the carpet and we should be good." She whirled to the door and came back rolling the hassock.

I watched from my propped position against the headboard. The cramps came regularly every ten minutes. Carol Ann timed them while working on our birthing set.

I panted and wiped my brow when welcome relief came in between the contractions. *Thank you, God, that I escaped Margot and Aaron! Thank you for Carol Ann and her help birthing...I need a name for the bairn. Graeme will do fine.*

Arriving at Carol Ann's house later that afternoon, Bran brought the medical supplies she ordered earlier. The two of them talked over the situation. I faded, unable to hear their conversation, just an occasional change of tone.

137

I dozed for an hour before the really hard pains hit. I leaned over the hassock, my knees on the shower curtain. Having the hassock to hold onto was a blessing.

Carol Ann coached me through the steps. "You're doin' great! We're down to two minutes between contractions. I want to examine you and be sure you've dilated. After that we'll just wait for the little beggar to poke his head out."

The agony continued for another hour. Finally the intense pain commenced. I felt like my body had gone into overdrive on its own. I had no power over the convulsions that took control. I panted and pushed and suddenly I felt him slide free.

"That's it, girl!" Carol Ann proclaimed. "Come 'ere, tiger. Welcome...to our world." She lay him on a towel and cut the cord that bound us together for the past ten months. She turned him on his side and patted his bottom.

He cried softly.

I turned and looked at him. He looked like his da would when he reached eighty. Wrinkled, dark, with black hair and black eyes squinting up at me. "I thought they were supposed to yell."

"He's breathing fine. I don't see any reason to slap his bottom. Here, let's get him to your breast and see if he'll take the little bit of milk you have. I'm glad he held off for us to get some fluid in you."

I tucked him up to my breast and watched him adjust his mouth. He sucked well, if not me, then his own fist. He was content—and very small.

"How much do you think he weighs?" I couldn't tear my eyes away from his beauty.

"Um, less than five pounds." She cleaned up the mess into a pan set in a trash bag, wrapped and secured it with a rubber band. "He's too small, Lizbeth. I wanna get him on an IV and maybe send Bran for formula. What do you think?"

"That he needs to be healthy. We'll use the formula until I produce enough milk for him. I don't ken how we'll take formula and bottles across, but I'll figure out something."

She squatted on her haunches and looked directly into my eyes. Her voice softened. "Sugar, he needs to stay at least a few days and you do too. Give me five days and then we'll reevaluate both of you and decide when it's a good time to go."

I inhaled. "Where will we stay?"

"Here, with me. Look, Bran's taking care of things. He's gone to get word on what's happened at your brother's house." She reached for my shoulders. "Don't panic. We'll be fine right here. This is no castle in the Highlands, but it'll do you for a few days."

"You'd do that for me?" I couldn't believe my luck—blessing.

"I will. I had suspicions about what was happening the day you were released from the hospital. Bran completed the paperwork for admissions and included his phone numbers. I called him. He was at your brother's house every week when he came back to town. They wouldn't let him see you."

I nodded. "I heard his voice a few times after the doorbell rang. I tried making noise but couldn't make enough for him to hear me from that—tomb." I looked down at my wee lad. He slept—content for the moment.

My breasts were far from full and I needed to be able to feed him on my own before crossing. It wouldn't hurt to stay and heal in this precious woman's care.

"Tell me what you think." She prodded my belly to be sure there was nothing left inside to cause infection. My hip bones protruded.

"That we'll stay. Bran will reimburse you for the expenses and...."

"That's not an issue, but he already told me money was no object. He really cares a lot about you." She glanced away self-consciously.

I reached a hand out to her. "It's not that way, Carol Ann. Bran and I have hung out and irritated each other for years. I married his brother and wished I hadn't. Bran's...I don't know. He's smart, funny, ridiculous. He has no common sense, but I love him anyway...as a brother. Truth be told we're closer than I've ever been to Aaron. I can tell by the way he looks at you, he's wild about you." I smiled. "I hope you two marry. He needs someone to ground him and pull him in out of the rain to keep him from getting soaked or drowning."

She grinned. "Thanks for the reassurance. I'm crazy about him too, or maybe just crazy."

We laughed together. I hadn't laughed in ages. It felt strange to my face and my heart.

****

I dozed on the soft bed, my son tucked under my arm, when I heard Bran's voice. I began to push myself up before he tapped on the door and peeked in.

"How you doin', sis?"

I straightened the covers. "We're wonderful. Come say hullo to your nephew." I scooped up my tiny boy and held him so Bran could see his face.

"Man, he looks like his da." He leaned over my son and brushed his fingertip over Graeme's wee nose.

My son stretched and wrinkled his forehead. "He does. He's lovely and not stable enough to leave, Carol Ann says. She recommends staying for a few more days. Tell me what you heard about Aaron."

"I have a friend at the police department. He says that Aaron is in hospital, so is Margot. Aaron told police that his wife stabbed him and must've fallen on the knife when she ran out the back door." He grinned.

"Really? What about me?"

"Aaron told them you left right after they fetched you from hospital and he wasn't sure where you were. I think he realized the game was up. It was also an excellent way to rid himself of that lunatic he married." He shook his head. "I don't get it, Lizzie, how could he stay in that kind of relationship?"

"She's worn him down over the years. I don't think she started to get nuts until they'd been married a while. Looking back, that's when everything about Aaron changed. He's always been pious and a bit of a strange duck, but she drove him deeper into her lunacy."

"So, do you think it's safe to bring Graeme over? I can go across tonight and bring him back."

I shook my head. "It's best not, Bran. Before Mom's funeral I noticed that both of you have sustained cellular damage. Some of that's from the static electricity of the crossing. Graeme appears worse than you do and I think it's caused from the pollution on this side."

"He won't care abou' that, Lizzie. He'll want to see his son and that you're...escaped and doin' better." He frowned.

I knew he didn't understand my concern, but there was more. "I'm not sure he'll have me back, Bran." Tears clouded my vision. "I'm not ready to know for certain. Give me a few days. I'll feel better and have a clearer prospective." I swiped my cheeks.

He crossed his arms. "I think you don't ken your husband. He won't like that I canna go for him, lass."

"Trust me on this, Bran. I have to protect 'im."

"I'd like to be a fly on the wall when you try to sell that idea to 'im." He turned away and left me alone with my child.

****

Bran found Carol Ann in the kitchen making soup. "Hey, you. How's our patient?" She turned a smile towards her favorite beau.

He grinned. "Fair, you lovely Yankee seductress." He slipped a kiss on her cheek. "What are you makin'?"

"Vegetable soup, Momma's recipe."

"Carol Ann, I need to confide in you. If I disappear for say, two days, can you tend to Lizzie?"

"Sure where you goin'? I'm sorry." She blushed and studied the soup. "You don't have to tell me that. It's personal."

"Nay, it's not a mystery, but I feel it's necessary." He glanced back to be sure Lizbeth hadn't joined them. "I'm goin' across, lass. I wanna see Graeme, try to work out the situation Lizzie might face if she returns. If she's not welcome, I don't want her to leave here."

141

"I understand." Her face blazed. "Bran, be honest with me, do you have…romantic feelings towards Lizbeth?"

He chuckled. "You've only witnessed a very mild side of my sister-in-law, love. She's a close friend and confidant. She's also threatened to kill me on more than a few occasions. I ken she loves me like a brother and I want to be good to her. When she married Garrett, my eldest brother, it was no time atall before he was runnin' round on her." He shook his head with a grimace. "He didn't take marriage seriously, but Lizzie did. It broke her heart. She never even dated after he died."

"I see. Well, I just didn't want to be in the way, you know. You go, do what you think is right and I'll hold down the fort. The police *not* looking for her should relieve her anxiety. But there's also the side of her that's a scientist and she knows the damage done to her body and her baby's."

"Whatever you need, get it. If you want to hire someone to come in and help, do it. I'm off without my checkbook, but I'll drop one by to you on my way out. Think I'll take the castle route. Less chance of bein' mistaken for an invadin' brigand." He grinned and reached for Carol Ann, pulling her into a hug. She snuggled into his arms. "When this is over, you and I need to have a long hard talk about the effect you're havin' on me, woman. I'm a changed man since we began."

Carol Ann looked up and smiled. "Really?"

"Aye, I'm serious; no' stringing you along, lovely lady." She stepped back and he smoothed a tiny crease on her brow then kissed it. "I'll see you in a tick. Make whatever excuse you need to Lizzie. I'll back you up."

She nodded. "I'll take care of her and her beautiful baby."

"You're in Scotland, lass. We have bairns not babies." He chucked her chin, playfully, with his knuckle and left.

****

142

Graeme's son was still hungry and I was dry as a bone. Carol Ann brought us a warm bottle and I teased his lip with the nipple. He acted interested and took the flat rubber into his mouth. He drew a long tug and made an awful face.

Carol Ann burst out laughing. "Oh, my goodness, he knows what he likes and that's not to his taste."

I tried again. He hesitated, but hunger won out and he sucked the formula like it might get away if he didn't hurry. I settled back in the rocker and held him close to imitate breast feeding.

"Your da likes his food, too." I admired the black fuzz covering his body. In a few days it would be gone. That laddie was my heart. I wanted a child with Garrett, but abstained because of his wishes. Now I finally had a son and his father loved him from the moment of conception and we couldn't be together for this wondrous introduction to our firstborn.

****

Bran circled the castle for the third time, a stop watch in hand. It was his excuse if a guard accosted him. He'd say he was timing the circuit. No one paid him any mind. He opened the portal to the secret tunnel and lit the torch inside the door. He carried it to the curve and waited.

A moment of brilliant light flashed the stacked stone crevices, no trees waving in the distance or the sound of wind and eerie voices.

"Hmm...well, all that." He glanced around, tucked his head and made a beeline to the old opening. He surveyed the stack of rocks blocking that entrance. He shook his head and watched the light fade. He studied the dark that fell and pondered the problem.

Why would Graeme close the tunnel off? He relit the torch he'd extinguished a few minutes before and trod heavily to the portal. *Unless it's to keep us from crossing back into his world. Oh, Lizzie! All you've been through, lass, and there may be no way to go home.*

Bran loped to the passage entrance, anchored the extinguished torch and eased the portal open. He checked for movement in the dim light and passed through, dusting himself off. He ran his hand through his thick brown wavy hair and sauntered around the castle towards the car park.

A guard making rounds approached him. "Excuse me, sir, wha' business have ye here at this time o' night?"

"Um, I was timing the circuit of the castle." Bran produced the stopwatch and held it out for inspection. "Sorry, it was the only time I was free today to get it done."

"Check in at the front desk from now on. We can't have folks wandering round here on their own now, can we?"

"Guess not. Didn't think to let you know I was here." He waved his hand as he passed and continued to his car.

****

I stirred when Carol Ann opened my bedroom door and eased through.

"Are you awake, Lizbeth?"

"Aye, come in." I checked my son and moved him over so I could sit up. He stirred and promptly stuck his fist in his mouth. Sucking noises began.

Carol Ann chuckled and gazed admiringly at my tiny lad. "He's a beauty."

"You should see his da." I sat on the side of the bed.

"Let's check your vital signs. Any pain or discomfort?"

"Nay, I'm well. I think I'm getting more energy too. The vitamin shots and intravenous feedings help. I ken I have more milk, I feel heavier."

She wrote down my blood pressure and pulse rate on a log she kept by the bed. She opened her mouth and said "Ah."

I followed suit. She stuck a thermometer under my tongue and I sat quietly while she knelt at my feet to poke my injured leg.

"The wound will clear up now that it's sanitized and we've got you rehydrated." She patted my thigh. "You're on the mend, milady."

"Where's Bran? Have you seen 'im?" I turned to scoop up my bonnie boy.

"He said he'd be out o' pocket for a day or two. He'll check in with us when he returns. He didn't want to leave, but had to." She glanced away as she spoke.

"He's gone over hasn't he? I know Bran well. He wasn't happy with me."

Carol Ann met my eyes. "I figured you'd think that, but I promised not to tell."

"Bran's as transparent as a cheap pair o' nylons. The fact he disagreed wi' me was enough. He left me in a huff and I figured he'd be away at dusk. I'm glad to not be disappointed." I smiled.

"Did you want him to go?" A half smile teased her mouth.

"Nay, I'm not ready to leave. My son and I need your help for a little longer, then perhaps. I'm not sure Graeme will have me, Carol Ann. I sent him home last time with orders not to return. The crossings and pollution in our air and water have taken a toll on his system. After a few months he appeared to have aged ten years. It's affecting Bran too, but he's more accustomed to fighting off the contamination here." I looked at the floor. "It's best if I make the crossing when we're able and throw myself on my laird's mercy."

"Are you sure that'll work?"

"The laird's laws require, regardless of the offence, that if I plead his mercy, he'll hear me out. Highland hospitality extends even to our enemies, when requested. If nothin' else he'll send me back...without my son." I sighed.

"That's an awful risk to take, Lizbeth."

"I know, but if he'll allow me just to be his son's nurse, it'll be enough."

She sat on the bed beside me and wrapped her arm around my shoulder. "Let's hope Bran brings good news."

The doorbell rang.

Carol Ann left me to answer. I heard Bran's voice and dragged the IV pole out to the living area where they spoke in low tones.

"You don't have to whisper on my account." I stood there in my gown, shoeless, my malnourished son tucked into the crook of my arm that wasn't hosting a needle.

145

Bran sighed and studied the carpet edging the stone floor in the foyer. He glanced up at me, more serious than I'd ever seen him.

"You didn't make it over. Why?" I studied him.

He squinted but met my eyes. "I can never keep a secret from you, can I, then?" His hands propped on his hips while he bit his lip.

"What's happened, Bran?" I insisted on knowing the truth that he was now privy to, regardless of the pain it would cause.

"The tunnel in the castle's blocked, Lizzie. That just tells me Graeme's angry. He's the only one who could make that decision."

"Aye." I peered down at my son, no longer treasured by his family or his da. I returned to the bedroom, lay down, curled around my bonnie boy and cuddled. Maybe I couldn't go back and be accepted, even as his nurse. How could I live in Graeme's proximity and watch him love someone else?

It was back into the cellar again with us.

Carol Ann tiptoed into the room and rested her hand on my shoulder. "Bran's going to try the other route tomorrow, Lizbeth. Maybe it'll be open."

I wept. All the hopelessness of the cellar prison washed over me again. I teetered on the verge of losing the will to breathe and pondered trying to stop my own heart beating and my child's. If Graeme closed me out of his world, there was nothing left in this one for me either.

I could start over, I suppose. Bran had the funds from the estate sale, the house, and car. I had the trust fund Mom left. I had provision. It would be alright, somehow.

I pulled a pillow over my head and sobbed.

Chapter Twenty-three

Detective Chief Inspector Martin MacKay reviewed the evidence found at the scene of the stabbing he'd been called to a few days earlier. One thing stood out forensically, the cellar was full of Lizbeth Walker-Macpherson's fingerprints. They were also on the knife used to stab Aaron and Margot Walker.

He previewed her information, mumbling, "An environmental scientist would ken to wipe her fingerprints off an object." The cellar smelled like a rotting mess, but there was no indication she was anywhere else in the house except for one partial they picked up from a bottle of hydrogen peroxide, in the hall bathroom.

Strange, but stranger still, was her brother's insistence she'd been gone for three months. There was no dust in the cellar over the prints. They were fresh. He tapped the chart on his desk and reached his conclusion.

Lizbeth Walker-Macpherson was dead. He'd need a warrant to dig up the grounds around the Walker house, but his gut led him to believe that was where he'd find the elusive scientist.

He picked up the desk phone and dialed a number he knew too well.

****

Bran carefully shone the torch into the shadowy places of the wood surrounding the cavern in the park. He didn't want to happen upon a group of gangbangers. The area looked deserted, but he checked the interior of the cave as well. Empty.

He started the sunwise trek, hoping his timing was right and that he wouldn't be mugged before making the journey. He dashed into the cave as the brilliant light flashed and roaring echoed loud enough to make him plug his ears. He ran full out through the static electrical curtain and stumbled onto Macpherson land. He looked around the stone hut and crept towards the low entrance.

147

The door to the woodcutter's bothy cracked open. Agnes peeked through the small opening. "Aye?"

Bran put on his best salesman's smile and nodded deference to the tiny seer. "Ma'am, I'm Bran, Lady Macpherson's cousin. I've been around a few times. I need to get a message to The Macpherson and wondered if I can borrow a horse for a few hours?"

Agnes opened the door wider and stepped out. "Me man'll be home in a tick. He can see to that fer ye." Her strange pale blue eyes watched his every move. "Ye're him what saved her, ain't cha?"

"Saved who, ma'am?"

"The Lady Macpherson. Ye helped her escape the dungeon, dae ye no'?" Her ragged head tilted to one side. "Yer carriage is the color of a robin's egg?"

Bran looked on the woman with renewed respect. "Aye, that it is, ma'am. I came in milady's stead. She gave birth to their son yesterday and is fairin' fine. Tha's wha' I wanted to tell Graeme, uh, the laird."

"Aye, aye, he ain't about. He's by here two nights ago to see about his wife. He's on his way to Inverness to war council. He ain't home."

"Ah, I see. Well may I leave him a note with you or should I go up to the castle?"

"Take a horse fer yerself and hie to the castle, then." She stepped back inside and slammed the door, bolting the latch.

****

Bran found tack in the small shed near the corral. He started towards Lizzie's horse, Daisy. The gray studied Bran as he stalked her. She reared her head and nodded.

He called her, speaking sweetly. "Daisy, come on, lass, you remember me. I rode you a time or two and find you the sweetest gal on four feet." She dropped her head and ambled to him, hay dangling from her black muzzle as she chewed.

"There now, sweet Daisy." Bran ran his hand over her neck and slipped the bridle in her mouth when she dropped her hay. He saddled her and led her out of the corral. Once the gate closed, he mounted his ride and left for the castle.

Bran tore through the countryside without noticing the depth of snow against the treeline. He didn't have an ear for the osprey's cry, as it fished the partially frozen loch. He gave Daisy her head and let her take them to the sweet hay in the castle stable.

****

I cried for hours, hidden beneath a soft down pillow. I heard Carol Ann come in and leave again every few minutes. When my son needed me, I bared my breast and lamented that I'd brought this angel into a cruel world with so little hope.

His dark eyes studied me, a hazy film blurring his view. He looked so much like his da it was almost too much to bear. I glanced away and closed my eyes, reliving a moment of bliss with Graeme, in my mind, and knew deep in my heart of hearts that I must, at least, see him. Even if he removed our son from my care and cast me out, I had to try.

My bairn's suction broke. I peeked down to see him smile, his eyes almost closed, dozing. I rubbed his back. He stretched, stirred, and began to take my breast again with renewed vigor, tiny fists pressing into me as though the milk would flow faster.

I prayed for Bran to be successful getting through. I prayed he'd bring back word of my treasured husband. I prayed the worst was over.

****

Ann answered the kitchen door at the castle as Bran stood on the back stoop. "Hullo, Ann." Bran smiled his greeting.

The pretty blond curtsied and bowed her head. "Hullo, sir. Why're you here at the back instead o' the front door?" Her frown made her even prettier.

"Well, I thought I might have a word wi' you or Mary before I speak to the Macphersons. I need to leave a letter for the laird." He stepped inside as she widened the doorway.

"I'll fetch Mary then." She strutted away, narrow shoulders thrown back.

Mary came out of the kitchen with a drying towel in hand. "Wha's this then?"

Bran smiled, but she pursed her lips and gave him a sour look. "Mary, I'm testing the water to see if I'm welcome with news of my cousin, Lady Macpherson."

"Ah, I see." Her expression changed to amusement. "No one will slay the messenger, sir. Come on through and I'll have Ann take ye to Laird Tomas." She turned and proceeded through the kitchen, giving Ann instructions and shooing them out of her kitchen.

Bran followed Ann through the massive dining room, into a hallway, and tapped on the first door.

"Enter!" Tomas boomed.

Ann opened the door and introduced Bran. "Master Bran to see ye, sir."

"Bring 'im." Tomas shook his great head full of unruly ginger colored hair and smiled. "This should be entertainin'."

Bran entered the room and bowed deference to Tomas. "Sir, thank you for seeing me. I have news of milord's wife and child. They are well after his son's birth."

"Are they then?" Tomas poured a tank of mead. "Come sit and tell me of the other side, my friend. I've been too many years in this prison chair and long to hear yer tales." He lifted another tankard. "Mead?"

"Aye sir, tha' would be welcome." Bran accepted the tankard and sat on a nearby chair. "I thought ye kenned, but Graeme never told me of your goin' over except as a child."

"Aye, it's where I saw a wheeled chair and was fascinated, never suspecting I'd be in one fer the rest of my days." He poked his dead limbs. "Smithy helped me, but I could never figure out the front wheels that turned this way and tha'."

"Round parts." Bran made both hands into fists, stacking them in the air and rotating in different directions. "They move together, yet independent of each other."

Tomas laughed. "Ah, I see. Well, if ye care a fiddle about me, bring 'em or send 'em over with Lizbeth when she can travel."

"I'll do that, sir. She should be well enough in a sennight or so. She was captive in her brother's dungeon for these long months. She was without water and food and they beat her regularly."

"Her kin did tha'?" Tomas frowning was a terrible sight. He had none of his mother's fine looks.

"Aye, they did. I was by once a week hopin' to catch sight of her." He shook his head. "To no avail for they locked her away. She'd told me not to try to get her out because she had an awful infection...well, she was very sick and needed a physician. She was afraid of the crossing. That she might die and lose the bairn." Bran glanced up at loops of rope hung strategically round the room from joists.

Tomas used them to move about, even to hoist himself into bed.

"Daed ye not kill 'em?" Tomas leaned forward.

"When I saw her at the physician's place, after she'd been there a fortnight, she asked me to wait for her call and then come. I fetched her clothes and carried them in my car...carriage waitin' for her to find a way to be free." He leaned back. "She was so sick by then I thought she'd die before we escaped and found a place to hide. She did great violence to her brother and his wife and for a day we feared them dead."

Tomas shook his head. "Why *fearin'* them dead?"

"If they died it might come to light that Lizzie...uh, Lizbeth stabbed them both with a kitchen knife and ran off to the wood where I met her. As it was, her brother said his wife stabbed him and fell on the knife herself. He claimed he had no idea where Lizbeth had got to, but she'd been away for months."

"So her brother lied to protect her after he beat and starved her. Hmm, strange one, that." Tomas pondered the conundrum. "She's with a friend of mine who kens medicine. My friend is tending her wounds and tryin' to get her strong enough to cross and bring little Graeme."

"Little Graeme?" Tomas' brows rose.

"She couldn't think of a name and chose to call 'im for his da. She's not well in her heart. Her courage fails her just now."

Tomas nodded. "I suspect so, lad. It's a hard thing to stab a man with a short knife. I killed a man once with my sghian dubh. Blood spurted all over me and I liked to not pulled the damn thing back outta 'im. I'd've cut him wide open to get that knife back. Da gave it to me on my twelfth birthday."

"How old were ye when tha' happened?"

"Mmm…fifteen summers. It was a minor skirmish with a clan of brigands. My da, his champion, and me were riding the circuit of clans on our land. Ye must check on alliances regularly to be sure there's no wont in yer people and everybody's still on yer side. We weren't far from the Grants, when outta nowhere, a posse of a dozen men rode upon us. Da left there wounded, but his champion carried him out."

"What abou' you?"

"Oh, I was fine. Da hid me behind a large careg. When he was wounded I ran out to help. I killed two men tha' day. My first. I vomited fer a sennight, couldn't keep the potions Mither made fer me to drink. Or maybe tha' made me puke." He grinned, a gap toothed smile.

Bran nodded. "I can fight, but I never killed anyone. When I was a lad, my da gave me a small caliber gun. I was so keen to shoot somethin' I went outside and spied a juvenile rabbit. He was dumb and scared. He froze in place while I blasted 'im to bits. I vomited and cried. My mam took the gun and locked it away until I was old enough to understand how precious life can be." Bran sighed.

"I guess ye daen't eat rabbit, eh?" Tomas wore the forbidding frown again.

Bran chuckled. "Ah, well, I get hungry too, you ken."

"Aye, that I dae. Dae ye wanna pen a letter to Graeme and I'll send it by messenger?" Tomas rolled the chair backwards and set paper and quill on the desk. "Here ye are, then. I'll call fer Quinn to saddle 'is horse and head fer Inverness."

Bran studied the paper for a moment before writing.

Sir, I crossed to tell you your son is born. Lizbeth is alive even after being beaten and starved. If you want to cross, I'll drive past the cavern in the park in her old car every day at dawn and dusk for the next fortnight.

Lizbeth is in hiding in a safe place with a friend who cares for her and your son. It will be days, mayhap a fortnight before they may travel, depending on how quickly they both recover and can do without modern medicine.

Your Servant, Bran Macpherson

Bran stepped back while Tomas sealed the letter, dripping dark wax on the edge and pressing his ring into the hot mass. Tomas handed the letter to Bran.

"Answer the door when Quinn knocks. Let's get 'im on 'is way. He can reach Inverness by tomorrow." Tomas rolled away from the desk.

Knuckles rapped on the door. Bran opened it to the young squire.

Tomas gave Quinn directions. "Find Graeme at once and deliver the message. Tell 'im the messenger has left us, but hasten home, if at all possible. We await his arrival with a plan to fetch Lady Macpherson. Got tha'?"

"Aye, sir."

"Good lad, go wi' God."

Quinn loped away. Bran waited and watched him cross the yard from Tomas' window.

"Sir, do you think Lizbeth belongs here?"

Tomas studied the web of ropes that gave him mobility. "There's room here for intelligent women. She's wanted. What I'm sure of is that my brother will die before his time if he fails to reunite with 'er." He rolled his chair forward and studied Bran. "Graeme's wastin' away. There's no spark of life left in 'im."

"Aye, Lizbeth's the same. I tried to come through the passage in the castle only to find it blocked. When I went back to check on her I had to tell her. I've never been good at keeping things from her."

"Graeme was angry when a moneth passed and she'd not returned." Tomas nodded.

"She was shattered afresh when I told her he'd blocked the passage." Bran studied the landscape and wondered about the brotherly feelings of being her protector. "It's an awesome responsibility we have to help our loved ones."

"Aye, 'tis that. Let's get ye fed and ready to return home, Bran. We'll send Graeme as soon as he can go. His heart's sick over losing Lizbeth. Are ye sure she'll have 'im?"

"Aye, sire, she waits anxiously for word. She couldn't change the circumstances of her kidnapping and did only what she thought best, at the time." Bran returned to his chair. "Did your brother tell you what transpired his last trip over?"

"A bit, but tell me yer version. The runt's bad to hold onto secrets."

Bran began the tale, that he played a starring role in, taking most of Graeme's angst upon himself.

****

Bran hastily circled the cairn three times and ducked inside just as the portal opened. Blazing light illuminated the dope smokers on the opposite side. The turbulent wind blew into his face. The cavern reeked of hashish smoke when he stepped through, but the lads were busy scurrying for cover.

He cautiously made his way out and through the park. *Hopefully Lizzie will still be awake and I can tell her of my talk with Tomas. Then all will be well AND Bran will have saved the day…again.*

He ducked into a bow before the audience in his mind's eye, just as a young man with a knife jumped from cover and challenged him. Bran backed up and into another lad with a similar knife. His head dropped. He studied the ground for a tick then flew into the lad in front of him feet first, he swung into whatever stood before him with all his might, yelling at the top of his lungs.

Chapter Twenty-four

I rose and threw off the cloak of self-pity I'd wallowed in for two days. My lamb slept in a knot in the warmth my body left behind. I dragged the IV pole with me to the bathroom and dared a look in the mirror.

I covered my mouth to keep from screaming at my reflection. No wonder Bran hadn't recognized me when I got in the car. I was sure I'd vastly improved since he picked me up. My cheeks were hollow, eyes sockets sunken, and what was left of my hair was matted and stringy. I scared myself.

Carol Ann walked into the bedroom and found me in the bath. "Mmm, I hoped you wouldn't do that just yet."

"What?"

"Look in the mirror. Honey, you look great compared to what you were when I got to the hotel room four days ago." She leaned in the doorway. "I have a girlfriend who does hair. I could ask her to come by and take a shot at tryin' to fix that mop."

"Thank you. I'd love to meet her *and* her scissors." I turned this way and that trying to find a side that didn't have a bald spot evident. "Well, I knew it was bad, but I haven't looked into a mirror in months. I was right not to; it's disheartening and I'm already depressed."

"You want some help with that? Is it post-partum depression or 'oh, my gosh I've been fighting to stay alive for the past four months'?" She watched me closely.

I knew that look. "Yes and I appreciate the help. There's really nothing I can take that won't affect my heart, in there. No chemicals for my bonnie boy."

Her blond curls bounced when she nodded her head to the side. "There's that. I thought an iced herb tea with a shot of single malt Scotch on the side might improve your outlook."

I chuckled. "Can I just have the Scotch on the side of a glass of water?"

155

"I can do that after I get you to eat another bowl of soup."

"Gladly. I'll shower first though. Do you mind keeping up with the cute chap in the bed?"

"I love being asked for those kinds of favors. I'll fetch you a clean gown." Carol Ann pulled the door closed.

I started the shower. The hot water felt lovely on my palm and I stepped into a steaming waterfall, soothing the sore aches on my spent body.

Thank you, God, for hot water, good friends, and an almost healthy bairn…as far as we know.

I stepped out of the shower to hear Carol Ann's voice cooing to my little guy. I peeked through a crack in the door to watch her tease the side of his face with her fingertip and study his timing as he turned back and forth trying to catch her. He was very slow. He'd need months to recover from lost nutrients and dehydration.

I wished Margot *had* died.

Carol Ann's hairdresser came in the door with a flurry of salon scents clinging to her uniform jacket, her case full of tricks in hand and a smile on her well-made up face.

I was off the IV well on my way to recovery. Truth be told, I'd been up for more than an hour and felt faint.

I ate soup and sipped water and waited to be done over into someone who looked human again. I almost felt human.

Tammy parked her bum in the chair beside me and grinned. I smiled back. "Wha' I'm here to do, luv, is straighten out the mess you look right now, ken?"

"Aye, I'm Scottish too. I've been in prison for four months and my hair's been ripped out in places. What can you do with this?" I lifted a shank off my shoulder. "It's okay if you have to cut it really short, but I'd rather have enough length to put it up. I play Medieval Festivals around the area."

She squinted through heavily made-up hazel eyes and grimaced. "Well, have ye thought about a wig?"

"No, but it's an idea—if I must."

She tenderly sorted the hair across my scalp. "Ye must consider a wig. There's not enough here to do a comb over. I hope the bitch that done this is dealt with harshly."

"Aye, as do I, Tammy." I winced when she touched the most tender spot that hair was ripped from, what four days ago? It seemed a lifetime yet the wounds were fresh, inside and out and would lay open for years before I was healed enough to cope with memories instead of nightmares.

"Okay, I'm goin' to leave it as long as I can, but that won't be more than an inch or so. We won't style it 'til yer scalp heals. I'm not a magician ye know."

Carol Ann cackled. "Pity's sake, Tammy, I told her you were the best and here you are decrying your fame."

The hairdresser cut a glance at Carol Ann. "So happens we can't all have the perfect head o' hair that God blessed *ye* with, lass. Most of us spend hours a week just tryin' not to scare small children." She turned back to me. "I wouldn't have it any other way as then I'd be outta business."

She reached into her case, extracted scissors, and chopped what was left of my hair off. No more than a good handful was long enough to pile on the floor. Margot had done quite a job of rending my glory. I hadn't had short hair since first form; I was six.

She stepped back after a moment and inspected her effort. She tilted her head to one side and straightened an errant tress in back, trimming it to length with the rest. She pursed her lips and studied the area where new hair was coming in slowly. I'd felt fuzz but hadn't looked at the spots.

"In about six months it should be recovered. Who kens? In a year or two it'll be long again. No dieting." She waved a finger in front of my face. "Ye need to gain some weight and extra protein will make your locks thick and strong. Take care o' yer body."

"Aye, I'm plannin' on it. Thank you kindly, Tammy."

She snapped off the plastic cape, winked, and gathered her equipment; then swept up the little bit of hair in the laundry's floor and dumped it in the bin. I watched, with tears creeping up on me.

Tammy squeezed my hand. "Hope you feel better soon. Call me anytime."

"Ta, I appreciate you comin' here, as I'm not able to go out yet."

"No problem, then." She fetched her case and shimmied out with the same energy she had when she came.

Carol Ann handed over my bonnie boy and looked closer at the hair cut. "In time you'll like it because you don't have to do anything to it."

"Because there's nothing much to do unto." I tried to smile, but the tears slipped free, like summer raindrops splattering my clean gown.

****

My bonnie wee lad and I were napping when Bran arrived. He opened the door a crack and whispered my name. "Lizzie?"

I turned quickly and sat up, throwing off covers. I reached back for my son and held him close. "What did you find out? Did you see Graeme?"

"I didn't because he was in Inverness, darlin'." He pulled a chair around to face me. "I spent the day with Tomas...."

"He's alive!"

"Aye, thanks to the medicine you sent to him. He credits you with his full recovery and sends his love. He directed Quinn to Inverness with a letter I wrote to Graeme. I told 'im I'd check the cavern every mornin' and evenin' for the next two weeks. If he cannot come over, I'll take you to him, if you can travel, in less than a month or come back with word."

I nodded. No news of my precious, but his brother would welcome me. Tomas had a great deal of influence over Graeme, so I felt better about returning home. I looked up at Bran and smiled. "Well done." My voice broke and so did the dam of tears, waiting for this moment.

Carol Ann, lounging in the doorway, left it to sit beside me on the bed and hold me while I once again lamented life. She cooed and soothed, but my wee lad picked up the bad vibes his mother released and began to howl. I sniffed and brushed the tears away and knew I had to control the outbursts or upset him to the point of colic...or worse. He had enough to overcome without the burdens of my emotional rollercoaster.

"There, there, wee one. It's alright." I held him up to my neck and rested his head against my shoulder. He sniffed, whimpered, and went quiet, sound asleep again.

Bran eased out of the room and waited for a calmer female to join him.

I didn't qualify.

****

Warrant in hand, DCI Martin MacKay tapped on Aaron Walker's hospital door. He pushed it open to find a nurse bandaging the patient.

Aaron snapped. "What do you want?"

MacKay raised his brows at the rude parson and handed him a copy of the warrant. "I'm searching your premises, *Reverend* Walker. We'll be diggin' up your fine lawn and flower beds."

Aaron paled. "Why?"

"After reviewing the evidence we found at your house, I've concluded you've lied about your sister bein' there three months ago. You see, we found her fresh fingerprints on everythin' in the cellar, a few on the knife that stabbed you, and one more. I'm interested in what you and your wife did with her body." The detective watched for a reaction.

Aaron waved the nurse off. "Lizbeth's not buried out there. I told you, she left. I stand by my word as a man of God." His chin lifted a notch higher and his voice took on a reverential tone. "Margot and I did our best by her. The ungrateful woman that my sister is, well, she's not mentally stable, so there's no telling where she's gone."

"Is tha' your last word on the matter? You'll no' come clean with a confession? 'Cause I ken you're lying." MacKay's face was passive.

Aaron studied the situation for a moment before he relented. "I'm sorry, sir. I was just trying to protect Lizbeth. She has

159

serious…difficulties. We tried to help her, but she became harder to control. My wife lost her temper a few times and hurt her. Once she fought back and broke my wife's wrist, grabbed a knife and tried to stab her. I wrestled the knife away from Lizbeth and my wife took it to try and stop my sister from damaging herself. She ran out of our home and Margot fell on the knife when she tripped." He closed his mouth and conjured up a few tears.

MacKay grinned. "You might be gettin' warmer to the truth, but you've no' told me everythin'. I believe I can find out more by diggin' up your fine lawn." He turned to go but Aaron's voice stopped him.

"Sir, have you ever tried to help someone who wouldn't have it? A thankless person whose very *life* causes you sorrow?"

MacKay looked back at the reverend. "Aye, I'm a copper. I'm lookin' at a man who's so accustomed to spinning yarns he doesn't ken the truth. I'm diggin' up the lawn." He pulled the door handle.

Aaron's tone became desperate. "Talk to Bran Macpherson. Lizbeth married his brother and has had an affair with Bran since his brother was killed."

MacKay stood in the open portal. "Aye, I've spoken to Macpherson. I'm diggin' up your lawn."

MacKay chuckled to himself as he hastened down the corridor. "I'll be buggered if we don't find a thing in tha' man's yard, but I'd bet my pension we do."

****

The Macpherson, riding in the company of his champion, John Tempest, and Quinn hurried to Clary Castle a day and a half after Quinn left to fetch him. As the trio neared the cairn behind the woodcutter's bothy, The Macpherson studied the sky.

"Ye go on ahead. I'll be along directly. I want to check with the seer for news of my wife." He turned to cross the pasture.

"Sir, we can wait fer ye." John offered.

Graeme looked back. "No need, I might be awhile. Tell my brother I'll come when I can." He goosed his stallion's rib and the beast leapt ahead to the house of the seer.

The following morning, before the household stirred, when all was quiet but Mary in the kitchen, Graeme slipped in and up to his room. He undressed, dropping his clothes in the floor and wearily climbed into bed.

Several hours later, he rose hurrying to find Tomas for counsel. He rapped on the oak portal and waited for the shout to enter. It failed to come so he searched the lower level for him.

The library door was slightly ajar. Graeme pushed it open to find Tomas dozing, with a book in lap. He harshly squeezed his brother's shoulder and sat opposite him.

Tomas looked round and chuckled. "There ye are, runt. What news dae ye bring from the council meetin'?"

"We voted not to spank English arse, but made threats and sent a contingent of higher office, disagreeable covenanters to offer them a word of advice." He sighed. "They raided Aberdeen again two days ago and took about two hundred women and children on board their slave ships."

"The bastads!" Tomas struck the arms of his wheeled chair with a burly fist. "They've tried fer centuries to breed us out. Now they steal our future. Damn!" He focused on his brother for a moment. "Ye received the letter from Bran?"

"Aye. It's why I'm here. Council's still arguing whether or not to side wi' the king. I left our vote wi' The Mackintosh. I need to see to my family."

"I thought ye might feel tha' way, but I think it too dangerous." Tomas pressed his lips together and studied his brother. "What say ye to this: send John along to meet wi' Bran. Ask that he be taken to Lizbeth to guard her with his life until she's ready to come home."

Graeme pondered the idea. "I like all but the part that John goes instead of me. She's *my* wife."

"Aye, but like I say, it's dangerous. Bran says the sheriff's around asking questions and she's hidden fer now. As soon as

161

she's able to cross, she will. She suffered terribly at the hands of her kin, bro. They need to be tended to, should the law fail to bring her wrong to righteousness."

"I agree; however, I still think it my place to be dolin' out the justice, not John's." Graeme left the chair to back up to the peat fire burning low in the hearth. "John may be overcome with all the noise, lights, and people. I'm more familiar with it and shan't be caught unawares."

Tomas nodded his great head. "Bran said Lizbeth was afraid fer ye, that the crossings are daen ye harm."

"She's mine and I aim to get 'er back home where she belongs."

"Give it a day or two and think it over. Move in haste and yer plans come apart. Rest up and tell me abou' the meetin'. Ken?"

Graeme shot his brother a sidelong glance and grimaced. "I've already lost three days gettin' the message and ridin' back."

"A day, two days, we shan't be so much older that we can't be careful." Tomas rolled his chair back and yanked the bell cord. "I fancy a bit o' mead. Ye?"

"Aye." Graeme sighed again and raked his hand through his hair.

****

DCI MacKay listened to the phone ring in his ear until the answering machine picked up.

"This is Bran's phone." The cheery voice made Mackay madder. "Leave your number and I'll return your call soon."

He waited for the beep. "I don't ken what soon is to you, Macpherson. This is Martin MacKay *again*. I need to ask you a few questions about Lizbeth Walker-Macpherson. Call me at once!" He cradled the phone and collected his file and briefcase. Maybe a ride out to the Walker place would relieve his tension. The lawn in front of the house was almost gone and there was no evidence found. Yet.

As soon as he made the office door, his phone rang. He hurried back to it. "MacKay."

"Hey, Martin, it's Bran. What's up?"

"I need to talk to you about your sister-in-law. Where are you?"

"Just outta the shower, at home. Wanna swing by?"

"Aye, fifteen minutes." He hung up the phone and left with a smile.

Bran answered the door to his apartment dressed, but barefoot. He held socks in one hand and a cup of coffee in the other. "Come in, come in. What news of the Walkers?"

"Ah, we're digging up the lawn. I just ken her body's out there." He removed his trench coat and plopped into an expensive, under-stuffed, contemporary chair. He crossed his legs at the knee and studied his friend.

"Lizbeth's body isn't buried in the lawn, Martin." Bran pulled on socks.

"How do you ken tha'?"

"She's not dead. She's very much alive. She's a mess, but breathing."

"Why'd you not tell me this?"

"You didn't ask. I thought you'd settled on the Walker's story, last we spoke."

"Aye, until I looked at the evidence of her fingerprints all over that cellar, a partial in the bath and a full set on the knife imbedded in Margot Walker." He leaned forward. "Where is she?"

Bran studied his friend. "I picked her up off the road in a copse of wood behind the house. I took her to a motel where she showered, for the first time in months, and found a safe place for her to birth her bairn."

"Where is she?"

"With a friend. Tell me what you want and I may take you to her if I like the answer. If not, she's no longer in town."

MacKay jabbed his stubby finger at Bran. "I want her account of wha' happened in that house."

163

"I can tell you that. She was taken hostage; beaten, starved, lashed wi' the cat-of-nine-tails and mentally tortured. She escaped with her life, but barely. Anythin' else?"

MacKay sighed and leaned back into the hard chair. "I need to speak with her. That's all, just talk. Will you take me to her?"

"In my car, my rules?"

"Whatever I need to do to talk to tha' woman."

"Aye, I'll do it, but if you make noises about arresting her and such....I won't be left with legal options on how to deal wi' you."

"You're threatening an officer of the law?"

"Call it what you will. She's climbing outta the pit and I'll not have her pushed back in, eh?" Bran slid his long narrow feet into handmade Italian loafers. "Well, come along then."

Chapter Twenty-five

Rhonda answered the doorbell in Carol Ann's townhouse when she saw Bran through the peephole. "Hey you!" She stepped back at the sight of DCI MacKay. "Oh!"

Bran smiled. "It's okay. He's a friend, Ronnie. Is Lizzie awake?"

Rhonda backed away, a watchful eye on MacKay. "I'll check."

"Just tell her I'm here, if she is." Bran closed the door behind them and motioned to a divan, his voice low. "Sit there, Martin."

Rhonda stepped back out. "She's just finished feedin' the bairn. She'll be out directly."

"Thanks, could we get a cuppa, love?" Bran stayed on his feet and moved closer to Lizbeth's bedroom door.

"Aye, I'll put the kettle on, then." She beat it to the kitchen.

Lizbeth stepped out with her son on her shoulder. She wore pajamas and a robe. "Hullo, Bran." She smiled, her eyes heavy with sleep.

"Hey, sis." He kissed her cheek, temporarily blocking her view.

MacKay was on his feet in a flash.

Bran held Lizbeth's free arm, steering her towards the living room. "This is my friend from the police I told you about. DCI Martin MacKay, this is Lizbeth." He felt her go weak and began to tremble. "Come sit, Lizzie. It's alright." He steadied her with an arm round her shoulders.

****

Bran lowered me to the couch beside the detective. I was scared witless. He might have read the quivering of my body as guilt.

165

Martin MacKay extended his hand to me and I took it briefly.

His voice was cajoling. "Lizbeth, I need a minute or two of your time. I have questions about your brother's house and neither he, nor his wife, will answer them. I thought you might help me piece a few things together, so we can get this case closed and off my desk. I'm not here to hurt you, lass. Be calm now." He nodded and smiled.

"Okay. I'll do my best." I wanted to vomit but held myself erect.

"I'm diggin' up the lawn at the house looking for your body and Bran tells me you're alive." He grinned and shook his head. "I was relieved to hear about your rescue."

"Don't stop looking at the house." I shifted my sleeping son into the crook of my arm. "Don't stop digging the lawn. It occurred to me a few times that maybe I wasn't the only one they tried to use as a surrogate mother."

"That's what they were after?"

"Aye, my wee bonnie boy was what they wanted. Margot's cracked, if you haven't figured that out yet." I patted my son.

"How long have they lived there?" He settled back, making notes.

"About three years ago my mother became ill and moved in with me. That's when Aaron wanted the house for himself and his wife. If he just had the house, Margot would be happy. Well, she wasn't. She wanted a child. There have been others kept in that cellar. I know because I helped Mom store her things down there when she moved in with me." I took a breath.

"Was somethin' missing?"

"Nay, it wasn't. There was a presence about the area. You ken when other people have been somewhere they shouldn't? That cellar was no place to live, but others had slept on the cot, covered with that wool blanket. Body odors were thick in the ticking of the mattress and on the blanket. Fear has a distinct scent. I thought at first Margot had picked it up at a tag sale, but then I realized it had been in the cellar for years. It was army issue. Da was in the army, Black Watch."

"I see." He looked away and pondered his next question.

Rhonda arrived with a tray for tea. She sat it on the table in front of us. She motioned towards my son. "Do you want me to take him?"

I looked down and back at the detective and shook my head. "Thank you though." I turned a glance in the policeman's direction. "There were etchings in the backside of the steps. I thought the words were carved into the wood with a nail. About five years ago I replaced three treads worn down over the two centuries since the house had been built. I substituted that fine hard oak with pine to save money. It was soft enough that someone scratched out several messages."

Rhonda smiled and poured tea, preparing mine the way I like it, a spoon of sugar, and a squeeze of lemon. She set it near enough I could reach it and plated two biscuits for me.

I smiled thanks as well as I could and waited for the questions to begin again. I sipped tea and tried my best to swallow.

Bran watched me struggling and patted my arm. "It's okay, sis. Don't be alarmed."

I tilted my head and gave him my best incredulous look.

MacKay stirred his tea. "I ken this is hard, but can you tell me what transpired the day you escaped? Bran's given me his version, but I need to hear yours." His pager went off and he checked the number. "Excuse me. May I use a phone, please?"

Bran stood and directed him to the instrument nearest his seat. They swapped places. Bran patted my arm again and whispered. "Please don't be upset, Lizzie. I've kenned Martin for years. He said he just had questions and he wouldn't lie to me."

"Okay. I'm trying." I nodded and shifted my tiny bundle to the other arm.

MacKay turned back to us, brows raised. "That's the sergeant I left in charge of the lawn digging operation." He looked at me. "Seems you're right. They just hit pay dirt. Two bodies have been uncovered in the rose garden."

Bran was on his feet. "What?" He paled.

"The sergeant said they found two bodies. The coroner's there now. We'll know more in a while." He picked up his tea cup and sipped the cooled brew. "Well, if you don't mind, let's get back to the question of the day you escaped them."

"I scrubbed the bathroom floor. Margot came in and began a ruckus. She'd been manageable for several weeks, without a lot of overtly violent behavior. She still had her fits, but they were just sparks of anger rather than a day or two of tirades. Week before last she bit me on the shoulder as punishment for breathing." I touched the spot, still tender but healing.

"May I see?"

I bared my shoulder, slipping the robe and pajama shirt down my arm a bit.

He peeked at the scabbed and bruised wound and glanced away to take a breath before making notes. He cleared his throat and spoke softly, "Go ahead, Lizbeth."

"That day she slapped me twice while I was in the floor. I didn't respond to her, just kept scrubbing the tile. Then she hauled me up by a handful of hair and tried to bite me again." I touched the scabbed spot under the turban I wore. "I used the momentum of my body clearing the floor and forced her arm into the door jamb. Her wrist cracked. Aaron dragged her out to the car and they left. He forgot to lock me in the cellar.

"I called Bran then pulled on one of Margot's shifts and a pair of her shoes. I started out, but they'd returned. Aaron grabbed at me. I snatched a knife out of the butcher's block and stabbed him. Margot was at the back door when I opened it. I ran past her, but she threw herself at me and I...I held the knife out and it slid into her gut like butter. I pushed her off me and ran." I looked up into MacKay's eyes.

He nodded and leaned back. "Tha's fine then. I don't think we'll need your testimony as we now have bodies, but may we talk again if there are questions?"

I nodded and tried to swallow. "Sure."

He smiled. "Thank you, I'll be ready to go, then." He stood and glanced back. "One more thing, Bran, why did you not call me when you thought she was being held there against her will?"

Jumping in ahead of him, I answered, "There are extenuating circumstances, sir. I asked Bran to give me time to sort it out for myself. I was wrong to discourage him when he found me at hospital a few months ago."

"Aye. ye were, lass. Well then, let's go look at the crime scene."

Bran was on his feet, delighted at the prospect. He kissed my cheek and nuzzled my lad. They left together.

****

The lawn was a mess. It was raining when Bran and DCI MacKay arrived at the Walker house. They stood back and observed the coroner carefully lifting out remains of one of two women found in the rose garden.

The sergeant walked out to greet them. "Sir, the coroner says one of the women was pregnant, almost full term as the child's skeleton was well-formed. The other, he's not sure. We've started on the flower beds and—."

"Sir!" A shout from one of the officers digging, dragged their attention away from the sergeant's report.

"Aye?" MacKay shouted in response even as his long legs carried him to the site.

"Looks like an infant here, sir." The coroner's assistant announced from a hole almost five feet deep.

MacKay stared at the tiny bones of the doomed child. He nodded his head. "Keep looking, lads. I need a body count to make formal charges. I'll be back at the station, finishing paperwork." He headed for his sergeant. "I want you to send a team inside with good lights. There's supposed to be some words etched into the back side of the cellar steps on the newer pine treads. That may help identify these girls or others like 'em."

Bran looked on aghast. "That could've been Lizzie." He bit his lip to keep tears at bay. "The bastard was going to bury her in a flower bed after the bairn was born. And if Margot killed little Graeme in one of her fits, he'd have wound up here too." He turned away and made tracks for his silver-blue Mercedes. He opened the door and climbed inside to wait for his friend.

After a few minutes, MacKay joined Bran. "First time seeing a child's remains?"

"Aye, and hopefully the last. That was the plan Aaron and Margot had for Lizzie." Bran leaned back in the seat.

MacKay nodded. "Looks like it right now." They sat quietly in the light rain. "Well, all good things must end. How 'bout dropping me off at your place for my car? I wanna get those two charged before the day's done. Give my regards to Lizbeth, but don't go into detail about the bodies. It'd be too much to bear, to ken for sure this is what her own brother had in mind for her."

"Aye, it's almost too much for me. I'd love to get my hands round that preacher's throat right now." Bran cranked the car.

"Me as well. But wanting to do it and actually doing it is the difference between us and them." MacKay waved to his sergeant.

****

Graeme slept later than usual the day after returning home. He went to the great hall to hear judgment, but couldn't keep his mind on the problems of the crofters and tenants. He left the hall and headed for his brother's apartment to say he was leaving to cross.

He tapped at the wide oak door.

Tomas boomed. "Enter!"

Graeme opened the door and found Tomas preparing for a journey. "Wha's this?"

"Ruane wishes to visit her family. There have been attacks on the church and the minister who married us was killed. I'm leavin' instructions fer ye in a few matters that I passed judgment on whilst ye were in Inverness."

"I wanna go across and bring my family home, Tomas." Graeme frowned into his brother's upturned face.

Tomas smiled. "I ken. That's why I think now's a good time to leave fer Ruane's clan. If I'm not here, ye have to be."

170

"I'll just leave Niall in charge." Graeme turned to the door, fuming.

"Nay, ye won't do tha'. Think about it, runt. We'd come home to bedlam. Mither would be running the place. We canna have tha'." Tomas grinned.

"Why're ye set on keeping me here?" Graeme's large hands parked on his hips.

"Because I love ye. Because Bran said he'd bring 'em home when they were well enough to travel. Because I daen't want anything else bad to happen to ye and Lizbeth said ye were getting sick from the poison in their air an' water."

"Ye vex me sorely, brother." His head dropped and he turned to the door.

"Daen't ye wanna hear what I'm leavin' ye laird over?" Tomas acted hurt.

Graeme didn't even look back. "I daen't *give a damn*, Tomas." He opened the door, passed through, and slammed it shut.

****

We had almost healed. My bonnie lad gained a pound. I gained five and had a bit of shiny hair again. Tammy brought a wig she found very close to my dark brown hair color. My complexion cleared of the problems brought on by too little soap and clean water. I felt good. I wanted to make plans to cross.

Bran came by to check on us. "Lizzie, I'll be away a few days. I have to run down to London."

"I wanna cross, Bran. I think we're well enough to go home. As kind as Carol Ann has been, I'm sure she'd love to have her house back to herself."

He frowned. "Aye, we'll talk about it on my return."

"What's wrong with now, today?" I looked around and gauged how long it would take to pack the few items we could take.

"My flight leaves in two hours. We'll go when I return. Carol Ann's talking 'bout goin' with us. We'll see. We may have to wait for her to get her new schedule. Anyhow, give us a kiss and we'll be outa your hair." He puckered up to kiss my cheek and stooped down to my son for a snuggle on his neck. "You be the lad round here while I'm away and we'll go see your da in a few days." He looked into my eyes and whispered. "I can't wait to get back, Lizzie. I've ordered Carol Ann's engagement ring, especially made for her. I'll pick it up while I'm in London." He grinned; fully aware he'd shocked me.

"Good, very good, Bran." I smiled.

He nodded and waved his fingers at me. "Aye, I think so. Remember: no telly, radio, or newspapers."

"Aye, knowing Margot's dealt justice is enough. I don't need the particulars." I hefted my son to my shoulder.

We walked Bran out to the door of Carol Ann's home. A neighbor was leaving for work and looked back. I smiled and waved. Bran stood in the door gazing at us. He looked so much like Garrett in that moment; it made me take a small step backwards.

"What?" He grinned.

I shook my head. "You remind me of your brother sometimes, especially as you age. You need to stop crossing. The trips are taking a toll on you that may steal years from your life."

"I'll consider takin' you home as the last one—maybe. Bye, Graeme, bye, Mommy."

"Bye, Bran." I closed the door and found Rhonda watching me.

"How about breakfast, Lizbeth?" She smiled as she dried her hands on a tea towel.

"I can fix something."

"Carol Ann left a high protein menu and mentioned packing a few more pounds on you." She turned back to the kitchen and we followed.

"Right then, breakfast."

Chapter Twenty-six

Graeme slouched in the high seat listening to complaints. His gaze drifted to the back of the hall.

John Tempest sauntered in, taking note of the occupants and mood of the room. The champion's fierce green eyes roamed and gauged the potential for trouble from those waiting for the laird. Hands on his narrow hips, the protector of The Macpherson surveyed the queue of disgruntled villagers and crofters.

Maybe Tomas is right. I could send John and, at least, ken tha' Lizbeth is in good hands. Bah! What rubbish! He'd be like a lamb led to slaughter. Better if I go myself, but.... He saw Niall enter the hall and head for the kitchen. *No, I'm stuck until my brother decides to bring his arse home. If I leave Niall in charge, there'll be a full scale revolt before a sennight passes.* He sighed. *Lord, guard my wife and son. Keep them safe from harm and bring them home to me soon.*

He leaned towards the crofter who posed his difficulty to the laird. "Kennan, take yer wife and child to her people and eat at the hall while she's gone. If ye need help protecting yer cows, hire a lad or keep watch at night and sleep days. I'm sure ye're capable, man, if ye daen't have to be worried about yer home being attacked. I'll ask John Tempest to see to ye." He waved his hand and sent the disgruntled farmer on his way.

Tempest looked up and Graeme motioned him to the high seat. "John, talk to Kennan there, about putting a guard on his fields. He's got troubles with lads settin' fires and stealing his livestock and it needs to stop now."

John nodded and followed Kennan to the door.

Graeme motioned the next man in line forwards.

"I needs to speak privately to ye, laird." He held his hat in hand, turning the blue boineid round, curling the brim as he went.

Graeme motioned him up the dais.

"Me name's Marcus Gunn and I hale from a village nearby. Ye visited there regular, a few summers ago."

Graeme's eyes narrowed as he felt an eerie shadow fall. "Wha' dae ye wan'?" He scowled.

"Well, sir, it's jest me lass, the one ye…seen, is fallen ill." He twisted the hat round again.

Graeme's voice was low. "Tell me wha' ye wan' from the laird, Marcus Gunn."

The man grimaced displaying a mouth full of rotten teeth. "Alms fer the lass, sire. She's in a bad way."

"Have ye a healer in yer village?" Graeme leaned back in the high chair.

"Aye, sir and she seen to her, says she's dying. The lass kent ye mi' help her old man out, ye ken?" He twisted the hat again.

Graeme nodded and pondered the request. *If I give 'im coins now, he'll return time and again wi' his hand out.* "Is it money ye seek or help?"

Marcus Gunn looked down at the twisted hat. "Money, sire."

Graeme's manner roughened. "Fer wha'?" He cast a glance around the hall. John Tempest was gone.

"Amends, sire, fer the loss of me family. The lass kept herself fer ye and daen't marry or have bairns. I got no more family."

Graeme sensed a trap. "Wha' barred her from having a man these last four years?"

Gunn studied the stone floor below the dais. "She fell ill with heart sickness when ye left her. She stayed to her bed wi' no life left in her."

The laird's eyes narrowed. "I'll see to her in a few days. I'll come myself and see wha' the lass needs."

Marcus Gunn nodded. "Well, she'll welcome ye, she will." He nodded again and hurried down the dais and away from the hall.

****

Graeme paced the library, considering Marcus Gunn and his request. He'd often wondered about the fair lass he'd kept for two years. Gwyneth was a beauty, that one, long red hair, fair skin. She smelled like sweet peas and lilacs on a spring morning. He'd been her first lover and took great care not to make the mistakes of his da and leave a string of illegitimate offspring in his wake.

He scrubbed his fist over his chin and recalled the last time he'd seen her. He'd had no intention of leaving her, even though Mither found him a bride. When his betrothed died on her way to the wedding, the dreams began. It became a nightly ritual of meeting Lizbeth and loving her.

Gwyneth quickly became a distant memory. Her realness failed to compare to the woman in his dreams. He sent her a missive and money, explaining he would no longer visit her. She was free to marry, with a handsome settlement.

So, why did she not? She had the dowry I provided. Why send her father now to collect more dues? Daen't make sense atall. Ah, where's Tomas when I need 'im?

Raking his hand through his silvering hair he made another round about the library and burned with need for his wife. He rang the servant's bell.

A page appeared promptly. "Bring ale." He sat in front of the fire and stared at the low flames of burning peat.

Graeme and John Tempest rode the snowy path between three villages and pulled up at Marcus' cottage. Clean laundry flapped on the clothesline in the chilly breeze. The men dismounted. Graeme studied the surroundings. The place was still. No noise came from the cottage. He removed his gloves, leisurely, and approached the door.

John held the horses and guarded their backs.

Graeme tapped at the door and listened. No stirring about came to his fine hearing. He started to the rear of the cottage.

"Graeme!" John's voice stopped him.

"Wha'?" The Macpherson glanced back.

"Towards the village." John nodded down the lane. A tall red-haired woman sauntered their way, wrapped in a wool cloak, a basket on her arm.

Graeme approached his horse and waited for the woman to come alongside them.

She held her arm up across her forehead shading her eyes from the morning sun. She stopped to study her visitors from a distance. After a moment she covered the gap to Graeme quickly.

"Milord." She dropped her chin in deference.

"Gwyneth." He nodded.

"Wha' dae ye mean coming here, sire?" She shifted her basket to the opposite side, squinting in the sun.

"Yer father came to visit me."

"*My* da came to *ye*?" She was clearly surprised and not sickly, in the least.

"Aye, he said ye were ill, dying. He asked for compensation. I came to see fer myself." Graeme felt his cheeks burn. This was obviously a mistake. Something more was afoot.

"Well, as ye can see I'm no nearer my deathbed than the last time ye saw me. I daen't ken wha' he told ye or why." She shrugged her shoulders, a half smile on her lips. "Ye wanna come inside?"

Graeme's gloves slapped his palm. "Nay, woman, I wanna ken what yer father's about. Hae ye married?"

"Aye, three years ago. Michael's a seaman. He gave me two wee ones." She smiled and rocked back on her heels. "I daen't ken what games my da's playing, sir, but it hasn't a thin' to do wi' me. If ye ain't coming in, then I'll bid ye goo' day. I have chores to dae before me lads wake."

Graeme watched with a frown as she proceeded to the door, opened it, and entered, after a quick smiling glance back.

He mounted his horse and turned to John Tempest. "I daen't ken what's happening, John, but we'll take a different route home."

"Tha's wisdom, sir." They turned in the direction of the village for a pass through, before navigating the hills.

Graeme and John rode around clusters of thatched huts, through the edge of the wood, and beyond Clary Castle to approach from the west. They found no trouble along the route until they neared home.

Picking their way through the tree line of the burn, they found the purpose of The Macpherson's lure to the distant village.

A siege of Clary Castle was underway.

Chapter Twenty-seven
The Siege.

An armed encampment of a hundred men surrounded the castle on three sides. They had recently arrived. Fortifications were taking place on the ramparts of the castle.

The two warriors stepped deeper into the treeline and studied the situation.

"Guess they didn't like the vote I left with The Mackintosh." Graeme grinned.

"Mayhap they've come to change yer mind." John offered a mirthful look. He checked his weapons.

"Aye, appears so." Graeme scanned the lay of the land behind them. "I wonder if Niall is still afield fer the day. We can make haste fer the woodcutter's cottage. I keep a few horses there. We'll make a plan and return. Nightfall may be our better opportunity to impress them with our displeasure."

We can't enter through the back; a wall of rock blocks the passage. So much fer my fit of temper.

John and Graeme turned back to the east and slowly progressed to change horses.

Graeme knocked on the cottage entry. Agnes opened the wood door a crack and peeked out. Her voice was sharp. "Me man's out."

"I wanna swap horses, Agnes. I'll dae it myself." He turned to the stoop.

"Ye're not here about yer wife, then?" She eased out the opening without widening the crevice overly much.

Graeme whirled to face her. "Wha' abou' her, Agnes? Is she well? Wha' of my son?"

A smile creased her leathery face. "She's healin' nicely and longs to return home."

"My son?" He insisted, hands on his hips.

178

"The boy's improving." She nodded her raggedy head. "He looks jest like ye, sire." She opened the door and eased back through the narrow gap. She slammed the solid oak and locked it again.

Graeme pondered her words for a moment before setting off to the corral. John Tempest had caught the gray and swapped the bridle and saddle from his horse.

"Tha's my wife's horse, John. Her name's Daisy."

"Would ye rather I not ride her?"

"Nay, she's a gentle one, though. No war horse that." Graeme rubbed her muzzle. "Yer mistress will return to us soon, old gal."

John removed his saddle and chose another. The bay backed up at the sight of the saddle. John murmured soft words. Graeme watched as the gelding stood off for a few seconds, then ambled to John and took the bit.

Graeme whistled and a white steed loped his way. He transferred his tack and began to plan their evening. "Let's wait 'til after dark. They'll post guards away in the hills if they're to have cover. We'll remove the alarms at our leisure and enter the camp around midnight."

John nodded as he mounted the horse. "And what dae we dae about supper?"

Graeme grinned. "Fish. I'll gather a few herbs from Agnes' garden."

"Fish? I feared that'd be yer answer. I believe I'll opt fer hare, if I can catch one." John chuckled.

"Well, then let's hie fer the hummocks and have our supper while we can." Graeme situated himself in the saddle and followed John into the hills.

The Macpherson shed his brogues and waded into the burn. The icy water caused every nerve in his body to shrink in rebellion. He shook off the discomfort and soon lost the sharp ache, enjoying the crisp current. He hovered over the middle of the stream and poised himself to catch a salmon attempting to swim between his thick legs. John left to hunt his supper and soon returned with a brace of rabbits in one hand.

He stopped on the bank and watched the laird catch and toss a four pounder onto the shore.

The champion reached down for the prize as Graeme reenacted his strategy on another unsuspecting salmon. He tossed a three pounder on the shore and climbed out of the water to catch it before the fish flipped itself back into its natural habitation.

His feet and lower legs had begun to blue when he sat to pull his wool stockings and brogues back on.

John had a fire built under a leafy tree to break up the smoke. "I've cut some cedar spits fer ye, laird."

"Thank ye kindly, John." He squatted and leaned on a nearby rock, looking up into the tree above them. A smile spread over his handsome face. "Dae ye ever wonder how many nights like this we miss, bein' too busy wi' life?"

John joined Graeme to watch the first twinkling stars and planets appear in the indigo sky. "Aye, I'd rather be up here than in the finest castle in the land." He grinned, his green eyes merry. "When's yer wife returnin'?" He rotated the spit to blister the skinned rabbits on every side.

Graeme met his friend's eyes. "Soon, John, very soon."

He busied himself cleaning and spitting the salmon. He lay strips of herbs inside the fish and strung them closed with sharp twigs. His side of the fire burned down to a bed of hot coals which grilled the fish to perfection in a few minutes.

The two men ate silently, occasionally taking a moment to study the shimmering sky. A half-moon rose and lit the landscape around them enough to make out shadows and movement. They cleaned up their camp and doused the fire with sand from the shore.

"We've about an hour's ride. The sentries should be comfortable by the time we arrive. We'll leave the horses at the caverns, outta the way." Graeme scrubbed his damp hands down his kilt. He resheathed his sghian dubh in the top of his sock.

"There may be enough light to see them before we get too close. 'Tis a crystal clear even." John checked his weapons, adding a second sghian dubh to his wardrobe. "What'll we dae after we breach their perimeter?"

"Find the men in charge and send 'em on to their maker. Cut the head off the snake, ye ken?" Graeme mounted the white gelding and turned him towards home.

****

The Macpherson studied the area. He spotted John, as he took out the guard closest to his position on the west side. Graeme watched the rocks for any movement to give away a watchman. He was surprised it came from directly in front of him, less than ten feet away.

The two men methodically executed seven men and felt sure they had eliminated the opposition's sentries. They circled the assembly from a distance, studying the layout from a different angle than above, in the rocks.

Burnt powder tinged the air and a few bodies lay outside the boundaries, covered with shrouds.

Graeme moved in like a cat on the prowl. A shelter occupied the center of the encampment. It was taller than the surrounding lean-to structures and sported a Bruce of Earshall clan pennant at the peak of its roof.

John closed in from the west side of the camp and Graeme from the east. They crept towards the main structure to a chorus of snoring men. Four fires burned, crowded with men sleeping on kilts and blankets.

Graeme spotted movement behind John and dropped to his chest.

John did the same, scanning his rearguard. A man stood and walked to the edge of the camp to relieve himself. When his back faced John, the champion rose and crept to his position. He grasped the man from behind and slit his throat, lowering his body to the ground without a sound.

On his belly, near the damp ground, Graeme watched the activity in awe of John's silent, deadly movements. When the champion returned, facing camp again he slipped towards the large tent quickly. The flap shifted and John was in the den with the enemy, whoever he was.

There's too small a contingent of men fer it to be The Bruce of Earshall himself, probably one of his rabid Anglican generals. The Macpherson assessed the situation as safe and joined his champion.

John recoiled, dirk in hand, when Graeme opened the tent flap. His champion held his palm out and jerked his thumb and head at the flap. Himself heeded the warning and slipped back through. He stole through the sleeping men and returned to the treeline at the burn, keeping a wary eye for John Tempest's return. Mist thickened on the ground to a depth of several feet, perfect cover for a man moving on his hands and knees.

Chapter Twenty-eight

Day dawned grudgingly; the sun peeked through dark stormy clouds while a cloak of foggy mist covered the area. Graeme circled round through a field of barley to the hills and horses. John had not reappeared. No alarm sounded in the camp. All remained quiet through the night.

Graeme found the horses as they left them, safe inside the entrance to a cavern. He saddled them both and rode back to the woodcutter's bothy.

He turned the horses out to graze and sat on a rock watching, as light brightened the crisp, cold air and the mist began to dissipate.

More than once his notice fixed on the cairn. *It'd be so easy to go across, find Lizbeth, and bring her home. Of course I must deal with the Anglicans before I can get into the castle.*

"Milord?" The woodcutter's voice violated the deep silence.

Graeme turned. "Aye?"

"Hae ye need o' something?"

Graeme studied the horses again for a moment. "Ye ken any other way into the castle than the front gate or the secret passage in back?"

The old man smiled and sucked on his pipe. "Aye, lad, git yer horse and we'll go there."

"An armed camp of Anglicans has sieged the castle." Graeme responded quietly. "John and I were caught outside. We went into the camp during the night and did a good deal of damage to their soldiers. John daen't return."

The old man nodded. "He'll be fine…er dead, then." He tied a lead on a mule and led him out of the gate to saddle the beast.

"Aye, just saying I lost 'im." Graeme uncrossed his arms and whistled sharply. He saddled his black stallion, leaving John's behind.

183

The woodcutter joined Graeme, astride his old mule. "Ye may hae to lead tha' studdly beast through the rocks so he daen't break 'is leg." It was the most words he had ever heard Agnes' man speak at once.

"Tell me when." Graeme smiled even as his heart tore for the loss of his friend and champion.

****

The woodcutter took off at a fair pace to the burn. They crossed to the other side and cut back in the direction of the castle. In about two hours they'd picked their way through careg outcroppings and thick brush to arrive at the mouth of a cave.

"Now, I ain't been up 'ere fer more than twenty summers, but there's a place where the former laird met his ladies. Daen't tell yer mither."

"Aye, sir, I shan't," Graeme agreed as he dropped his stallion's lead on a low branch.

The woodcutter led the way deep into the cavern after lighting a torch at the entrance. Graeme glanced up gauging the massive amount of rock bolstered above him. He followed his guide.

The woodcutter started up steps cut into the stone rising in the direction of the castle above. After a few minutes of circling, they encountered a rock slide.

"Uh!" The older man turned to Graeme. "'ere's where yer youth comes in handy."

Graeme stepped forwards and pulled enough rock out to slip by the pile while the woodcutter held the torch high. He dusted his hands off and they proceeded to climb.

After an hour of scaling the narrow steps, stopping regularly to clear the path, they arrived at a portal.

"This 'ere shou' open to yer da's chamber, if it ain't blocked." The older man leaned into the wall and let Graeme try the entry.

The Macpherson put his shoulder to the door without success. No amount of coaxing moved it to open.

There was no handle to turn, so the key that moved it was recessed somewhere into the wall or ceiling, if it even worked anymore. He pressed, pulled, and felt around in the shadowed spots for a lever of some kind. He found a wooden handle, barely reachable, imbedded amongst the rock and wiggled it before choosing a direction. He grasped the device at the point closest to the rock and gave it a tug.

The door scraped a few inches. Graeme put more muscle into it and the solid oak slid open a foot. The gears of the apparatus were almost rusted shut. He seized the portal and put his shoulders into action and managed another foot. Something blocked the opening on the other side.

Graeme dropped his head and remembered the layout of the room. It took a moment to get his bearings in a room he hadn't been privy to until he entered to say goodbye to his da on his deathbed. Desperation drove his next action. He put all his weight into pushing the object straight ahead. It fell forwards, stopped by the bed in the center of the room.

"Well, I be leavin' ye here, lad." The woodcutter turned and started down the steps.

Graeme glanced back. "Thank ye, sir." He smiled through the dust covering his face and hair. "Watch fer smoke from the tower and wait by the burn to lead the men who respond up this path."

"I'll dae that, lad."

"Take my horse back wi' ye then?"

"Aye, will dae it." The old man stepped down the stairs as slowly as he had on the way up.

Graeme scrambled over the backside of the downed wood chest. He found his footing and righted the furniture, sliding it out of the way. He dusted himself off, looked around, and set out to find the rest of the household.

Nellie answered the tap at his mither's door. "Oh, praise God! Ye're alive. We been worried sick o'er ye, master." She opened the portal and he stepped through to find his mither and Niall consulting before the fire in her parlor.

"Thank ye kindly, Nellie." He waited for his mither to dismiss her maid.

185

Esperenza smiled. "Part o' me knew ye were fine and part o' me's been scared to death through the night." She rose, laying her shawl aside and approached her middle son. Graeme met her for a kiss on his cheek. "That's all fer now, Nellie." Her maid disappeared through the bedroom. "Shall I order ye a bath?"

"In time, Mither." He turned to Niall. "I wondered if ye'd made it home before the Anglican henchmen arrived."

Niall nodded. "I thought I saw ye in the camp last even. Was John wi' ye?"

"Aye, he didn't come out though." Graeme winced at the thought of his friend's loss.

"Then it *was* him goin' into the tent?"

"Aye, I followed but he waved me away. I pray my impatience daen't cost him his life." He spied scones on a plate and sat. He buttered a scone and bit into the soft center.

Niall poured tea into a fine china cup and set it in front of Graeme. "It's probably best Tomas isn't here."

"He went to Ruane's family because they'd already had to deal with the tyranny of the Anglicans. I fear we shan't hold 'em long if their reinforcements arrive." He wolfed down another bite and sipped the tea.

"How'd ye get in here?"

"Secret passage from a cave beneath the cliff. Had to move a piece o' furniture in Da's room to get inside." Graeme buttered a third scone and ate it in two bites. He sat back, propped his ankle on his knee and gazed around. "We lose many men?"

"Not one. We gave 'em hell when they demanded we turn over our parson. They wanna string 'im up fer preachin' God's word, ungoverned by that King o' theirs." Arms crossed, Niall stared into the fire.

"Well, let's go out and give 'em some more hell and we'll send 'em packin'." Graeme rose and called out, "Thank ye fer tea, Mither. We're goin' now."

Niall stood with him. "Cora's scared. She's never been through anythin' like this before, her family bein' so much higher in the mountains."

"Aye, but they'll get a share if the zealots have their way." Graeme opened the door and the brothers left to prepare for the coming battle. "We'll call a war council. Fetch every man under seventy summers and every lad o'er twelve," Graeme ordered Niall. "Build a bright fire on the roof of the tower and take enough water for smoke."

Chapter Twenty-nine
Lizbeth

Bran returned late at night. We crossed two mornings later. I was anxious to be away, yet part of me didn't mind lingering. But I missed my husband. Studying my braw boy helped, his hands were like his da's, his face a tiny mask of Graeme's.

Carol Ann knocked on the door and opened it to peer inside. "How're my patients today?"

I smiled, confidant that I no longer looked quite so ghoulish. "Fine, very fine. How're you?"

"Good, it was a long night. I'm hitting the hay. Rhonda's here if you need her and breakfast's ready."

"I'm coming then." I slid my feet over the side of the bed and into soft slippers. My boy tucked into the crook of my arm, I headed for nourishment.

****

Bran came by to take Carol Ann out to dinner. I had seen her ring when he returned and knew she'd be stunned. A carat and a half oval cut diamond on a platinum band awaited her fine, skilled hand in his jacket pocket.

He was delighted with himself. I've never seen him so happy or handsome. He wore a black suit with a blue shirt, the color of his blue green eyes. He bounced on his toes as he tried to stand still to talk to me.

Carol Ann took her time coming downstairs, but she was definitely worth the wait. She slowly descended in a black tea length gown that fit in all the right places. She wore a simple silver rope chain at her neck and diamond teardrop earrings.

Bran, eyes glued on his beloved, nearly drooled. I bumped him and said, "Swallow, silly." I dabbed at my son's wet mouth with a cloth diaper.

He bent to kiss her. "Milady." He bowed.

She took his arm and they paraded to the front. I followed, with my son, as far as the entry. They proceeded to Bran's car. He opened her door, closed it, looked up and waved to us. I waved back and fastened the inner door. My son and I were alone for the first time in the four and a half weeks we'd been free.

I bathed Graeme and propped his sleepy, cuddly body in an infant seat Bran brought. I sat him in the floor of the bathroom and ran a hot bath for myself.

Soaking, I daydreamed about going home. On the morrow we'd cross to my husband's family, leaving this world and all its shortcomings behind. I closed my eyes and remembered the touch of my husband's hands, his rich full voice, and the sound of his laughter.

I prayed he'd have me back, love me as his wife again. I glanced down at our son, so like him, and swiped tears away. I bathed, got out and pulled on a fresh, soft gown and remembered the gauze gown I slept in at home.

Home. On the morrow we'd be *home.*

****

Graeme led a group of men along the wall to inspect troops. The opposition set up two cannon pointing directly at the gate. He glanced down the wall and knew he didn't have the manpower to stand up to the bombardment if they arrived with a wagon load of balls and powder.

"Men, we're facing odds we couldna foretell. We're fighting fer our lives and our faith in God. Keep a steady heart and a claymore at hand. I wan' the finest hunters along the walls. Use ammunition wisely and be cautious of the lads who load fer ye." He gazed at his ragtag group of farmers, hunters, and anglers. "God be wi' ye all and save us from this scourge of Anglicans." He turned back to the fortification. "Take yer places, lads."

He strode to the buttresses and checked on his cannon. "Be ready, men and keep fixed. Daen't retreat even if the wall feels like it's crumbling beneath ye. It'll hold. Be sure to dae the same."

The young men, in each group, nodded agreement and answered in unison. "Aye, laird."

Graeme left them to check the tower and its fortifications.

Niall hurried to him. "The woodcutter brought twenty more men over. I fear we must cut off the passage before the enemy infiltrates."

"Aye, tha's wise. Make it so." The Macpherson paused. "What of the parson?"

"He's in the keep with the women and children." Niall scanned the newcomers, marching into the barmekin with whatever they owned that could be used as a weapon.

Graeme laughed, a thunderous noise echoing 'gainst the stone. "Damn, man, ye might as well hand him over to the Anglicans as leave him with Mither."

Niall chuckled. "When last I saw to them, Mither begged he be surrendered or she'd hang 'im herself."

"Archers!" The laird shouted, "Here!"

The men scrambled up to the top of the wall.

"Ye've brought a quiver full of arrows and the smithy and fletcher are turning out more as we speak. Shoot high and let the air be filled with yer volleys. We wanna keep their men bunched as much as possible for the cannon. Any questions?" His hands rested on his hips.

The men glanced at each other and shook heads in unison.

One lad answered. "Nay, sire. We're good enough to put food on our tables. We'll give ye wha' ye ask fer."

Graeme grinned. "Aye, then get along to the front line and disperse yerselves. When we lay down fire we wanna hit 'em with all we have. They need to see we won't roll o'er fer 'em."

A young lad, about fifteen summers, shouted. "Aye, sire, we ain't scared!"

Graeme nodded. "Keep yer heads down. May the good God o' heaven bless every mark and make yer arrows sure."

He left them.

Graeme checked the wagons pulled against the gates, loaded with everything that could be found for ballast. He checked the men arming themselves from the castle's armory. Tall, short, thin, heavy, his army molded into a formidable rival to the fanatics who besieged them.

"Thank ye kindly fer comin' to our aid." He shook hands with every man. "Some of us'll meet our Maker this day. Repent while ye have a chance and be prepared. There are women in the keep to protect from the adversary, should they overcome us. I'd appreciate it if five of ye guard the entrance at all times. Choose among yerselves." He marched away to the next fortification as men volunteered for the last stand.

Graeme's long stride carried him to the back gate past the smithy, pounding out arrowheads. Loaded wagons stacked against the smaller rear gate. Four archers stood along the wall, prepared for a fight. The narrow shelf of rock, skirting the back of the castle, was defensive terrain, impossible to launch more than a few men at a time to bombard the entrance.

Niall paced the wall in front calling orders to archers and men armed with muskets. "Hold steady, men!"

The younger lads sat nearby to reload and run errands. A volley fired into the invading horde. Graeme had no desire to see the action from the wall. But the keep, where his mither, the parson, Cora and the maids held fast was another matter. From the parapet he could study the layout of the enemy's formation and command more effectively. He turned towards the keep when he heard a commotion.

Niall shouted, "Graeme, here!"

He loped along the fortress ledge and leaned on the front wall to watch as John Tempest was paraded in front of the castle. His hands were tied and he was covered in blood, stumbling along.

A shout was heard from a mounted captain, strutting his horse to and fro before the castle gates. "We'll trade ye yer man fer the parson."

191

Graeme glanced down at his old friend and shook his head. "Kill 'im if ye mean to do it. He's of no account to me."

The emissary looked up at The Macpherson. "He's yer champion."

"Aye, he was before he betrayed us."

John Tempest turned fiery eyes up to him and spit on the ground, with a sneer.

Graeme continued. "'Twas ye who sold us to our enemy, eh?" He grinned. "I figgered it out early this mornin'. The woman was a mistake, John." Graeme turned to the archer nearest him and spoke quietly in the pre-battle calm. "Kill 'im."

He left the wall as the shooter took aim, lodging an arrow in the champion's heart, slaying Graeme's childhood friend.

The Macpherson hurried up three staircases with a spyglass in hand. He watched for a half hour as wave upon wave of attacks left men dead and wounded before and behind the castle walls. When the enemy laid a ladder against the back wall, at great cost, he took action.

He scaled the steps down from the keep to the rear wall. Graeme drew his claymore and battered every man who attempted to scale that entrance. He heard Niall's shout at the front gate and turned away to his brother.

An arrow caught Graeme's left shoulder. He shuddered, peering down at the protrusion. He glanced up to see the archer hidden among the treetops. Six arrows struck the archer at the same time.

Graeme turned back to the ladder and swung his claymore, almost severing the head of a man foolish enough to try to breach a wall with a dozen men in defense. He glanced down at the blood staining the arm of his tunic.

The commander of the archers shouted, "Sir, ye're wounded!"

Graeme roared, "A small thing, this. Take 'em all, men." He swung the claymore again with one hand. A man fell to his death on the rocks. The laird leaned over the barrier to the limit of his reach and pushed the ladder away, sending two more men to the boulders below.

He left the wall and scurried down the steps to the front gate. A battering ram slammed into the ancient thick oak, loosening the iron hinges and latches more with every blow.

Graeme shouted to Niall, "Can we hold 'em?"

Niall answered likewise, "Aye, I believe it so. Shall we take the fight to 'em then?"

"Aye, with thirty ready men we'll open the gate. Wipe 'em out!"

"Ye're hit, brother. Go! Let Mither tend the wound. I'll finish this." Niall turned away and began to round up men with any kind of weapon at hand to pound the enemy rushing through the gate.

Graeme ignored Niall's advice and joined the men on the ground. He roared at the gatekeeper, "Loose the latches and get back!"

The gatekeeper climbed aboard the wagon and opened the locks, bailing off the side as the wagon jerked away from the entry.

A dozen invaders ran across the ground on either side of the ram rolling freely into the barmekin.

Graeme and his men fell on the trespassers with claymores, dirks, and swords, slashing their way through to the boundary of the walls and into the enemy attempting to enter. The ambush successfully captured the ram and slew every man who stepped into the barmekin.

Niall, on the wall above, called the men to fall back. They closed the gate against the few crusaders left outside and barricaded the opening again with the battering ram as a brace.

Graeme leaned against the cool stone of the inside wall and slipped to the ground. He heard shouts, but failed to distinguish the words. Alarmed, Niall hurried from the ramparts and knelt in front of him. The Macpherson swallowed and glanced down. Through fuzzy vision he inspected the dirk protruding from his upper thigh. It was the last thing he noticed.

****

Niall had five men shoulder the burden of a sling carrying Graeme inside the keep.

Esperenza hurried to meet her sons. She spotted Graeme and began to wail. She shook as she screamed. Nellie stepped up to support her, wrapping her strong arms around her mistress.

The men laid Graeme on the dining table. He still breathed.

The physician followed them inside and bent over The Macpherson. "Fetch the healer, lads."

Quinn left at a trot for the former master's room and the tunnel.

Darkness fell and with it, calm. But inside the castle, emotions roiled. Niall paced and his mother wept.

Chapter Thirty

I was awake before three o'clock and packed a few small things to take across with us.

Bran slept over last evening, but was up with coffee when I stepped out of our room with my son in my arms and a small bag of baby items.

"Mornin'." He smiled at me and reached for Graeme. I handed over the bairn and went for my own coffee—for the last time.

Carol Ann came down the stairs in a medieval gown and period shoes. She stopped in front of me. "How do I look?"

"Verra good. How's your ring finger holding up?" I held out my hand for hers.

She draped it in front of me before laying it in my hand.

"Beautiful. Do you like it?" I grinned.

"I do, and I was a little surprised, to tell the truth. Think I ought to leave it here?" She twisted the ring on her finger and frowned.

"It's probably best. For one thing, the place we're going to pass through is full of gangs on this side and when we arrive, we're in the middle of not too much in the way of population." I smiled, offering assurance.

She slid off the engagement ring, looked around the living room, making tracks for an ornate painted box and opened it, depositing the ring inside. She winced. "I feel naked already."

"It's best for now, my love." Bran assured her. "You can put it back on when we get home tonight."

"You're only staying the day then?" I began to feel nervous about the prospect of being on my own on the other side.

"Aye, you'll be fine, Lizzie. We'll get you to the castle, visit a while and come home at dusk." He lifted my wee son and kissed his cheek. "Lad, I'll miss you like I'd miss my own breath. You'll need to see to yer mam and take care not to let the lassies go wild

195

o'er you. You're a handsome fellow and there's many a trap set to catch you off guard. What say ye?"

My smiling bonnie boy cooed, a stream of spit flowing from his lower lip. I looked at the clock. "We'd better go." I busied myself gathering last things and took my son from Bran.

We headed out to the cavern in the park.

Crossing was easy enough. I believe the gangs decided to steer clear of Bran. He was unpredictable. We drove my old car and parked it under a streetlamp. I tied my son into a sling across my body. We loped to the cavern and ducked inside while Bran circled sunwise three times. The static curtain appeared.

I would see my husband soon. Before dark I'd know my fate, mother to my son or his nursemaid. If the latter I'd return with Bran and Carol Ann. As much as I cherish my son, I could not watch my husband love another woman.

The portal opened and we passed into shadowy silence. There was no wind and the sky darkened with threatening clouds. We glanced around and spotted the woodcutter walking towards us. Dread spread through me as he failed to meet my eyes, speaking only to Bran.

"Me woman said ye'd be coming over. I'm to take ye to the castle straightaway." He muttered something else I couldn't hear. "The Macpherson's dying if he ain't dead already." He shuffled past us for three horses and a mule, saddled and ready to ride.

After crossing the burn the terrain changed. We climbed over rocky paths and picked our way across a narrow ledge, leading the horses. Bran and I exchanged looks, wondering why we approached the castle this way instead of through meadows and fields along the burn. Upon reaching the mouth of a large cavern, we were informed of all that had transpired the past two days.

"Castle's under siege so we going in through an ancient tunnel. Mind yer steps as the path's rocky." He looked at me for the first time. "Milady, hold yer bairn close, some of the switchbacks are tight. I daen't wan' ye to lose yer footing."

"Aye, thank ye kindly." I watched him warily as he led us into the cavern hefting a flame tipped torch, up winding steps carved into stone.

I stumbled once and caught myself on the wall. Bran followed behind Carol Ann who was behind me, while I clutched my wee lad to my chest.

When we reached the top, our guide turned to Bran. "Sir, I'll let ye open the door, then."

The three of us stepped back to allow Bran to pass for the door with no knob.

Bran looked back at the woodcutter. "Is there a lever or stone to push? How do I do this?"

The woodcutter pointed with his walking stick. "Through tha' hole yonder is a lever ye pull, if ye can."

Bran reached up, stretched on his toes, and caught the tip of the lever pulling with all his weight, his feet clearing the stone floor. The door slowly creaked partially open. Bran grasped it with both hands and widened the gap, so we could pass through. When he flourished his hand to the woodcutter, the old man shook his head.

"I'll be waiting out 'ere, 'til I'm needed." He sat down, producing a piece of salt tack and his sghian dubh.

I glanced around the room we were in and shrugged. "I don't ken where we are." I headed for the door feeling sure it would lead to the hallway. Opening the portal I stuck my head out. "Through here." I waved Bran and Carol Ann along.

We heard voices from below and went to the stairs. Niall looked up from the gallery. "Lizbeth?"

The three of us hurried down. "Aye, 'tis me. Niall, where's Graeme?" Shivering with fear and dread, I wrapped my arms around myself and my child.

He glanced at my bundle. "The physician's with 'im. Come." He led us to the dining room where Agnes and the medical man discussed the situation.

Carol Ann stepped forward and glanced at me. Mither looked up and left her chair for my side.

"Mither, this is a medical woman." I held out my hand to Carol Ann. "Her name is Carol Ann. She saved my life. Mayhap your son could benefit from her knowledge."

Mither nodded. "Please, examine The Macpherson and see if there's aught ye can dae fer him."

I translated for Carol Ann.

Agnes stepped back and so did the physician. The old man spoke quietly. "There's nothing more fer 'im. He's abou' gone."

Standing by my husband's head, I brushed my fingers through his hair, wet with perspiration. "Please don't leave me. I only just arrived, Graeme. I brought our son to see his da and stay here forever with you, my heart." I lay my hand along his planed cheek.

Carol Ann pulled at Graeme's clothes around the wounds. "Get me boiling water, a sharp knife, and a needle with the strongest thread you have."

Niall repeated her directions, in Gael.

Cora left her seat against the wall. "I have needles and thread." She ran for the backstairs and her sewing room.

Carol Ann turned to Bran. "I need that knife in your sock."

He produced the sghian dubh he carries all the time. "Here, what d'ya wan' done?"

"Cut away his clothes. I need to see what's going on. We may have to reopen the wounds to sew him up inside." She pulled the garments apart as Bran sliced them with the razor sharp knife.

When Graeme's chest and thigh were exposed Carol Ann began to probe. She addressed the physician and healer, but looked at me. "What sort of weapon made the wounds?"

I passed on her question in Gael, then translated their answers. "An arrow in the chest and a dirk, knife with a twelve inch blade in the thigh." I listened to Agnes for a moment. "Agnes says they removed both and wiped the area with clean rags." I glanced down at beloved. "The problem with the dirk is not knowing what it's been used for previously, skinning a dead animal or some such."

"This'll be tricky then. He's burning with fever. His pulse is slow; we may be too late."

Bran shook his head. "We can't be. This isn't supposed to happen." He glared at Graeme.

I kissed my husband's forehead and raked his hair back with my fingertips while I muttered a prayer. "Please, God, don't take him from me."

My son stirred from slumber and stretched. I scooped him out of the sling and held him close. Mither approached and pulled me away from the table.

She held onto my arm. "May I hold my grandson?" Tears spilled down her craggy cheeks.

"Aye, Mither, I'm sorry. Of course you may hold him." I laid my bonnie boy in his grandmother's arms.

She gazed at him, her mouth open. "He looks like his da, exactly like Graeme looked the day he drew his first breath." She smiled, pulling our bairn up to her face and snuggling him, her eyes closed.

Carol Ann labored away for more than an hour cleaning Graeme's wounds. He had not stirred. His heart rate slowed further. There was blood on the table, trickling to the stone floor...far too much blood.

When I looked at Carol Ann, she soberly studied me for a moment. "Lizbeth, there's nothing else I can do." She cleaned her hands of the mess of dead tissue and dropped the bloody rags in a nearby pan.

I felt strong hands on my shoulders as Niall pushed me down into a chair. My body fell into the, now familiar, vibration of deep shock. I sobbed and slid to the cold stone floor.

Chapter Thirty-one

Quinn entered and whispered in Niall's ear. Niall nodded and stood to make an announcement. "The siege is lifted. The King's men have left us, fer now." He went to Graeme and stroked his hair. "Too late fer ye, brother. But ye fought them like a man gone mad, ye daed." Tears slid down his cheeks. "But fer ye, we'd've been overcome by 'em. If they return before Tomas gets home, I'll be lost without ye to give me direction."

His shaky hand covered his mouth as his lovely blond wife offered solace through a touch, leaning her face into his chest.

****

I felt numb as I dressed for my husband's funeral. Carol Ann helped me button on my clothes. I slogged through the quick sand of grief, delicately balanced on the edge of the darkness waiting to swallow me.

We went through the motions and slowly descended the stairs.

There were thirty silent people in the gallery. No sound was uttered until my bonnie lad began to wail. We followed the hide and pole stretcher that my husband's body graced.

When we left the gallery for the barmekin, a breeze blew Graeme's beautiful black and silver hair. How odd, that even in death that small glimpse of life stirred my heart to hope. I would never forget every moment we shared, in love and companionship. The passion that blessed us had to last me a lifetime.

Bran and Carol Ann walked on either side of me, my son propped on my shoulder, sucking his fist. He fretted occasionally, perhaps from his mother's misery—yet again.

The tomb was a small cave, ready to receive Graeme's body. He was lifted onto a stone shelf by four strong men. I wanted to die with him. But for our child, I'd join him.

We watched helplessly.

Goodbyes were spoken aloud and many left, grieving in hearts and souls.

A young woman with red hair approached me, but Niall stepped between us. He spoke sharply to her and she sadly turned away, two red-haired toddling children clinging to her skirt.

We walked back towards the castle as dusk settled. I glanced at Bran, realizing they'd missed the chance to cross. Barely intelligible words flowed from my mouth and he responded.

My last memories of that day were through a filtered lens of tears and pain. My feet moved one in front of the other, but I don't recall the path.

Chapter Thirty-two

"Cuisle mo chroi?" A voice called from far away. "Pulse of my heart, come back to me." The deep resonant tone of Graeme's voice washed over me.

I felt a gentle hand brush across my cheek.

"Please daen't cry, Lizbeth. I'm right here." A heavy sigh followed.

My eyes opened to light. "Hmmm?" I was bone dry.

Beloved smiled, his merry black eyes meeting mine. "There ye are, mo chroi. I was getting tired of waiting fer ye to wake."

The bright light pricked my scorched eyes. I managed a noise. "Heaven?"

He chuckled. "Nay, lass, no' even close." He nuzzled my neck. "Ah, wife, ye scared the wits outta me."

"How's 'at, sir?" My tongue felt sluggish, preferring to cling to the roof of my mouth. I had to close my eyes against the glare of light.

"I was afraid I lost ye." His warm hand rested on my exposed arm, achingly cold.

"Canna go anywhere." My own voice sounded strange to my ears.

His voice sounded divine. "How dae ye feel, my sweet?" He sniffed.

"Headache." I mumbled.

"Aye. Ye had a tumble, lass. Your car flipped off the bridge into the loch. You suffered quite a blow to yer head." His dark hair, streaked with silver, gleamed in the harsh sunlight streaming through the sterile white blinds of a hospital room. He wore the silky tresses pulled back with a leather thong.

"Wha' abou' our son?" I squinted his direction, hating to take my eyes from him.

202

"He's small but growin'. He was born almost two months ago. I'm sorry, Lizbeth, I ken ye looked forward to feeding 'im but after the accident, well, not this time."

My eyes closed as I struggled to stay with him. If I slept again, he may be gone upon my waking. I heard other voices in the room, but couldn't respond.

Bran said something.

Beloved chuckled. I felt his lips on my cheek.

Carol Ann came into the room, touched my wrist, and wrote on a metal foldered chart. She kissed my forehead.

I fought to stay with them but succumbed to the blanket of unconsciousness waiting just off to the side of my muddled mind.

****

The room's light softened. Dim lamps broke up the darkness. Bran was visible from the slightly raised head of my bed. Graeme moved into view. Bran said something so quietly I couldn't make out his words. He handed my husband a packet of papers. Graeme accepted it and stuffed it into his satchel.

Was he leaving me? I tried to speak. No words came out of my mouth. Graeme turned to the bed and smiled. He took a few steps and leaned over.

"Hullo, my love." He smiled, then bent to kiss my cheek and nuzzle my neck.

"Where you go?" I sounded like a drunken sailor.

"Nowhere. Ye fell asleep last time I tried to tell ye. We have a place to live across the road. Bran secured it fer us. I go to bathe and change. A...nurse is there tending our bairn. Bran and Carol Ann took care o' tha' too." He brushed his fingertips over my cheek. "I miss ye, mo chroi." He smiled.

I tried to smile back. "Miss you." Tears flowed, as I knew this was all a dream. My husband was dead. I'd watched them stack rocks in front of the door to the tomb to protect his body from wild animals.

"Shh, now ye mustn't take on so, Lizbeth. Everything's better. Ye're getting well and soon we'll go home. I promise." He kissed my mouth.

My teeth felt wooly. I would turn my head if I could, but my body was gripped into position by iron. At least it felt that way.

Bran walked towards us. "Lizzie, how you feeling?"

"How's 'is real?"

He shrugged and looked at Graeme. "Do you know wha' she means?"

Graeme shook his head. "I daen't ken."

That's when I noticed his clothes. My husband wore a solid color pullover and jeans. He seemed so natural in the strange attire. Then again, he looks great in everything...or nothing.

Graeme glanced back at me.

I worked to form words. "D'ya recall how we met?"

He nodded. "How cou' I forget tha'?" He winked. "We met in a dream, my love. Three years after the dreams began we met at ceilidh at the castle. Dae *ye* remember?"

"Aye." My eyes closed. They burned with unspilt tears. I managed to choke out another word. "Aye."

"There, now." His hand rubbed down my arm. "I wish I kenned what I could say to ease yer heart."

I smiled. "I know." I drifted off again, holding fast to the idea that he'd be there upon waking.

When I opened my eyes again, I thought my brother, Aaron, was in the room.

I gasped and tried to move.

"Lizbeth, calm down." Bran pushed his palm at me, then turned away and walked to the door. "Nurse?"

The blur of a white uniform with dark hair flew into the room. She called out loudly. "Mrs. Macpherson?"

"Aye." I wanted to say so much more. All I could do was tremble. *Why's my brother in here? He tried to kill me. He's in prison awaiting execution for the women he and Margot killed. Where's Graeme?*

She couldn't read my mind.

The sunlight hit Bran's hair again, causing the chestnut gleam to lighten.

It wasn't Aaron. It was Bran.

Graeme walked in and grinned at Bran. "Hey, man." He slapped him on the back in a familiar gesture. "How's the house comin'?" He watched the nurse check the monitors around the bed and frowned.

"Good, the roofers finish today. Next they'll repair plaster and the wood floor. I told them I'd be back up to check on progress in a few days. Don't worry abou' anything. You have your hands full here." Bran glanced at me. "I think I scared Lizzie a while ago. She went into a panic."

"I wonder what she's thinking, ye ken? When she fell asleep again, I left fer a shower. Carol Ann working?"

"Aye, she'll be off in about an hour. We can tend the lad tonight if you want to stay here."

"If yer wife doesn't mind cooking fer us?" Graeme watched the nurse at work.

"I imagine she can scare up a meal or two. She's quite the chef. She misses Lizbeth though."

"Me, too." I interjected. My body vibrated, the beep in the heart monitor raced.

Graeme's handsome face filled my vision. "Mo chroi! How dae ye feel?"

"Verra tired." The words oozed out as one slur.

He grinned. "It's okay to sleep, my sweet. If I'm not in here wi' ye it's because I'm with our son. The nurse will call me when ye tell 'em. Just now ye need to rest. I fed Iain, ye still call him Graeme, just a little while ago." He smoothed the pillow beside my face, barely touching my skin. "He's a handsome lad. I'll bring 'im by again in a bit. He's been here, nestled up to ye. Ye just haven't been awake fer it, lass."

I wept, then slipped away again. My last conscious feeling was his fingers drying my tears.

An infant screeched in my dream. I felt hands upon me and opened my eyes to see my husband laying our tiny son against my neck. The bairn's face, so close, felt wonderful, but his cry rent my heart. He was nestled beside me, propped with a pillow.

205

Graeme pulled something soft from under my thigh. I caught a fuzzy glimpse of a baby blanket. He lowered his face to our son's ear.

"'Tis yer mam, Iain Graeme Walker Macpherson." My husband's breath was soft against my skin, whispering encouragement to both of us. The warmth sent a shiver through me. He kissed my neck and raised our son to swaddle him in the small blanket. "Tha's wha' she smells like, lad. Da's wrappin' ye in the fragrance of yer mam."

"See 'im?" I hoped he understood my drunkenness.

"Aye, my love." He turned the bundle around to face me, stretched the length of his da's forearm.

"He's beautiful."

"Aye, but he looks like his da just now. How's the ache in your head?"

"No' as bad." I managed. My eyes were too heavy to hold open. "Love you too."

He kissed my dry lips. "And I ye, my sweet."

I woke with a start, alone in the white room. I heard noises far away and wondered about them. Nothing was discernible.

Carol Ann stepped inside with her nurse paraphernalia. Sashaying to the bed, she smiled. "I'm glad to see you awake. Every time I make rounds you're sleeping or dopey."

I smiled back. It's contagious. "Mouth's dry."

She hefted a glass with water and a straw. "Don't get in a hurry, sip it."

I followed instructions and studied the tubes and cords attached to me. "Wha's all this?"

"We have to monitor you closely. You took a bath in the loch. Did Graeme tell you?"

I shook my head. "No."

She put her stethoscope in her ears. "Deep breath, darling." She moved it. "Deep breath again." She tossed the stethoscope over her shoulder. "Can't have you getting pneumonia."

"Why am I tied down?"

"We had a little trouble with you thrashing around. Some of the monitors were disconnected. Of course that was immediately after the accident. I'll call the doctor and see if we can unhook a few of them. Do you need anything?"

"A mirror?"

"Not just yet, Lizbeth." She patted my hand. "We had to shave off what was left of your hair to stitch up the cuts on your scalp. There's one, high on your forehead. When your hair grows out it'll cover up nicely. You have a lot of bruises." She glanced away. "You could have died, had Graeme and Bran not been standing in the yard when you left. It took both of them to get you outta that car. Bran said the steering column broke. I was inside the house with Iain. I didn't know about the accident until Graeme fetched me. "

"I'm sorry. I don't remember."

"The kind of head trauma you're suffering tends to result in lost memories, even fantastic imaginings. Now that you're awake you can go home soon. You'll need to return daily for a while until you're sure of your footing. Don't worry about it." She kissed my cheek and left me, as Bran came in, pausing to squeeze her arm.

As more days passed, I was in and out of consciousness, until I opened my eyes one morning and knew where I was, why, and that sunshine flowed into the room. There were two vases of roses standing nearby, one studded with lavender. My eyelids were back under my command. My body ached from lack of motion.

The door opened to my husband.

How? Graeme died. I watched his body laid onto a shelf in the tomb.

"Lizbeth, ye're awake this time." He kissed me and stood beside the bed, taking my hand in his, smoothing over my palm. "Tha's good because we need to talk 'bout a few things."

"How are you here, alive at this moment? I saw you die."

"It was a ruse. The seer gave me a potion to drink and brought blood from slaughtered sheep to the castle. I was wounded in battle, but she sent everyone away and dosed me with her elixir and poured the blood round me to make it look far worse than the damage done. Two days after they closed the tomb, I left it and met Bran at the cavern." He paused and took a deep breath. "I had to leave, Lizbeth." His voice softened. "It was important that my family believed me dead."

"Why?"

"Bran crossed over and sent a letter to me in Inverness, dae ye recall?"

"Aye."

"In his letter Bran said he'd check the cavern every morning and night. On my way home, I passed near the cairn in time to cross, so I did. He waited for me in the park. He brought images of you and our son. It was all I could do not to go directly to you and never return. We spent several hours concocting a way for me to leave my home and family to make a life wi' ye here."

"But why? We were going to live there, Graeme."

"It had to appear that I was dead. There was no way Tomas or Mither would've allowed me to escape. Mo chroi, life is very hard there. I thought of our bonnie laddie and losing him to the constant battle to survive. I considered my home...." He searched for a word, in Gaelic, to express himself. "Bran helped me see, that in ways, my home was superior to yours, but in many ways, it was not." He frowned. "Daes tha' make sense?"

"Aye, but you couldn't come talk it over with me?" I tried to not feel jealous of Bran's input in our future, but Graeme would never have considered me as an equal partner. He was my protector and provider.

He stroked the side of my face. "My treasure, had I seen ye in the flesh, I would not hae been able to return to my land." He held my chin in two fingers. "Had my eyes witnessed, that day, what Aaron had daen to you, I'd have found a way to kill 'im." He paled and his eyes held a cold glint.

Until that moment, I had not seen my husband for the warrior that he was, meting out justice as The Macpherson would, even across time.

I nodded. "I ken."

"Good. We're going home as soon as ye can. I love ye, lass. I mean to tell ye more, but I see ye and my mind goes blank." He kissed my palm. "Ye'll always take my breath away." He smiled that gap toothed smile that made me smile.

"Bran sold my house. Where's home now?" I was confused, my heart uncertain that I knew my own mind, or history for that matter.

He grinned. "Carol Ann and Bran found a manor wi' a bit o' land in Badenoch. We bought it. There are nice prospects. It has a burn and it's near a loch." He leaned close and whispered, "He's handling the details. He said something about replacing his brother."

I considered the declaration. "Ah, that makes sense. Good. He'll get papers for you. We're never returning to your castle?"

"Lass, my home's wi' ye. When I was in Inverness, at the council of Chattan members, I decided I couldn't put ye through a war. This world may no' be as good, in some respects, but the death...mo chroi. I daen't wanna raise my sons to die in senseless battles with belligerent Englishmen *or* Scotsman, ye ken?" His face screwed into a frown. "I wanna raise our children to be brave, strong, and true, not fodder fer a cannon. I wanna wake with ye ever' mornin' and sleep wi' ye ever' night. 'Tis all I wan' from life."

"You're never leaving me again?"

"Nay, lass. Ye're looking at me, such as I am and I'm all yers." He brushed my cheek with his fingertips. "My love, we have a lifetime to dream, but this much is real now."

I smiled, feeling the stitches on my forehead pull. "Tell me about the car going into the loch."

He winced. "I'd crossed two days before. Bran and I were out front of Carol Ann's home, talking. Ye left for market. It was yer first journey on yer own. We heard yer old car hit rocks. We both made fer the bridge, fast as we could and I dove in. Bran went in the opposite side. The loch was deep there and the car was still sinking when first I saw it. The current was strong, pulling the car away from us. I went back up for air. Ye were...." He searched for a word, "not aware? We had to pry yer door loose to get ye

209

free. It was all the two of us could handle. I had my sghian dubh and cut ye from the hold of the strap."

"Seatbelt."

"Aye. Once we had you ashore, Bran breathed into yer mouth until ye coughed water. I ran back to the house fer our son and Carol Ann joined Bran in helping ye live. I waited, onshore, having no idea what to do. Lizbeth, it made my decision firm, um—I kenned it was right to live in yer world. The knowledge here, the understanding I have to learn....Please, tell me ye can accept my reasoning."

"Aye, sir, I ken your thinking."

He appeared relieved. "The physician said ye may go home a few days after ye wake. Bran's watching over the workers making our home ready. I've seen it only once, but he'll show ye images when he returns."

"I look forward to it, milord."

He touched my lips. "None of that, wife. I'm just yer husband and it's all I wan' to be."

Chapter Thirty-three
Nine years later....

This afternoon we walked over a new footbridge across the burn, behind the manor that is our home. We picnicked on the bank of the icy water with our lad and lass.

Work on our home, while I was in hospital after the accident, renewed the brick and stone structure, a mere three centuries old. It backs a lovely open field that now pastures horses. The cattle and barns are located on the west side of the property.

In our greenhouses, we grow organic vegetables and fruit, for market. Our freely-roaming chickens produce four different coloured eggs for market as well. Our beehives give us far more honey than we can sell, so my husband and Bran make mead. For themselves, of course.

Carol Ann and Bran have two delightful children and built a holiday home on the other side of The Macpherson's land. Bran still dabbles in the world of high finance. I'd never have dreamed he'd make such a devoted father and husband. He's full of surprises.

The Macpherson and I have two more children, besides Iain, who never fully recovered from the malnutrition of my pregnancy and the static electrical fluxes of the crossings. His small body was wracked with arthritis, his vision needed correction when he was only two and he could never play with other children for fear of shattering joints. His da carried him for miles every day and kept him close, no matter what task he was about.

Our son's pain reminded me hourly of the hell we lived through in Aaron's cellar. We lost Iain when he was three years, two months and four days old, to pneumonia. His lungs had never fully developed.

Two children are adequate in this world; we needn't make allowances for the number lost to war, famine and pestilence.

The Macpherson trains young men in the art of battle, just as it was fought three hundred and fifteen years ago.

He built cabins at the farthest end of his land for training seminars. Bran rounded up quite a few gang members from the park we passed through in our early days. He conveyed them out to our farm and they learned something more useful to life than drugs and robbery.

Four lads and one lass stayed on to work our greenhouses, the market, and help with the animals. Graeme set up a scholarship fund for young people wanting to leave gang life behind.

My husband provides a fine legacy for our family: honesty, patience, empathy and kindness. He taught me to grow vegetables, grains and our bairns.

Carol Ann taught me to cook.

Leaving the city and the crossings behind, his body adjusted to breathing our air and drinking our water. His hair has turned almost solid white but his skin slowed aging.

At market a few weeks ago, two women discussed a program on telly about crossing through rifts in time. As they chose their favorite tomatoes and marrows, Graeme sacked their selections.

He listened, a half-smile on his face. "How would ye ken should someone pass from another time?" His brows rose as both women studied the handsome man before them.

"Perhaps the way they dress?" One woman ventured.

He shrugged and responded, "No' so different as ye may think."

They left our stall slowly, glancing back after a few steps. I slapped his arm.

He turned and laughed. "I could no' resist. I'm sorry, mo chroi."

"You're a rascal at times, Macpherson."

Another customer handed over a batch of kale and reached for a bucket of purple potatoes. Graeme cheerfully tended them.

Part of me will always treasure the time I had with Graeme's family. But they've become a distant memory. We searched out records to find where they were buried and when they passed beyond their world.

Now, we visit their gravesites and trace names carved by a stonemason's chisel. The rocks still cover the entrance to the cave where Graeme's body was placed upon a stone shelf when he died to that world.

Graeme shares stories with our son, Tomas, who is seven, of battles he fought alongside his da and brothers. He tells his yarns in Gael, to make learning the language easier. Tomas is blond, like his namesake, but looks like his da.

Graeme spins tales of knights and fair maidens for our daughter, Maggie, who is five-years-old and has her da's dark coloring. She's learning our native tongue, as well.

I listened at her door tonight while Da told her the tale of a knight in shining armor, her true forever love, whom she'll meet in a dream.

Well, maybe someday.

Glossary of terms for Scottish books

A **bairn** is a baby or baby doll.

The **barmekin** or bailey is the plaza inside the castle walls. The operations necessary to fortify the castle against sieges and provision for everyday life lined the interior walls. The streets were generally cobbled or stone to keep wagon wheels from sticking.

A **bard** is the keeper of the oral history of a people, through song, poetry, and the telling of legends. It is an ancient tradition. He had to know the clans' history and keep track of new events amongst the people, writing songs and poetry for future generations.

A **boineid** (bonaje) was a Scottish bonnet, fitted around the crown of the head, puffy on top with a pom in the middle. Ribbon allowed for the adjustment of the crown. Lowlanders wore the ribbon dangling. Highlanders preferred the ribbon tied into a bow.

A **bothy** is a small cottage or shack.

Men usually wore their clan's **breacan** or tartan plaid in a kilt. Women also wore kilts, but often wore the **breacan**, plaid, in the form of a cape or shawl pinned over the shoulder with a brooch.

A **brochette** is a rotisserie set over fire in a large hearth.

Brogues are boots or shoes.

Burn is water, a creek or stream.

A **cairn** is a rock hut. Believed to possess magical or miraculous powers, a large number of castles built towers, the first construction on those sites. Abbeys, in particular, built over cairns with the idea they'd control the activity.

Careg is rock or gravel.

Ceilidh (kay-lee) is evening entertainment: musicians, jugglers, magicians, etc. in the great hall or bailey.

A **chatelaine** is the woman in charge of organization and operation of the castle and occupants.

A **cockernonie** is a woman's snood or bonnet.

A **dais** is a platform, in the great hall. The high seat of the chief, where he held judgment and the high table were on the dais.

Two weapons were constantly at hand, a **dirk**, a twelve-inch blade sheathed in a holster worn under the arm and a **sghian dubh** (skee-an dew), a six-inch blade with a short handle worn tucked into the top of the sock or stocking.

Erse or **Eireann** (air awn) is the Irish language.

Gaels and the **Scots** followed the Celtic calendar. An agrarian society, they lived off the land and closely followed the undulating change of seasons, celebrating each one.

- Candlemas February 1 or 11 celebrated Christ's presentation at Temple
- Whitsunday May 1 or 11 celebrated Pentecost
- Lammas August 1 or 11 celebrated first fruit harvest
- Martinmas November 1 or 11 End of harvest and St. Martin's feast

The actual dates vary by historian but generally fell on the first or middle of the month. The calendar changed in the 19th century.

The **great hall** was the communal gathering place for festivals, daily meals, and entertaining visitors. The council met in the hall, sometimes in a private room. Everyone in attendance went well-armed.

The definition of **ken** is yes, understand, or see. "I ken your ways." Past tense is **kent** or **kenned**.

A **kertch** is a headscarf. The type of daily head-covering indicated whether a woman was married or maiden.

A **kirtle** is a sleeveless cover, worn over the primary dress or a sheath. It can be linen for summer or wool or hair fiber for warmth in the winter. Much like a pinafore, it buttons in front.

Laird means lord.

A **leine** (lane) is a man's long-tailed linen shirt.

A **loch** is a lake. There are many small tributaries off the lochs. A lochan is a smaller version of a loch.

A **sennight** is a week, a **fortnight** two weeks. A **summer** accounts for a year of life.

Stays is a corset, worn on the trunk of a woman's body, stiffened with whale bone, and laced up to boost the bosom. An interesting historical fact; prostitutes were called 'loose women' because they did not wear stays, to save time dressing and undressing. A relaxed version, think sports bra, was made of leather and called **jumps**.

The Chattan was a large confederation of clans, a state unto itself. The power and influence the Lord of the Chattan held was widespread. However, if any chief failed to take care of his clan, he could be voted out or killed to remove him from power.

The head of a clan had many names like The Mackintosh, laird, milord or, my favorite, Himself.

The Lord of the Chattan reigned over a large number of major and minor clans.

The **hierarchy of the council** followed; chieftain, tacksman (taxman), minor chieftains.

The Highlanders occupied the mountainous regions and northern Scotland.

The Lowlanders occupied the plains, generally along the border with England, and lower coasts. Control of the shires or counties along the borders were hotly disputed resulting in frequent skirmishes between Scotland and England.

While each chieftain was head of his own clan, i.e.; **The Macpherson, The MacGregor,** he fell under the ultimate authority of the Laird of the Chattan who ruled at the pleasure of the council.

Terms of endearment: mo chroi (muh Khree) my heart. Mo a `stor or mo `stor (muh store) my treasure, cuisle mo chroi means pulse of my heart.

Trews are men's trousers, knee breeches.